THE EXCLUSION ZONE

ALSO BY ALEXIS VON KONIGSLOW

The Capacity for Infinite Happiness

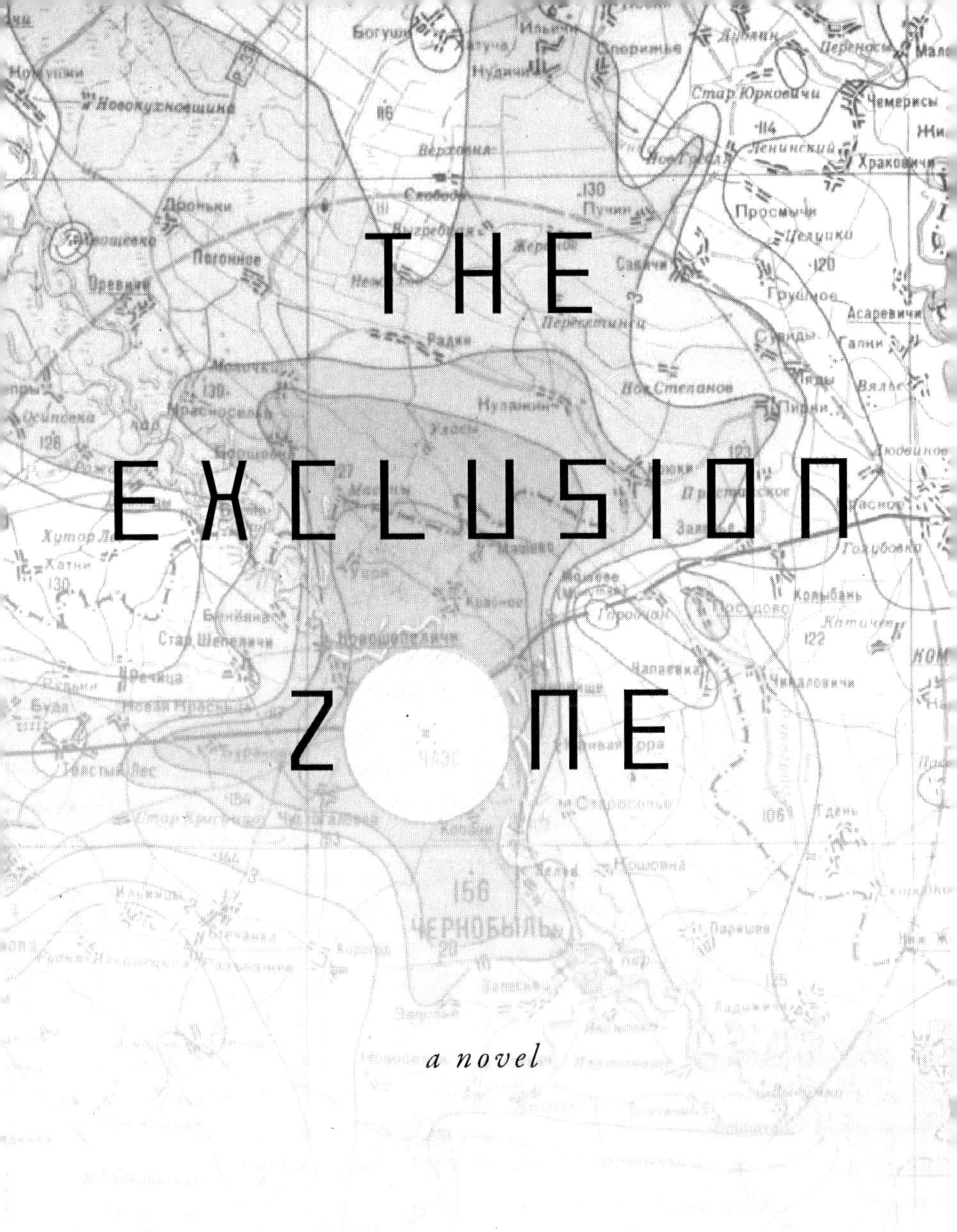

THE EXCLUSION ZONE

a novel

ALEXIS VON KONIGSLOW

Published by Buckrider Books
an imprint of Wolsak and Wynn Publishers
280 James Street North
Hamilton, ON L8R2L3
www.wolsakandwynn.ca

Editor for Buckrider Books: Paul Vermeersch | Editor: Emily Schultz | Copy editor: Jamila Allidina
Cover and interior design: Michel Vrana
Author photograph: Kier von Konigslow
Typeset in Garamond Premier Pro, Adelle Mono Pro, Evaglory
Printed by Brant Service Press Ltd., Brantford, Canada

Canada Council for the Arts
Conseil des Arts du Canada

Canada

The publisher gratefully acknowledges the support of the Canada Council for the Arts and the Ontario Arts Council. We also acknowledge the financial support of the Government of Canada through the Canada Book Fund and the Government of Ontario through the Ontario Book Publishing Tax Credit and Ontario Creates.

Library and Archives Canada Cataloguing in Publication
Title: The exclusion zone : a novel / Alexis von Konigslow.
Names: Von Konigslow, Alexis, author.
Identifiers: Canadiana 20250166119 | ISBN 9781998408160 (softcover)
Subjects: LCGFT: Novels.
Classification: LCC PS8643.O535 E93 2025 | DDC C813/.6—dc23

for Oliver, always: you're my best love too

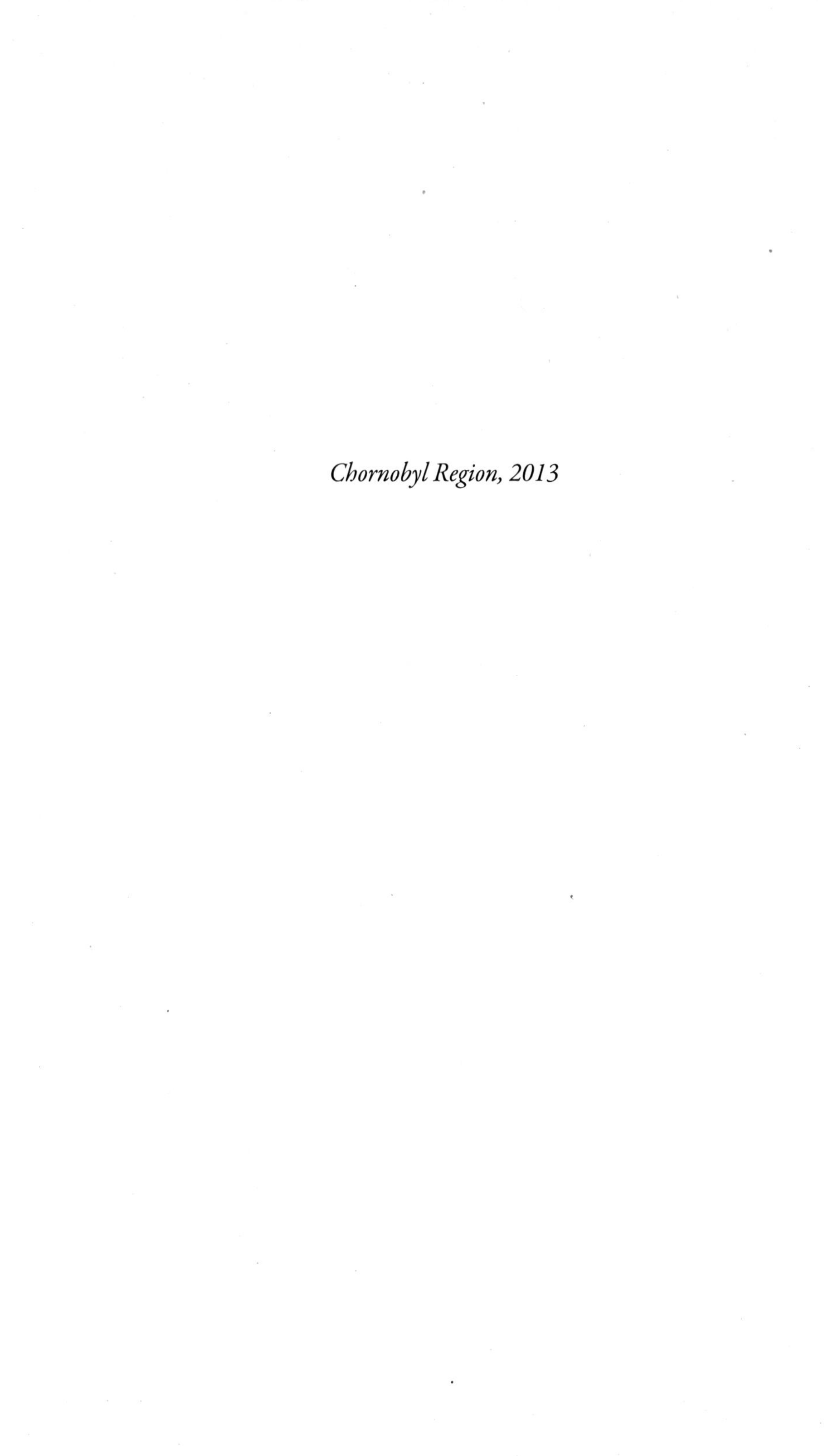

Chornobyl Region, 2013

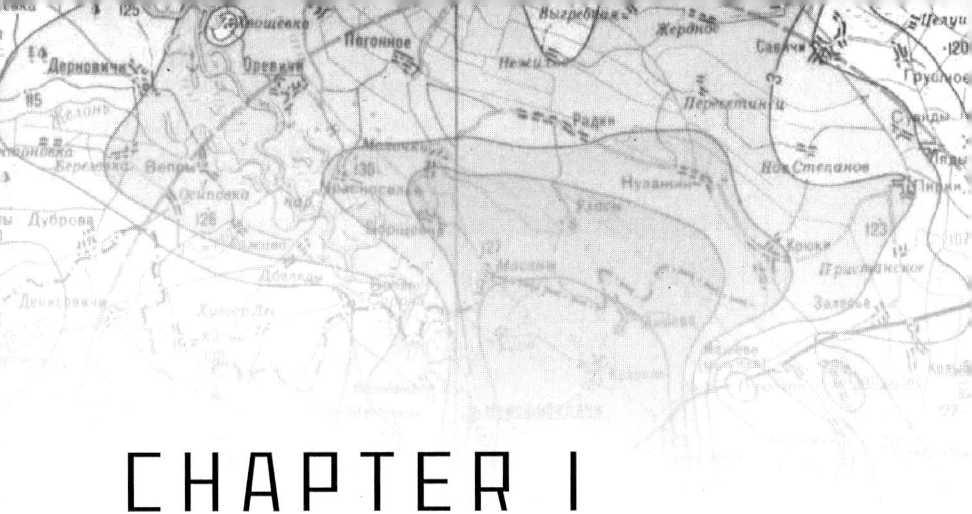

CHAPTER 1

MAYBE RENYA DIDN'T KNOW ABOUT THE THEORY OF EVERYthing and how all the building blocks of the universe fit together and all that, but she did know some things.

She stopped. The trail that she'd been following was blocked by a downed tree. She kicked at it. The outer layer crackled satisfyingly, but the trunk itself was sturdy. It gave her a foothold, so she threw herself forward, grabbed on to a knot of wood at the top and scrambled up. Renya stood. A rogue breeze lifted her hair and she looked up. The branches in the canopy looked like a circulatory system. The leaves bowed and shushed each other and made the lights dance. The patchwork of shadows and light through the tree cover, the shifting clouds through the canopy, made the forest feel like a church. This was a dead place, she reminded herself. The exclusion zone wouldn't be inhabitable for another five hundred years, so she probably shouldn't fall in love with it. Anyway, who knew what was in the wind here. She felt for the mask in her pocket, government-issued and already broken, she remembered, the elastics snapped within minutes. Had she packed tape or a stapler? She had not. Nick would have planned ahead.

She hadn't yet found this quadrant's researchers. Nick would probably know how to find them. He'd know what to do now. Renya could do some things though. She knew a lot. Nobody understood human musculature and facial expressions better than she did, and there was all that chemistry, and psych stuff, obviously. And she knew brain makeup a bit, and some behaviour-based cues. Those things were more practical. She could work backward, probably, and figure out at least something about the human mind. But Nick could probably do that too. He could go back to first principles and figure out brain electrons or some garbage, knowing him. And he didn't tend to have huge rants in his head. That would free up some time.

She should get to work. She was supposed to look for the other research groups so that she could take pictures of them at work and scan the photos later for emotional displays. She hadn't found anyone at all this morning. They were all late to make their way into this quadrant.

Renya could make some general observations. Nick was better at that too no doubt, but she did see some things. The dead tree felt harder than she'd expected. She rocked back and forth on her feet. It was long-dead from the look of it, so she'd expected sponginess, the give of decaying wood, but the log held her. The ground had felt spongy on her hike out though. Every time she'd strayed from the path, she'd felt like she was walking on folded blankets. There were a lot of leaves. Although that was foolish. She was in a forest. Forests have leaves. This forest was eerily still. She could detect a bit of birdsong, but not much. There was the odd crack. The place was spooky. That probably didn't need to be recorded. It would probably be assumed.

She pulled her notebook out of her pocket. Everyone had relationship problems, but she and Nick never had – until they did, of course. *We were great. We were the best couple.* Then all of a sudden, they were a catastrophe and it was all over. But for so many years, they'd stayed close while everyone else bickered. Why had these issues snuck up on her? Renya put away her pen. Marital problems should probably go in a different notebook. Ditto for her complaints about being married to a physicist. Ditto for fears about her partner's, well, probably ex-partner's, health. She shoved her observations notebook back in her pocket.

Why was she feeling so unbalanced? She didn't feel alone. That was why. She'd read about this place since she was a little kid, but it wasn't just recognition, she felt sure. She was primed to scan for ghosts here, but she wouldn't actually do it. That couldn't be the feeling.

Just then she saw movement up ahead on the trail. Then she saw him. There was a man here, and not one that she recognized.

Renya jumped off the log and dropped to her knees. The camera hanging from her neck knocked into the bark, and she grabbed it and held it to her chest. Her breathing was so loud. She craned her neck. The man was alone. That was a red flag. He was definitely not part of any of the groups scheduled to be in this quadrant.

She could just barely see the apparition over the log, the man standing behind two deciduous trees a bit past her trail. He looked corporeal. He'd stopped moving, however. He came into the clearing and just stopped. Renya grabbed the tree trunk.

He wasn't supposed to be here. Nobody was supposed to be here. These were empty woods in an evacuated area. This place wasn't going to be safe to even just visit for hundreds of years. He couldn't be a ghost. That would be illogical. And yet, if a ghost were to be protecting the Chornobyl region, this would be a great place to patrol.

She turned and ran, crouched at first, but then just fast.

Were there footsteps behind her? There might be footsteps. She focused on the crunch of worn earth and dead things under her sneakers, and she didn't slow down until she got to the stone path.

⊙ ⊙ ⊙

Seeing the research station beyond the crest of the little hill, Renya allowed herself to skid to a halt. The footsteps had stopped, but she didn't know when. There was no one behind her now. There were no human sounds at all, just the low murmur of the forest, the shuffle and pop of strange things in hidden places.

He might have been a chef or a cleaner, or a scientist out for a walk. In this one place, humans should probably be the least of her worries.

She let her heartbeat return to standard, her breathing normalize. Fear was her favourite of the six major emotions, well, top two for sure, but she wasn't used to experiencing it first-hand.

She looked up. The station was larger than she'd expected when she'd first arrived. It was eight storeys high, and the grandeur hit her again now. It was a huge building, with white brick and climbing vines, large windows, balconies and a gabled roof. There had been detailing too, but it was faded and crumbling now. This had been a hotel at one time, one of those spots that only rich people went to. The great ballrooms had been turned into command centres first, then labs, makeshift right after the accident, then built up over the years. The most exciting parts were the ground floor and basement, full of labs that were stocked and shining, with more variety of equipment than Renya had ever seen in one place, since so many different teams worked here, on rotation, obviously, because of radiation exposure limits. She still felt a thrill that tingled right into her fingertips, just picturing them. Her face must look indecently happy. Just being here, alongside so many different scientists, still felt so new and strange, so bracing. Located right by the blockade, the building was far enough from the explosion site that people could live here safely for short periods, close enough that you could walk or take ground transport to research sites in the outer ring of the zone of alienation or out into surrounding farms. And it was big enough, obviously, to allow all the scientists to live here while they worked, while they processed the data they collected on these short stints, and to also allow a rotating site-staff, cooks and cleaners who could live with them only long enough that they didn't max out their radiation exposure allowance all at once themselves. Maybe the support staff snuck out for walks sometimes. She probably would. Maybe that's who she'd seen.

The building loomed above her as she walked in the front door, the vines of winding leaves just starting to turn colours, waving slightly in the breeze. Imagine what she could accomplish here. Imagine what other people had already figured out, all the research in all the various pipelines.

She couldn't figure out emotions completely, obviously, not in any satisfying way anyway. People were too different. Their very electrons and circuitry were too individual. Nobody had managed to make a predictive model. She couldn't reasonably want that. But she could harness feelings, in her own small way at least. She could build a program to allow scientists to search for emotional displays, even short ones, hidden ones, emotional seepage as some labelled it, to look out for predictive patterns, especially among many faces. It was the numbers that would do it. If many people got scared all at once, for instance, that would mean something, especially if you were targeting specialized populations, scientists say. She could find the patterns. She could raise the red flags. Nobody would be able to downplay danger ever again. Nobody would be able to minimize, or gaslight, or falsely reassure. Nobody could lie about anything big ever again, not to themselves, and not to other people. She'd catch them all, if she had access to a video feed or pictures. She would harness fear. And this terrifying place would help her do it.

⊙ ⊙ ⊙

Renya tilted down her computer screen to stop the glare. Nick's beard had grown in and there was grey in it. He looked really good in that silver damned sexy way that men had. She shouldn't have called him. He'd cheated. She'd left. It could reasonably be assumed that she wasn't supposed to call him anymore. Also, she'd asked him to move out. That should really preclude her from using him as a confidant. But she did want to check on him. He'd had that heart thing after all.

"I want to –" he started.

"No." Renya didn't want to hear the rest. She didn't want to talk about the man in the woods, but she wanted to tell Nick something, even if she didn't know what exactly, and so far, he'd been the only one talking. She kicked her laptop farther away on the worn comforter. She wanted him to stop. And he had. They'd lapsed into silence, she realized. Strange. Silence wasn't Nick's MO. He seemed okay though. It didn't look like he was experiencing cardiac problems anyway, so there was that. "When my grandmother was growing up in Russia," she started, drawn to the past as she'd been since her plane had landed.

"Your grandmother wasn't Russian," said Nick.

"She called herself Russian." This wasn't true. She'd called herself Ukrainian, but for some reason she didn't want to admit her obvious mistake.

"And sometimes she called you by the cat's name," said Nick.

"That's unkind."

"Your grandmother was a nice lady."

"Thank you."

"A nice lady who grew up between Kiev and Belarus, what is modern-day Ukraine."

Renya wanted to slam her laptop shut in his ridiculous face. "When she was growing up, it was part of the Russian empire." And she'd had no love for Russia, but Renya certainly wasn't going to admit that now.

Nick paused. He was calculating. "Okay," he said. "I concede the point. Go on."

Renya rolled her eyes, but then she quickly dropped off the bed to explore the room once again. She opened a drawer beside her. Empty. It wasn't wood either. Everything looked like it was made of solid wood in this place, but nothing was: the finish was peeling off of everything, leaving warped clapboard.

"When your grandmother was growing up in Russia," Nick was saying. She reached for the laptop and angled the screen again so she could see his face. He looked repentant. Maybe he could read her as well as she read him. Or maybe he was just counting the atomic number or valence shells or whatever physicists did to guess at emotion. She walked off again. "Really," he was saying, "I want to hear."

Renya exhaled, then forced herself to count from one to ten. Frustration passed. It crashed over you like a wave and washed away again. "My grandmother used to talk about spirits in the forest," she said slowly. "She said there are ghosts here."

"By 'here' you mean –"

"They're the ghosts of the people who lived in the town maybe. I don't remember. Anyway, they come back to check on all the people, that's their job."

"That's a common thought."

"They howl through the trees. No, that isn't right – wind howls through the trees. It upsets the dust on the road, and the dust envelops the ghosts, so sometimes you can see them in outline, with their mouths open, crying." The last time she'd seen her grandmother, she'd been crying. Renya had been afraid. It was certainly not the time to bring out that old shrapnel.

"That's a lot of crying," Nick said after a moment.

"What?"

"The wind. The people. Sorry, ghosts."

"You're being unkind."

"I'm sorry, I just – I sympathize, you know? I just – People often make up these stories to help them get used to the permanence of loss. Not that –"

"Oh, and they also make fog."

Nick brought the computer closer to his face. "Nothing that's happened has to be permanent."

"When all the ghosts gather together, that's where fog comes from. That's what Baba used to tell me. And don't tell me where fog actually comes from because I don't want to hear it. I loved my grandmother. I know that's a ridiculous thing to say. I know everybody does. But I did. She was the only one in the whole family who was fucking approachable. She was the only one I didn't have to impress. Anyway, I keep thinking about those weird old stories when I walk around here. I know she didn't grow up here, exactly, I know that she meant somewhere else, but this is a landscape that is conducive to ghost stories."

Nick seemed to scrutinize his screen. "You could be anywhere in Europe. By the looks of it, I'd say France or Germany."

"I'm in Chernobyl." Or Chornobyl, more properly, as her, yes, Ukrainian grandmother would have called it. Renya leaned closer to the laptop. She'd told Nick the story of the protective ghosts, but more often, her grandmother had told her the story of *this* place. Her father had talked about it too. The three of them used to read through books and pore over the pictures. They'd talked for hours about the science behind it all. She didn't know why. Normal families had fairy tales and princess stories. Her family had a nuclear accident. Had she ever told Nick about that? "I had this idea," she said instead.

"What idea?"

"When the accident happened, everyone lied."

"It wasn't an accident, it was –"

"After the reactor at Chernobyl exploded, everyone obfuscated, every layer of government, every type of news media, and not just in Russia either."

"Oh *that* accident."

"First, the local officials tried to cover it up. Then the government lied. Then even the news tried to play it down so people wouldn't panic."

"I thought you were talking about –"

"But there's a reason for fear in a situation like this. Fear would have been motivating. Fear would have forced people to make better decisions."

"You don't need to –"

"The international community should have helped, first of all. They should have rushed in, but they didn't because first the Russian government hushed it up, then outright lied to people. Then all the surrounding countries lied to their populations as well. They all said, 'this is fine, we'll all be okay, this doesn't affect us all that much.' But if you watch the broadcasts from the time, you can see fear tells from government officials, from the broadcasters, from everyone. I found very clear fear displays in so many stills. What if I can create a computer program that looks for fear in governmental broadcasts, in the news? What if I can make a red-flag program to scan international broadcasts? The international response didn't have to take so long. People didn't have to be outside on all those days, absorbing radiation, getting sick and not knowing it. People could have been saved."

"So you're looking for lies?" said Nick. "Sorry, I'm trying to catch up –"

"Not lies," said Renya.

"Because I think they have those devices already."

"Polygraphs, you mean?" Renya set the computer on her lap again. "Those are different. They require subjects to be hooked to sensors, and they monitor, what, heart rate, breathing, perspiration? They can be duped, easily. A stubbed toe, a breeze through a window, any biological differences can make their readings obsolete. They don't work at a distance at all." Renya shook her head. "Anyway, I don't care about lies. Everybody lies," she said. Lying was difficult to *accurately* detect because so many individuals lied so differently. You didn't even have to step on a nail or whatever criminals did to fake out polygraphs on TV. You could choose to believe the lies, in part. You could hide from the truth. You couldn't hide from fear as easily.

"There was that researcher who said he could detect lies in people's faces," Nick was saying.

"I don't know how I feel about that," said Renya. There had been so much research into lies and facial expressions, multitudes of studies, reams of evidence, but Renya herself didn't understand the causality. She didn't really understand how lying worked. She didn't understand lies themselves. Some people told untruths, sure, but some people embellished and changed stories and fabricated just to make themselves understood. She didn't understand why people would have similar facial expressions when they told untruths or half-truths or embellished truths, especially when reasons and motivations and even understanding could be so different. Renya herself sometimes said slightly incorrect things to explain technical concepts to laypeople, or talked on and on to make sure she explained the whole truth, to ward against lying, but other people didn't seem to need to do that, and sometimes looked at her sidelong when she did. She had trouble making herself understood sometimes. She assumed others did too, even if it took different forms. She was more comfortable with emotions. Emotions were pretty stable, across time and across cultures. Charles Darwin called emotions adaptive. She believed they were adaptive. She believed that being able to read emotions and have one's own emotions understood had pushed humans forward along their evolutionary path. And she understood at least some of the connections to facial expressions. Fear triggered the amygdala, which affected the nervous system, which released cortisol and endorphins, which caused skin heating, eye widening, et cetera, et cetera, et cetera. She didn't understand all the emotion to emotional response links, but what she did understand just seemed to make more sense to her. Lies were so muddy in comparison.

"I don't like lies," said Renya. "I'm not comfortable with them. I need a better target. I need something more straightforward to detect."

"But seriously," Nick started.

"I'm being serious," said Renya. "Lies are complicated. They're contextual. You need to know what you're looking for and read between the lines. I can't figure that out with facial expressions. Polygraphs can't do it at a distance. They can't do it for crowds, and they can't do it for pictures and video feed at all. I can't program a computer to do that anyway. Fear is different. I can flag fear with pictures. And too much fear is a red flag. It's always a red flag."

"Yes." Nick was nodding. "I can see that."

"Anyway," Renya said, sitting up and looking at the clock. Time passed so quickly here. Time passed quickly when she talked to Nick, but she didn't want to think about that. She was already late for the big dinner. She should focus on that instead. She leaned away from the screen and strained to reach the clothes on the dresser.

"Can we talk about this more?" Nick was saying. "I want to hear more about your idea."

"Sure," she said. "Maybe. I have to go now."

"But later?"

She looked back. Nick didn't seem to be lying about his interest. "Okay." And Renya closed the laptop.

⊙ ⊙ ⊙

The clothes on the dresser were dirty already. She flopped back on the musty bed and watched the dust particles dance in the uneven lamplight.

Security, she realized with a start, a certainty come from nowhere. The man in the woods must have been security. People had been talking about patrols in the evacuated areas, started after the accident and continuing in all the decades since. There was talk about the cooking staff, about a dishwasher who could be paid to drive people to see the sarcophagus. There were also rumours of rebels, tensions with Russia, something or other brewing in the Crimea, but her political understanding was pitiful. She rolled over and patted for her computer, to look up the political situation.

There was no excuse for that kind of ignorance, especially since her family was from here.

But instead of searching for the political context, she let go of the computer and slid off the bed once again. She shuffled to the suitcase that she'd left open on the bare wooden chair. She stared into the twisted mess of clothes.

⊙⊙⊙

Renya walked slowly toward the great hall where she was supposed to join the others soon, now probably. She veered toward the window. She felt herself moving closer and closer toward the front door. She felt pulled outside, to a radioactive forest. How much direct exposure could she sustain? Everyone said that two weeks here would be fine, since they were in the outer ring of the zone of alienation, but people lied, that was the entire point of her project. In any case, how much *fear* could she maintain before she freaked out, because she would lose it eventually – under this much pressure, everyone did. Her thoughts felt lightning-fast already. Her head buzzed with calculations. Sustained sleep had not been possible since she'd landed.

She touched the windowsill, then scratched at the faux-wood finish. It was peeling off in a long ribbon.

Would the other scientists be scared? Was elation their primary emotion too? How fast were they oscillating? Her mind felt like a deck of cards being shuffled. And how much would she be able to find out about the others' experience? She had the daily surveys, sure, but nobody had admitted to much of anything yet, scientist display rules being what they were, and, again, people lied. Would the fear only be visible in pictures?

Renya pulled a bench from the entryway hall and moved it to the doorway. She'd set up cameras earlier so that she could catch the scientists coming and going, to calculate how much time they spent outside, to measure their emotions as they came and went. She'd caught unguarded moments. You always did in doorways. Doorways were transition areas. Colleagues who'd been cavalier about signing the release for photos and videos but were likely quite uncertain about the whole project and looked stilted and uncertain in other photo arrays had probably forgotten that they were being filmed here. She'd witnessed *real* emotion. She'd seen her colleagues steeling themselves to go outside. She'd caught the relief of making it back in. She touched the little cameras lightly. The red recording lights were on. She'd already checked the positioning on her laptop. In fact, she'd already run the pictures through her program: nothing for days, and then a few fear displays trickling in just recently.

A group of men and women walked through the stairwell door and toward the gathering, and Renya jumped down. As she looked up, Renya caught her reflection in the mirror. She was grinning. The other scientists, she noted, were smiling just as broadly. They walked in that same arc that veered toward the window. She hadn't expected this. She'd hypothesized there'd be a spike of fear when they arrived, then a flattening of emotion as they acclimatized. She hadn't anticipated the excitement, the new-place energy, the thrill of new possibilities.

There was danger outside. There was so much they could find out.

⊙ ⊙ ⊙

"Well, we're unbalanced," Renya heard a voice say as she manoeuvred toward the drinks table. A breeze from an open window ruffled her hair. She paused. Windows were supposed to be sealed. It could have been a blast of air from some hidden HVAC system or air filtration unit. The air was meant to be scrubbed here too. She turned, then turned again, but she didn't see any air filters, and she didn't feel moving air again. She felt unbalanced, certainly. She lost her previous train of thought and found, instead, a physicist talking to a group near the window. She edged closer.

"The windows are supposed to be closed, right?" she whispered to a woman with a ponytail she'd met earlier.

The woman shrugged. "I've seen people open them sometimes," she replied softly. "They probably shouldn't."

Renya shivered.

"We get energy from the sun," the man at the centre of the group was saying. "The earth absorbs some of it, and this warms us, obviously, and it allows plants to grow and all that, but the earth reflects a lot of the energy too, in the form of infrared radiation. We can't see this part."

A woman raised a hand.

"Humans can't see it, I mean," the man said.

The crowd that had formed around him chuckled. They were talking about butterflies and plants, she'd bet.

"But it gets a bit more complicated. The reflected energy doesn't just get blasted into space. I mean, some of it does, but some reflects back toward the earth again. It gets absorbed by greenhouse gasses then re-emitted back toward us."

"But some of that extra energy is necessary," said a man in a track suit.

"Of course," the physicist said. "Without this second step, this reabsorption, the earth would be too cold, and plants and animals, the plants and animals we have currently in this iteration of the earth, wouldn't have enough heat and energy to grow. But if there's too much reabsorption, then we have an imbalance. So what we've been doing is we've been sending up more and more gasses into the atmosphere, and these gasses reabsorb more and more of the sun's energy. So we have far less energy getting shot out into space and more getting reabsorbed by the world. That means we have an imbalance."

"We're heating up," said the track suit.

"We are," said the physicist. "The excess energy is adding up. It's not linear anymore. I'm concerned it might be getting exponential now. We've trapped too much energy in the system and it has nowhere to go. The northern hemisphere used to deflect more than it absorbed. That's reversed now, we think. We're trying to figure that out. We're trying to figure out why."

"But we're also transitioning to clean energy."

"The imbalance is still there. The extra energy is still unaccounted for. It's going to get absorbed, either by the oceans or by the land or by the ice in the oceans, which is dangerous, because once the ice has all melted, the oceans could get really hot, really fast. In any case, then the earth's temperature is going to continue to rise. Even if we never lit another fire, the earth would continue to heat. That energy would still be there. It would have to *do* something."

"Are you serious?"

"There's more to be afraid of than just radiation." The physicist cleared his throat. "That's all I'm saying."

The crowd that had formed around him dispersed.

⊙ ⊙ ⊙

Renya ambled toward another assembled group. "I'm excited to be here," a woman was saying. "I'm looking at many components of course, but I'll be paying special attention to sulphur."

"Right, because the shipping rules are changing," said a bespectacled colleague, a small-animal person Renya recognized vaguely.

"International shipping regulations haven't changed yet," the woman was saying, "but change is coming. Already companies are reducing the sulphur content of their shipping fuel because they're anticipating it too. I'm excited to see the consequences in the soil. I'm hopeful to see soil health and soil quality coming back again."

Renya edged away. Her project was so different from all the other research conducted here.

⊙⊙⊙

"I've published extensively," said the man, Robert, from the name tag hanging limply from his neck, large-animal, immune systems and broad-spectrum antibiotics, in smaller print just below. She'd been in the gathering for five minutes and she'd already been cornered. *Typical.* She'd almost rather listen to terrifying physics. "If you're interested, you should probably read through my work. You can find many articles online."

Renya looked at his face again, closely this time. She wasn't particularly interested, she wanted to tell him. She'd just been making conversation. Instead, she smiled. He smiled back of course, then looked away. The smile was forced, no muscles by the eyes activated. He looked down at her chest, but that wasn't surprising given his age, mid-fifties, likely. Sweat beaded on his forehead. The leer, when it appeared, seemed more dominance-based than carnal, but that made sense too. *But it's a compliment. Ladies are gracious in accepting any kind of good feedback. Professionals don't take these things so seriously.*

"You can order my books on Amazon," Robert was saying.

"I might do that," said Renya. She probably wouldn't.

"It's probably a good idea. You should, of course, have done the research before coming."

"Right." Because she needed to know about the immune systems of cows to go about her own work. Also, she was vegetarian. "I'll get right on that."

Robert's procerus and supercilii activated, drawing down the skin in his upper forehead, pulling his eyebrows in turn, but the scowl was gone fast. His eyes darted to the corners of the room and back again, feigning disinterest, but the sweat gave him away. He'd forgotten to inactivate the depressor labii inferioris in his chin so he was still pouting a bit. He noticed her interest and his smile reappeared fast.

"Good then," he said, his forced smile getting more and more ghoulish. "When you do, I'd be happy to discuss my work further." The expression, the body language, were clear. He wanted dominance-submission. He was trying to play the virile academic to her little-girl student. Forget it. She'd done it before. She'd had to do it a lot. There was no reason to do it now. She'd made it to Chornobyl. She'd gotten what she wanted.

"I'll review the material and decide," she said.

That got his attention. His dilator naris fired, causing his nostrils to flare. *Ha. Got you, doctor big-man academic.* He looked at her, finally, straightening to maximize the height difference between them. She smiled, looking straight into his eyes. *Who are you to me*, she telegraphed. *I'm short, but I'm smart, and you can't make me feel little.* He stiffened. Then she batted her eyes and he relaxed. It was remarkable how well that worked. Nick, for all his faults, was the only academic she'd known who hadn't fallen for the cute little schoolgirl doe-eyed routine. He used to help her sometimes, setting up the older guys and then playing straight man as she tore them down. And then they both smiled demurely until all was forgiven. The first time was almost an accident. He'd had an inkling, apparently, before one winter symposium, so he gave her a paper to read beforehand. You can't be married to a physicist for so many years and not know how to read a derivation, and the holes were in fact easy to spot. She hadn't needed his help with it at all, and, in his defense, he hadn't offered. Then at the cocktail party later, he'd lured the poor author into a conversation, let him condescend to her about 'soft science' first, and then lip gloss of all things, then let Renya ask pointed question after pointed question about math that didn't quite work out, but "maybe it was just her soft science experience," while Nick laughed into a napkin. Oh but that memory stung now. Thinking about Nick as an ally and all the games they used to play gave her an uncomfortable pang in her heart, and then that, of course, let loose an avalanche of other feelings. Why did she have to miss him? She blinked and made herself remember other incarnations of Nick: kneeling down to tell her about the affair, raging red-faced and slamming doors, hanging onto the doorpost pale and shaking, struggling to breathe, but no, that one didn't fuel her anger or self-righteousness or whatever emotion she was after. She shook her head, human-kaleidoscope style, and the images vanished.

Robert inched away and moved on into the room. He'd probably been trying to get away from her for a while. She made way for him.

She looked around.

This particular gathering was in the dining room. Well-dressed people were milling awkwardly on worn-out carpets, whispering to each other, clearly preferring to be alone. Many seemed to know each other. They all studied animals and soil and plants, and had probably run into each other at conferences. Renya didn't particularly want to be here either. She pulled at her jacket. Hiking chic was hard to pull off. They were all wearing the same tricked-out outdoor gear and sports jackets anyway though, just another type of uniform since they'd had to drop the lab coats, so she shouldn't have worried so much when she was packing. Anyway, clothes were beside the point. Worrying about how she looked was a waste of time. She was in Chornobyl, for God's sake. This was a once-in-a-lifetime chance, and she had no intention of coming back again. She'd rather be outside, exploring, or yelling at Nick, maybe, or composing angry emails in her head.

She scanned the room and everyone looked bizarrely familiar, like weird versions of the people she already knew. Except, there in the back corner, she spotted Tiv, a wolf researcher she'd sat with on the plane on the way here. He looked cornered and uncomfortable too.

There was one person who looked like someone she would want to meet, a twinkly eyed woman in the corner, who seemed to notice her too. She walked quickly toward her. She was Claire, according to the name tag. She had dark hair cascading down her shoulders. She seemed nice and gave the impression of being very honest, somehow. Renya approached, uncrossing her arms, working on open body language, to match Claire's.

"So you must be someone's kid," said Claire as they met in the centre of the room.

Renya stopped. She flushed all over. Five minutes in and she was already found out. She was usually better than that.

"Oh, I don't mean anything by it," Claire said before Renya could formulate a response. "I'm also someone's kid. My dad's a chair of stuff in California."

"My dad's a physics head in Canada," said Renya. "How did you know?"

"You're psychobiology, right? From what I understand, you're taking pictures of people taking soil samples. But this is a pretty dangerous place for that. And you jumped in last-minute. Someone had to buy your ticket."

Renya hadn't thought to google the list. She should have. She was going to be stuck with these people for a while. "I got lucky," she said. "I had an idea, and the funding committee jumped. The family name certainly helped me get the meeting though. And you're . . ."

Claire tapped at her name tag. "Oh, I'm birds all the way. But not these ones, necessarily. They're cool, but not the endgame."

"You have an endgame." Renya was living minute by minute, it seemed, especially lately. Even this project was just practical. She'd stumbled on the idea, and run with it, run off. If she were to be honest, she'd mainly only wanted the travel grant.

"I'm teaching myself to be cool in dangerous places," said Claire. "That's why I'm here." She gave Renya a hard look. She was smiling, sure, but the muscles along her lower jawline contracted to bare teeth, barely perceptible, but there if you knew to look. Renya, for all her faults, knew to look.

"Have we met before?" Claire asked.

"I don't think so." Renya had the impression that she was being tested, but she couldn't imagine what the parameters of the examination might be. Should she adjust to meet this too? Should she act playful but with an edge? Could she pull that off? Debatable. She could be edgy, she knew, but she wasn't very good at controlling it. Sometimes she could veer toward meanness accidentally. She didn't want to be mean. "I think I'd remember you," she said.

Claire's eyes widened, frontalis muscles activating to raise her eyebrows. That was surprise. You couldn't fake that. Well, you could, but the expression looked very real, and it would be hard to simulate that realistically.

Renya shrugged. She didn't know what Claire was looking for. "You're really pretty," she said. "And you seem fun. I think I'd remember if we'd talked before."

Claire's expression seemed to soften. Renya detected surprise again, but of a gentler sort. Could this be what disarmed looked like? Renya had never seen it, but that wasn't altogether surprising since she was usually wearing a lab coat. Lab coats usually kept people on edge. Even other scientists didn't tend to relax around them.

But Claire's shoulders raised again. "We haven't seen each other at Mensa?"

"Hasn't the idea of IQ been pretty thoroughly debunked?" And then Renya remembered where she was, who she was talking to, and that she *liked* this woman. "You must belong!" Oh God, she was always talking first, thinking after. These people postured, and sometimes you had to buy in to fit in, and it was fine if Claire believed in Mensa. "There's a lot of merit in those organizations, I mean, it's a place to, I don't know, have conversations and meet like-minded –"

"They're nonsense," said Claire, laughing.

Renya paused. She looked carefully at Claire's smile, straight at the zygomaticus major, no messing around. They were activated, pulling Claire's mouth into a smile. The muscles around her orbicularis oculi were activated too. That showed serious amusement. She'd bet on it. It wasn't just wishful thinking.

"My dad made me join when I was ten," Claire was saying. "Only child syndrome. I'm first-gen too. My parents are from Brazil. It was all a perfect storm meaning I had to be a prodigy and all that. I know how little it's all worth. I wanted to know about you. I saw how you were making Bob sweat just now."

"I don't mean to do those things," said Renya. "I mean, I do mean to, obviously, since I do it. I can get mean when I'm offended, or when someone's trying to embarrass me. I'm not proud of it though, that's what I'm saying."

"Every time I run into Bob, he congratulates me on my tan," said Claire, "usually in front of many people. I don't have a tan. This is what I look like. I'm not white, get it?"

"Oh no."

"So you can make him sweat," said Claire. "I have no problem with it."

"I will then," said Renya. "I mean, I'm sorry he does that."

Claire was smiling broadly now. "I think we're going to be friends," she said.

"I would like that," said Renya. She really did want to be this person's friend. But probably the old cues weren't going to cut it. There were no little espresso places with exposed walls. Claire didn't seem like the kind of person who would be impressed if there were. Maybe that was just a Toronto tick anyway, and maybe a bit dishonest since Renya secretly didn't mind chains. She could try something difficult: vulnerability. "I want to show you something," Renya said. She was a weird person and could be honest about that part too. This could backfire easily. But she hadn't come all the way here to leave unchanged. She turned and hoped that Claire would follow.

⊙⊙⊙

When Claire saw the vending machine in the little basement alcove, she laughed. It was a pure sound, like a wind chime. Renya liked her even more. "I can't believe it," she said.

"There's a thing I can't figure out though," said Renya. "Someone has to fill it."

"They're going to have to fill it more often now. I could live on Fanta." Claire fished coins out of her pocket and jingled them into the little slots. The machine rumbled and spat out a can with a hard thump. She sat cross-legged on the floor. "It's such a weirdly normal thing to find here."

"It's disconcerting," said Renya.

"Yes!" said Claire. "It's like life didn't just end here. But it did. Normal things shouldn't be able to just happen, shouldn't be able to just coexist. You can't just have ordinary soda machines that people come in and fill."

"And take out the money," said Renya, sitting beside her. "Does some Coca-Cola person really come to replace the cans? Does the company actually come all the way to Chornobyl? I mean Chernobyl," she amended, pronouncing the name the Russian way, the way all the scientists seemed to.

"You've been exploring too?" said Claire.

"I've walked through the halls a bit," said Renya.

Claire's frontalis muscles activated, raising her eyebrows questioningly.

"Okay," said Renya, "yes, I've opened all the doors that were unlocked."

Claire smiled. The skin beside her eyes crinkled prettily.

"I've snooped on every floor," Renya went on. "I've scoped out just about everywhere. I'm a child that way. I even rifle through drawers."

"I knew we would be friends." Claire was smiling widely now. Her orbicularis oculi had contracted even more, and her eyes were joyful crescents. That was what Duchenne called a true smile. That was textbook. "You're going to have to call me Clairesie now. It's a bit ridiculous, but neither of us has a choice."

"I have to call you Clairesie all the time?"

"Nope." Claire took a long drink. "You'll know when. So what is your research? I know that you're taking our pictures. I know that you're hiding. You've hidden cameras in the common spaces."

"Just entrances and exits, mostly," said Renya. "Not in your labs, obviously. Well, there are cameras outside the labs, but they point out, not in."

"What are you looking for?"

"Fear."

"Like this face," Claire said, making a mock-horror expression.

"That's the one," said Renya.

"We all make the same face?" said Claire. "I mean, when we're scared?"

"Mostly," said Renya. "I mean, there are always exceptions, and there are some small differences across ages and cultures, but by and large, we do. When you get scared, you trigger the amygdala, and that tends to release stress hormones like cortisol, for example, and adrenaline, and that gets your nervous system ready, and your body ready, to react. You can run really quickly. You breathe faster. Blood transfers to systems that need it more. Energy gets rerouted to your limbs. You get twitchy. Your corrugator supercilii muscles activate to let more light into your ocular system. So your eyes get really wide. You can almost see in the dark. All this activates predictable muscles, mainly in the forehead and face, so you can look for it. It's super fun. Fear itself is really fun. People often consider that there are six basic emotions, but fear is by far my favourite." Renya stopped, aghast at how much she'd been talking. It was like she was an overexcited undergrad again. She looked at Claire, but Claire seemed interested, if anything. That would be generous, if true.

"I read that fear produces dopamine too," Claire said.

"Yes!" said Renya. "It can cause pleasure, after. There are fear-chasers around."

"Are you one?"

"Well, by definition," Renya started, but then she stopped herself, understanding the question. "Oh! No! I chase fear *expressions*. I don't go after the emotion itself, except in little ways. I don't skydive or anything."

Claire laughed at this. "Academics," she said. "I'm like that too."

"I also look for short expressions or emotional slips," said Renya. "I slow down the camera to look through the thousands and thousands of stills, and I try to find the emotions that people are hiding, all those times that we slip up and show emotions that we normally don't want people to see, and I try to catch them before people can self-correct. We're socialized to put on a mask of calm, and, well, smiling happiness, most of the time. But sometimes the mask slips. I look for those moments. Well, I wrote a program to do that last part. Some of the displays can last seconds, so you can only really find them if you slow down the shots on high-speed cameras. So that's my project. I'll be tailing you guys and taking high-speed photo bursts to track emotional displays. But we're in Chernobyl. This place is scary by definition. I'll be focusing on fear."

"What will you do if you find it?"

"I'm trying to catch patterns," said Renya. "When we're working we tend to get into a flow state, of sorts. I record instances when we break out of the flow. I'm looking at what causes the breaks, and how often they happen, and for how long. I'm trying to find shifts in emotion and mood, so I can work backward to see what caused it. I'm working on the historical case as well. I've got a bunch of the old video feeds and pictures from the time of the accident." Renya was talking too much. She couldn't seem to stop, however. "Emotions are so useful. We have them for a reason. Charles Darwin called them adaptive, and I believe that. They're evolutionary. Sadness brings people closer to us. If you cry, people come and investigate and see what's upset you. It's hard-wired. Fear gives us bursts of energy to help us think quickly and solve problems and get our bodies to safety. Patterns in fear can give you a hint of what's happening in the wider world. We can use them to trigger red flags. If too many people are all afraid all at once, then there's clearly an issue. We have computers and cameras now, so I'm going to use those new tools to sort of push the adaptive use of emotions."

"I think the same way," said Claire. "Birds are useful to study too. Natural habitats also. They're interesting in and of themselves, but you can learn from them in so many contexts. You can see patterns. You can use those patterns to guess at other things and to get a wider understanding."

"What's your project?" said Renya. "What do you expect to see?"

"I'm studying sparrows, barn swallows, shrikes, warblers and some others," said Claire. "We're tracking them through the years to see how the subsequent generations deal with the radiation, because of course they have shorter lifespans, so generations go fast for them. But I'm keeping an eye out for larger patterns as well, not just birds, and not just radiation. I'm looking at their wider world as well. You might think that I'm overthinking, or overreacting, but I think that things are changing everywhere. I think that red flags are being raised whether we're recognizing them or not."

"What do you think you'll find?" said Renya.

"We've been finding smaller brains and a couple of genetic anomalies. I've seen a bit of altered behaviour. But we see them thriving too, living in a mostly human-free environment, so it's tricky. on strange findings in populated cities too though. I don't think that I'll find that much difference between Chernobyl and other built-up spaces. There are alarms *I* want to sound, to be honest. You talked about red flags. I want to put up red flags too."

"Wouldn't this place be quite different?" said Renya. "It's been destroyed. It's irradiated."

"We're blowing things out on a big scale."

"You mean in the whole world?"

"I'm just starting to understand it."

"You're talking about climate change?" she said. "Like that physicist."

"It's not just the climate. It's everything. It's much worse than I originally thought. That's what I think that I'm finding. This project is just a little piece of the puzzle. Just like one person's one emotion is just one part of their bigger emotional life."

Renya took a sip of her drink and sat back. That was true. One emotion *was* just a facet of a whole emotional life. She nodded as if that were a common consideration for her. Emotional life wasn't something that she thought about very often. She tended to hyperfocus too much for that.

Already, this trip was mind-altering.

Renya looked up. Claire was watching her sidelong. "I'm sorry I was so prickly just now," she said quietly, "asking about your dad and Mensa and all that. Sometimes I get nervous when I meet new people. I've always been like that. I don't mean anything by it."

Renya shook her head. She didn't know what to say. She really did want to be Claire's friend. "Don't worry about it," she said at last. "And now we're friends, so that sort of thing is allowed."

Claire grinned. She stood. "Do you want to explore?"

Renya scrambled to her feet. She absolutely did. Happiness might not be her top emotion to study, but it had its merits.

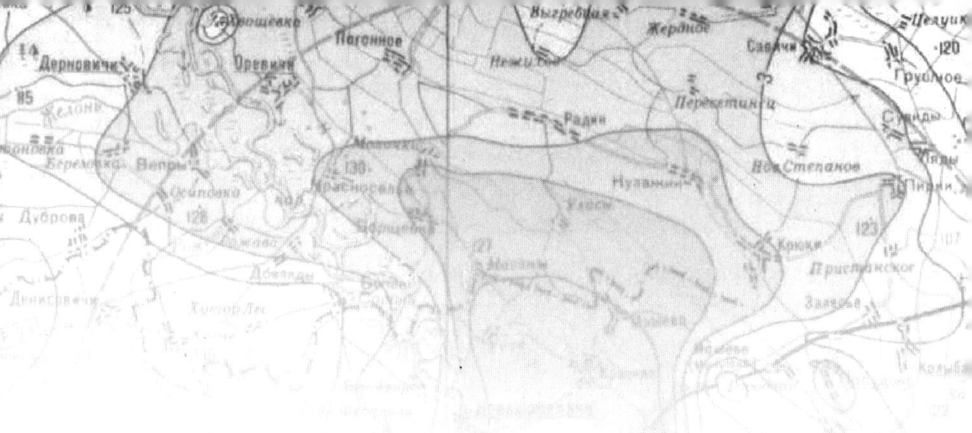

CHAPTER 2

RENYA COULDN'T REMEMBER HAVING FALLEN ASLEEP THE previous night, and the morning had come astonishingly quickly. She'd opened her eyes to a straining daylight, purple as an old bruise, and to a bleating alarm.

She filled her cup with the sludgy coffee from the decanter. The cups in the dining room were the tiny, hotel variety. She'd need a dozen refills. She considered just bringing one of the pots to a table with her to save time. She squeezed her notebooks under her armpit, and balanced her cup on her plate to see if she could carry the decanter too.

"You're up early," said a voice behind her. She wheeled around to find a sandy-haired man that she vaguely remembered from the orientation, and also from the gathering the night before. Had they spoken?

"I'm not surprised that you're up too," she ventured. Maybe if she threw him off balance, then they'd feel equally awkward.

"I was sure you'd be the sleeping-in type," he countered.

"I was hoping to walk around the grounds." And she was hoping not to run into anyone this morning before she went out, hence the early alarm. "Recon. You know."

The man chuckled, not entirely pleasantly. Renya bristled, but she couldn't put her finger on why. She was feeling that old red flag emotion, but she couldn't explain it. This man looked a bit like Nick. Charlie,

Physics, Radiation, read the name tag. Nick wouldn't know this person, surely. People here were researching practical questions and applications. Nick was as theoretical as they came.

Renya looked down, hoping to find her own name tag dangling, but of course she'd forgotten to put it on. The pastry she'd been struggling to hold steady on her plate wobbled. She straightened to keep her notebook clinched under her arm.

"Don't worry," said Charlie. "Renya. I remember."

"Oh." Renya looked around. Men at a nearby table were watching her with guarded expressions. She surveyed the room. Tiv, the kind man with the big family that she'd met on the plane on the way here, was sitting by himself in a corner by the window. He was watching her too. He seemed to be holding his breath. Again, that unquantifiable danger signal sounded.

"I know your husband," Charlie said suddenly.

Renya's coffee sloshed in her mug. She put everything on the table. She just wanted to get outside.

"Women always forget the name tags. Usually sleep in a bit more too, don't you? Need that beauty sleep?"

Keep your sense of humour, Renya thought bitterly. Can't you take a joke? Well ha-fucking-ha. Beauty sleep. Priceless. This wasn't how adults were supposed to talk to each other.

Nick might have met this man, but they couldn't be close. Strange vibes aside, this was all too *applied* for Nick.

"Come, you can sit with us." Charlie gestured to a table. "Regale us with your observations."

"That's too kind." Renya pulled away, grabbing her things and in the process spilling her coffee again, this time on her shirt. She wished she had some kind of retort for the beauty sleep bit. But she was more tired now, if anything, and she didn't particularly want to be baited. She just wanted to get on with the day. "I just realized that I forgot my good lenses," she said. "I'm going to eat in my room, then run. Nice to see you again this morning, Charlie."

Men weren't all like this, she reminded herself. Scientists weren't all like this. She'd have to cast around for another group. It was best not to be too isolated. She'd think about it later.

⊙⊙⊙

Renya walked farther out into the woods. She tugged at her shirt, damp still from where she'd scrubbed off coffee. She was still getting used to the thick and starchy material, the hiking aesthetic. She'd somehow expected, before receiving the packing list, that there would be industry-standard clothes, or that someone might have invented a spray to ward against radiation. Nobody had. The intro package had suggested snuggly-fitting hiking clothes with closely woven materials, closed toe shoes, that was all. She'd felt exposed when she'd first arrived, but she was getting used to it now.

She carefully followed the grid that she held out in front of her like a talisman. So far, her forays into the woods had seemed fairly anticlimactic. She hadn't expected two-headed animals and glowing trees, but maybe she'd been hoping for them. The red forest was apparently more dramatic, but that was in the inner zone, and she had neither the permit nor the courage to go there. You needed a special vehicle anyway, from what she understood, with properly sealed windows and doors, and with strict anti-contamination protocols, to protect the passengers from the intensity of the radiation. This forest seemed listless but devoid of freaks.

She stopped to kick at a tuft of grass. She rifled with her foot to look for damaged things, but she didn't find anything obviously deformed. She shouldn't disturb stuff, she knew. She shouldn't risk aerosolizing anything she didn't want to breath in. But she wanted to see closer. Maybe she was safe. Maybe she didn't want to be. She'd always erred on the side of caution. In science, you can test multiple hypotheses, but she'd only had one youth to play with, so it wasn't her fault she couldn't figure out how to live it. Nick was also better at visualizing outcomes. He'd never felt the need to play it safe.

Renya spotted a family of wildflowers. She crouched down to examine them, then touched each one lightly. Again, there were no visible irregularities. But it was still exciting. Even though the forest didn't look like she'd expected, even though she hadn't seen mangled trees or weirdo plants all growing with their roots in the air, just being here, just seeing it first-hand, was thrilling. She was in a place where very few people were allowed to come. She touched a blade of grass. It looked inert. It wasn't inert. It was living its own life, going through its own biological functions. What had the climate guy said last night? It was absorbing the sun's energy. It was working hard at photosynthesis, at the same time reradiating some energy back in infrared. It had its own experience of radiation, even though countless generations had come and gone since the explosion from its frame of reference. She touched the soil lightly. It was sandy and dry. It had its own understanding too, but it wasn't telling.

From her backpack, her old dosimeter popped suddenly, loud and arrhythmic. That was an indication of very elevated radiation. It was the strongest reaction she'd heard so far. She froze, her heart thumping. Pieces of the destroyed reactor had been buried in the earth, but not this far from the accident site, surely. Renya shifted. The dosimeter's alarm screeched. She shot to her feet and darted down the path. The alarm wailed.

Renya forced herself to stop. Not everything had to be regular. Nature couldn't want predictability. Butterflies bounced erratically to evade predators, so there must be at least a bit of evolutionary merit in oddity. And hadn't she just been hoping for signs of radiation? She noted the dosimeter reading, then jotted it down on her map, along with the time of observation. She walked forward one step, then another. Then the alarm stopped and the readings went back to normal. She moved to the left, then to the right, but it didn't go off again.

She didn't want safety, she reminded herself. She wanted change. She'd come here for a life change or a personality change or something. Risk was good. Her heart was galloping. Her fingers were buzzing with adrenaline.

She saw a shift in the grass. But nothing appeared. There were no more rustles. She walked on. Her dosimeter popped faster. She adjusted the map and noted the reading and time of observation again. After a while, the popping slowed.

Renya found some flora researchers and hid behind a yellowing deciduous tree. She uncapped her camera and snapped shot after shot. The men were crouched in the dirt, engaged in some kind of conversation although Renya couldn't hear them well enough to even discern the language. They'd taken off their face masks. Theirs had probably all broken too. She'd planned to work around the masks and to focus on the muscles around the eyes, but nobody was wearing them. She breathed carefully through her nose. The masks helped if they worked, but the government-issued ones were shitty and constantly snapping. She should have thought to bring her own. She wondered if the other scientists were nervous too. They didn't seem anxious currently.

One man stood up. He stretched his back. Renya focused on his face and snapped shot after shot. He turned to talk to the colleague still crouched on the ground. He was smiling, for sure. His zygomaticus major and minor muscles were activated, pulling up the corners of his mouth, tilting his lips into a crescent. But his eye muscles weren't stimulated at all. It wasn't a true smile. Renya had a student who called these lying smiles. Renya herself wouldn't label them as that. Some people used facial expressions for communication. Others smiled for social reasons like putting people at ease or making them feel good about their work or contributions to conversation. Still others smiled because of mimicry, and mimicry was a very natural response. But this certainly wasn't an emotional expression. It wasn't a voluntary smile. It wasn't triggered by endorphins, by neuronal signals. Those lit up full faces, activating a much wider array of muscles. But there was no fear anyway that she could detect. The man crouched down again.

She carefully focused her camera on one face and then on the next, and then snapped more pictures. She got full faces. They'd be easy to read. There was still no fear, that she could readily discern anyway. She'd have to run through the shots later to see if there were any subtle signs, or any short displays or so-called seepage. Her computer program could take care of that for her. She could easily have caught unguarded moments and just not noticed. She was just as interested in micro-expressions, the emotions that the scientists were trying to hide. In most of the pictures, the men were smiling though, broadly, it seemed to her, whether they were true smiles or not.

They weren't supposed to eat or drink outside, so she came back for lunch, sat by herself at the small table by the window and unwrapped a stale sandwich.

⊙ ⊙ ⊙

"Where are you really?" said Nick. His face on the computer screen seemed drawn, a rehearsed neutral. But unreadable was an expression too, especially if your wife studies emotional displays. "Are you really in the exclusion zone?"

"It's repopulated now," she said, "did you know that?" She wished she could stop calling him. She wished she could just stay offline or talk to someone else. When had she lost all the other people she used to confide in? She hadn't even been married for that long. Six years was nothing.

"That's not safe, that's behind –"

"Five hundred people come and go," she said. "Mostly scientists, some resettlers, apparently, off the grid, although I don't know if I believe that."

Nick raked a hand through his hair. "The effects of radiation are cumulative, Renya. The more you're exposed, the greater the chance of problems down the line."

"There's a hotel that's been turned into a research station. That's where we're staying. That's where we conduct the research too, obviously, or where the other teams house the equipment. There are labs in converted ballrooms, very postapocalyptic. The background radiation is a bit elevated, but apparently just above average for parts of Europe. We don't eat the local vegetables."

Nick got down on his knees. He leaned closer to the computer, which he'd set up on the coffee table, she noticed. "What do you hope –"

"I had an idea for a postdoc. Another one, I mean. A better one. I told you."

"The fear idea, I know, but you wouldn't really go. Would you? You could research that from here."

Renya reached for the disconnect button.

"Stop!" Nick was reaching, as if he could touch her hand. Something about the gesture was oddly familiar. It brought her back to their early days as a couple, to when they'd just started dating. "I just – I can't believe you'd really go there."

"You don't give me much credit. You don't think I'm capable of being brave."

"Of course I think you're brave."

"You think I have no drive, no ideas."

"I'm the one who has no original ideas."

"What are you talking about? All our conversations are about *your* career, *your* advancement, *your* place in your department."

"That's what I'm saying." Nick's hands had disappeared. Was he holding the computer? "I'm just following what other people do," he was saying. "My research is nothing original. You're the one who does new things. We both know that you were spinning your wheels, waiting for your next big idea. We both know that you're the one to watch."

Renya was taken aback. "How do we both know that?"

"You're the one who thinks you aren't brave."

"Fuck that."

"Just – I'm sorry. Maybe I wasn't as supportive as I should have been. Maybe I wanted to have big ideas too, so I downplayed yours. I am proud of you though. I know I should have said it more often."

And there it was. There's what she'd wanted him to say, for years, it felt like, forever. And he'd just said it? Renya opened her mouth. She closed it again. She'd wanted him to say that so badly, to admit to that exact thing, and now that he said it, she felt like she'd had the wind knocked out of her.

"Just promise . . ." he said.

"I don't have to do anything," she said quietly. "I don't have to promise you anything." She looked at him, at his searching face, then down at her own hands. She had no idea what to say or what to do now. "Anyway, I have to go."

"Can we talk later?"

"Maybe." Renya slammed the computer shut and found herself balancing with her elbow on the door as she pulled on her sneakers.

She didn't think she was a coward. Her series of safe and boring postdocs, her focus on Nick's career, that hadn't all been her own fault. But maybe it had been, at least partly. Maybe she *had* thought she was a coward. She hadn't thought she was a person who would actually take off and fly anywhere, never mind to an irradiated place. But here she was.

⊙ ⊙ ⊙

Renya jogged out into the forest so fast she felt air fill up the hood of her sweatshirt. She felt a boiling in her stomach. Eighty-three percent of respondents in that *Lancet* thing she'd just read reported feeling anger in their lower torso or bowels. That made sense. Anger caused increased blood pressure. It released adrenaline and noradrenaline. Anger diverted blood from the stomach area and digestive tract to get people ready for physical action. So she'd be physical. She ran faster.

Renya focused on the sound of her sneakers on the gravel. She watched the blurred greens and spindly trees wheel past her. She was angry. She was mad because Nick was dismissive. He didn't believe she could do it. He said he did just now, but he'd never said that before. No, she was mad because of the woman. No.

She paused, grabbed a tree and leaned against it for a moment as she stilled her breathing. The rough bark tickled at her forehead. Nick had admitted that he downplayed her accomplishments. He'd told her that he was proud of her. She'd wanted him to say those things, and now he had, and where was she supposed to go from here?

She felt hollow. She held on to the little tree.

Nick never watched documentaries with her. She kicked at the soft gravel and rocked the stones back and forth under her sneakers. That was an absurd reason to be angry. But she'd gone to all his functions, event after event after dinner after boring terrible gala, and never once admitted that she was miserable, and he wouldn't even watch a TV show. She watched his shows. He hadn't apologized for not watching hers. That was a ridiculous thought.

Renya took a deep, steadying breath, and launched herself off from the tree, jogged off the path this time. She couldn't be angry because of television-watching habits. She couldn't be that petty.

It had always been so easy to lie to herself. This was something that had always been on the periphery of her thoughts. Emotions were hard. Emotional honesty was harder.

⊙ ⊙ ⊙

Renya was hoping to find Claire at the vending machine, and there she was, sitting with a Fanta, her laptop open on her lap. Claire shut the computer with a pop, slid it into her backpack and scrambled to her feet. "We should explore," she said, gesturing to a hallway.

Renya followed. She had to jog to catch up. "What do you really want to research?" she said. "What are your endgame birds?"

"The demilitarized zone," said Claire, swinging down the staircase at the end of the hall.

"North Korea?"

"There isn't a place in the world that's that level of undisturbed," she said, looking up. "Nothing can touch it."

"There are also people who point guns."

"I'm learning to deal with difficult situations."

"Nuclear wasteland first, then war zone?"

"I'll cheers to that." And she amiably held up her Fanta can, dinged at the corner and shining brightly in the fluorescents. "My family wants me to go to the Amazon. That's where we're from. I don't know about that though."

"There are a lot of dangers there too," said Renya.

"Indeed."

"What do you think you'll find in all these places?"

Claire stopped at the bottom of the staircase. She pushed hair out of her eyes. "I think I'll find that we're on a trajectory. The undisturbed places are earlier on the journey, and this place is later, but we're all headed to the same place. I think that I'll find that birds are changing everywhere. Maybe life is changing everywhere. Birds are the canary in the coal mine. Ha!"

"Oh," said Renya. "That's interesting. You have perspective."

Claire laughed.

"Really though," said Renya. "I don't. I hyperfocus and forget to zoom out. In fact, nobody I know zooms out. We all get lost in the details. It's neat to meet someone with a wider view."

"I don't know that I had a wider view before I came here," said Claire.

"Sharing space with all these different disciplines helps," said Renya.

Claire and Renya wandered in silence, down another hallway, then another hidden staircase, before they finally came to a stop in a hallway Renya hadn't seen before. Claire opened a double set of wooden doors with a flourish. Inside, they found a giant, open room, easily four times the size of any of Renya's old student apartments. Like in all the other rooms in this place, the wallpaper was sun-bleached and stained, faded to a sickly orange, the floral patterns faded to almost white. The wooden floor was scuffed and marked. Renya crept farther inside. Drafts came from unknown sources and made the giant glass chandelier sway gently. It was as old and decrepit as all the other spaces she'd visited here, but it gave a hint of this station's former life. It must have been glorious. She could almost feel the balls that had been held here.

"This is beautiful," said Renya, touching the ornate fixtures.

"I thought all the big spaces had been converted to labs," said Claire, "but then I found this."

Renya walked to the giant table in the middle of the room. Her footsteps echoed eerily. "Something about this place reminds me of a church."

Claire turned sharply. "Do you go to church?"

"I did as a kid. It was fraught though. It was a community thing, and my stepmother was into it, but my father and I were both Jewish."

"Do you believe in God?"

"I don't know," said Renya. "You?"

"I went to church as a kid too," said Claire, turning away abruptly. "How do you deal with the off time?" she said, half-facing a window. "How do you get through the nights here?"

Renya's finger froze on the table. She shouldn't touch things anyway. She wiped her hands on her pants. "What do you mean?" she said. She'd been waking up in the middle of the night either worrying about Nick or raging at him. Surely, Claire couldn't mean that. How could she know? How loud had she been?

"I'm always happy during the day," said Claire. "But at night, I get scared. I get to thinking that I shouldn't have come. At night, I'm convinced I don't need to be doing this and none of it matters anyway."

"I have an outlet," said Renya. "I've been picking on my . . . on Nick. That's how I've been dealing so far, but I should find a better strategy."

"Picking on him how?"

"I don't know," said Renya. "I keep calling him." *I keep starting fights*, she didn't say. But Claire nodded as though she had.

"I keep calling my partner too. Do you talk at all? I mean, do you really get into things?"

"We argue."

"He doesn't think you should be here?"

"How did you know?"

"I suspect that none of our families think we should be here."

"I guess not," said Renya.

"Do you think we should be here?" Claire asked lightly.

"I'm trying really hard to believe that it's necessary." Emotions were not fundamental. They weren't fundamental forces. They weren't necessary to understanding life on earth, the laws of the universe or even the laws of people and how they interacted, not really. And yet she was drawn to them. She wanted so badly to understand them better. There were questions *she* needed to answer. Even if this was just for her, even if nobody else in the whole world would ever read her work, yes, it was needed. "It's hard to admit this," said Renya, "but I think it's necessary for me."

She turned to Claire, who'd turned back toward her and was nodding and smiling to herself. She seemed to understand.

"Do you think we should be here?" said Renya.

"I'm like you," said Claire. "I know that *I* need to be here."

"It's dangerous, but I don't always feel it," said Renya. "I know we're stuck, and we're on a bit of a hamster wheel of station to forest and back again, but I'm on a hamster wheel at home too. The world feels oddly bigger here."

Claire nodded, pausing to drink her Fanta again.

"Hey," Renya said after a moment. "I think it's not really done, but can I come with you for a bit some time? Check out your research? I'd love to see what you do."

Claire nodded again. "I'd like that," she said.

The world *was* bigger here.

⊙ ⊙ ⊙

After her walk with Claire, after Claire had retreated to her room, presumably to at least try to sleep, like a normal person, Renya still couldn't settle down. She wanted to explore. She grabbed a jacket and ran to the front door. She stepped out of the research station and froze. It was so dark.

A security light turned on and blasted the immediate area with a spotlight. Everything was white and grey with alarming dark shadows that seemed to outline each individual pebble. It felt like she could see the gravel in incredible detail. She forced herself to walk forward, down the path surrounding the hotel. If she stuck to gravel, she couldn't get lost. The light turned off again. She continued onward.

Night in the exclusion zone was absolute. It was like nothing she'd ever seen. There were no streetlights or lit houses. There was a forest and nothing else.

Claire was right. Nighttime hours bent and distorted everything. What had seemed essential in the day seemed foolish now. She couldn't figure out anything important here. She should never have left home. She should never have left physics. Her father was right. Nick was right. Physics was important. Their research was necessary. Her concerns were trite and trivial.

She rounded a corner and heard a bustle of voices. She stopped. Some of the scientists had gathered on the main porch. Claire was among them, on the periphery, talking to an aggressively beautiful woman in a fancy suit, and to that climate guy she'd listened to before. Maybe Claire couldn't sleep either.

Forget a night walk, Renya decided. She could just join them.

She climbed up the stairs hesitantly. She didn't want to interrupt. She didn't want to seem desperate for friendship from this woman who she did long to befriend. She hung back at the periphery.

"I'm interested in the Amazon too," the climate scientist was saying.

"It's not what it was," said Claire. "The clear-cutting changes everything."

"That's what I mean," the physicist said. "For me too. Clear-cutting changes the albedo. The albedo of the entire planet has changed. It's definitely all connected."

"Right, because different matters absorb energy differently," said one scientist.

"Colour would matter too," said another. "Different colours absorb and readmit differently."

"If you cut down that many trees, then the colour and makeup of the planet is different. That forest used to absorb the sun's energy. It used it!"

"Photosynthesis," said the beautiful woman, "but there are other processes too."

"Exactly."

"Now there's much less photosynthesis, for one thing. The amount of energy that gets absorbed versus what gets reflected is altered. The function of the absorption is altered. That's going to end up being important too."

"I'm looking at albedo too," said Claire's friend, "but from a soil degradation and weathering perspective, and what *that* does to the rate of absorption of solar energy."

"What are you finding?"

"I thought the soil would be improving," said the woman, "but that's not what I'm seeing at all."

Suddenly, Renya felt a cold hand around her forearm. She turned. Charlie, she saw. She smiled thinly. His front teeth caught the moonlight and made his smile look wolfish.

He thrust a drink into her hand. "Not too busy with your deep thoughts tonight," he said.

Renya opened the can. The beer was cold and tinny. She played with the condensation on her fingers. She could ask about his own "deep thoughts," but she didn't want to start an argument.

"I always see you puttering with your notebooks," he said. "It's very cute, of course."

Renya turned back again, to look for Claire and her friends, but Charlie took her arm again and squeezed. "Have you met our esteemed leader?"

Renya stepped back and brushed against another man, one she hadn't felt looming behind her. Telerson took her arm now. He squeezed, with a slightly unpleasant force.

"This is Walter Telerson," Charlie said lightly. Telerson didn't release her arm.

Renya felt her smile tighten. Still Telerson didn't let go. She looked around and noticed, for the first time, that she was surrounded by men. Claire and the other woman must have gone inside. The beer soured in her throat. How did she always get herself stuck like this?

"We've been introduced," she said quietly. She straightened, pulling down on her shirt. They'd met the first day. Telerson had introduced himself to everyone.

"But we haven't had a chance to get to know each other," said Telerson.

"This is Renya Eidelman," said Charlie. "Married to Nick Trotter, at Toronto."

"Oh sure," said Telerson, "I know Nick."

"Didn't take his last name though," Charlie was saying.

"Well, why would she? She's smart to keep her father's."

"Max Eidelman!"

"She's a smart cookie." And Telerson was standing even closer now. "Her father's name will give her much more power in scientific circles."

She'd always liked her last name. She wasn't playing games. Renya was moving backward slowly, backing up against the outer wall of the building. What could she say? What would a successful academic say? How would any grown-up woman respond to that? "It's spooky in the dark," she heard herself say. *Oh that was professional and grown-up.*

Renya made a fist around her beer can. She felt the cold metal in her hand crush a little. Her back was pressed against the wall now. She quickly took a deep drink and made herself cough and splutter. "I'm so sorry," she said, allowing Charlie to take her drink. "It must be the jet lag."

Telerson nodded, a looming presence above her, still way too close. "I've always said – it's hard on the female constitution."

"It must be," she said through gritted teeth. "In fact, I'd better go lie down." And she darted back to the door before they could take her arm again.

⊙ ⊙ ⊙

Renya eased quietly back inside and crept to her room. She quietly shut her door and locked it. She slid the deadbolt into place.

Then she lay down on her stomach on the threadbare carpet. She opened her computer and scanned through the results of the previous day's observations.

ALGORITHMIC OUTPUT

Target set: September 28, 2013 / Zone of alienation, outer ring, research centre interior

Dominants: happiness; fear

Displays discovered: happiness; disgust; fear

Statistics [fear expressions]:

Qualitative review of what was observed in the target-set material:
Target set includes video of researchers entering and exiting the centre on September 28.
Fear detected, sub-dominant, short duration/increasing from previous target set.

Fear made top-three today. That was interesting. Renya paused, finger on the screen. Until now, she'd seen mostly happiness, or, more specifically, excitement. She scrolled through the long-form report to see the raw data. The fear display durations were still not very long, especially compared to the other emotions detected. She didn't need to think about it too much then. The observation period for this project was ongoing anyway. She should work on the historical case first.

She arranged the laptop in front of her and called up the photographs. She had pictures and video feeds from the original Chornobyl accident, generously provided by the unnamed and unidentified suits from her funding meetings, acquired who knows how, and she was running them through her program as a proof of concept.

She'd put a batch of historical information into the system to run that morning, and the system seemed to have worked. It had generated red flags where she'd expected. Renya scanned through the detailed results. They weren't bad. The stats were off, obviously. The program still picked up all circular or oblong shapes and scanned them like they were faces, so that affected, what, number of individuals, percentage of fear responses? That was fixable. That should be fixable. None of the wall clocks displayed any facial muscle activation, so the glitch didn't affect any numbers that particularly mattered. It was lucky that she'd found the problem now, in fact, because it would have presented a major problem to her other project, the proposed road rage program: it wouldn't work well for anybody if subjects could just hold up a pumpkin to prove they weren't experiencing rage or anger. She'd figure out how to fix all that later. She'd enroll in more courses.

But the program had found fear. That was the important thing. It could calculate the number of individual fear displays, the length of the longest fear expression, the average duration. Even if the statistics, well, the percentages, were off, fear was fear, and these numbers could help, especially if you knew in advance how many faces there were supposed to be, and if you could program in the fear tolerance or expectation of the particular location.

She scrolled through the report. She just had to type in a description of the target set to finish the report.

She could also break the target set into smaller pieces and run each of them individually, to look at how the system worked with small time frames, and to confirm her thinking about the night of the experiment too. *Why not.*

She sat up and stretched. There was a dim sourceless light filtering in from the window, a lantern on an adjacent balcony maybe, and it was throwing long shadows that crept up the adjacent wall. And there was a hushed conversation from somewhere outside. Every few minutes, a raised voice boomed, though Renya couldn't make out any words.

She broke the target into discrete events. She ran the first.

ALGORITHMIC OUTPUT

Target set: April 26, 1986 / Chernobyl nuclear power station / scenery

---

Dominants: n/a

Displays discovered: n/a

Statistics [fear expressions]: scroll down

Qualitative review of what was observed in the target-set material:
Target set includes aerial pictures of the destroyed reactor of unit four, taken quite soon after the explosion, the fires still burning. The complex is seen from above. One side of the reactor has been destroyed, and concrete and steel spread outward. Subsequent close-up shots show a hole in the ceiling, visible reactor equipment, plumes of black smoke. There are no people in this video. The program detected no fear displays.

Renya opened the folder and looked through the pictures herself. Unit four looked like a toppled Lego building. It had crumbled. It looked unreal. She could see the giant ladders that scientists would run up shortly, to survey the damage. The pictures seemed to sizzle. The radiation had interfered with the film.

She hesitated, her fingers hovering over the keyboard. She should delete that last sentence. She shouldn't brag that the program hadn't detected people. That had only worked properly because of the magnitude of the destruction: the force of the blast had destroyed all regular shapes. Her program had scanned acorns before. It regularly zoomed in on clouds.

She decided to leave in the small victory. She'd fix the program later. She'd find a way. There would have to be a course for that, somewhere. She moved on to the next target set.

Renya pulled out her security stills. She'd been given some photographs of the night shift technicians on duty April 26. She scrolled through, just to look. In the first pictures, the technicians seemed calm, well, busy. One man looked excited, at least for the moment. She circled the subject, the clear zygomaticus activity, the corners of his mouth pulled out and up. The next pictures were grainy, but the expressions could still be made out. Many of the faces looked bored – at first glance anyway. Maybe, the technicians were posturing. There was a thrust-out jaw, some tensions in posture, but not much of note before the explosion.

ALGORITHMIC OUTPUT

Target set: April 26, 1986 / Chernobyl unit four / pre-explosion

---

Dominants: happiness

Displays discovered: happiness, excitement; limited zygomaticus area activation

---

Statistics [fear expressions]:

Qualitative review of what was observed in the target-set material:

Target set: unit four technicians, pre-explosion.

Subjects display some excitement, but show mostly neutral or neutral-leaning expressions.

Emotional display lengths estimated using time stamps.

The night shift shouldn't have had to deal with this. It wasn't supposed to be their problem.

The day shift technicians had devised the experiment. They'd planned to disconnect from the power grid, then stop the reactor to see if the reaction's own spin-down could power the cooling system. Usually they had backups, obviously. They wanted to know if they could stop the reaction without if they needed to. It was in case of attack, or in case of fighting in the area of the Chornobyl and Prypyat region. They suspected they could do it. The experiment itself wasn't considered particularly dangerous or controversial. They wanted to try it out, just in case, with a backup right there to plug the cooling system into, if needed.

But then there had been problems on the day that the experiment was set to take place. First, another power plant in the region had had to be shut down, so they couldn't afford to turn off reactor four and disconnect without causing local blackouts. So they pushed off the experiment to the night, when fewer people were awake, running fewer lights and appliances, so the whole thing went to the night shift. That explained the technicians' excitement in those photos, she'd hazard.

Renya skipped through the pictures of the night shift technicians, highlighting facial muscles, scribbling notes.

At the same time, the reaction itself had been acting oddly during the day. It had been generating extra by-products and not producing enough heat, so they, the day shift technicians that was, had had to make the reaction faster by adding more neutrons to split extra uranium atoms. They decided they'd make the night shift go ahead with the investigation anyway.

But then, that night, the experiment went wrong. The technicians were supposed to gradually decrease reactor four's power. But when they hit the target of five hundred megawatts, the power output suddenly dropped much lower, to about thirty megawatts. It could have gone down as low as three. That wasn't enough energy to power cooling. They couldn't let the system fail. They had to cool the reactor. If they let the reactor heat too much, the core could boil away all the water that surrounded it and expose the fuel rods. Then the fuel could meltdown, or go critical. The technicians scrambled to find a way to generate more power. Renya found the corresponding pictures. They weren't panicking. That was clear. But when she zoomed in on their faces, she saw that they were afraid. She circled the stress, the tension, the unmistakable fear.

ALGORITHMIC OUTPUT

Target set: April 26, 1986 / Chernobyl unit four / moment of explosion target set one

Dominants: fear

Displays discovered: fear; activity in supercilii muscle group

Statistics [fear expressions]:

Qualitative review of what was observed in the target-set material:
Target set shows technicians in the control room. Subjects display fear expressions. Action indicated. More information required.

Renya flipped to the next set.

The technicians were working at their consoles. They tried to get the power back up to normal levels. They tried to make the reaction run hotter again, so they could still power the cooling system. But then something happened. Maybe the by-products suddenly burned away. Renya wasn't sure. She didn't know if anyone knew for sure. The reactor's *output* spiked. It suddenly generated a massive amount of energy. The reactor exploded. Then, two or three seconds later, there was a second explosion. It knocked the steel and concrete lid right off the top. There were bits of reactor and graphite everywhere.

The people in the building didn't know that yet. They just knew that the world had moved under their feet. It had felt, technicians said later, like an earthquake.

And there it was, the startle. In the photos, the figures displayed wide eyes, wrinkled brows, arms out and reaching. The primary reaction was mainly in the limbs. First, the technicians' expressions were puzzled. There were some raised upper eyebrows. One man had tense lower lids. Next, they showed fear, so clearly that anyone could make it out. She circled the proof, the muscle activation clear in the pictures.

ALGORITHMIC OUTPUT
Target set: April 26, 1986 / Chernobyl unit four / moment of explosion target set two
Dominants: fear, terror
Displays discovered: fear; major activity in supercilii muscle group
Statistics [fear expressions]:
Qualitative review of what was observed in the target-set material: Technicians shown in control centre post-explosion. Subjects display extended and uniform fear expressions in a low tolerance area. **Action indicated. More information required immediately.**

Renya scrolled through the generated data. Sure, the stats were a bit off. There were a handful of people in that room, but the program had detected dozens. It had counted circles, like the clock in the corner, and the old-fashioned slightly rounded computer displays probably. Maybe it had counted coffee mugs. But the computer had detected fear, and because of the number of subjects, the uniformity of the emotional expression, the assumed length of the displays and the vulnerability factor of the location itself, it had generated a red flag.

She loaded the program's message: multiple scientists in a high-risk environment had displayed out-of-character facial expressions and body language that indicated fear; the number of targets and the duration of the fear expressions warranted further inquiry.

No joke.

She'd done it.

Here was precisely where the program would be useful. It would recognize fear expressions in technicians. It would find the safety signals, tolerances and protocols programmed for this particular location, and it would flag the situation for more observation. Then it, and the observers, would look for more input to confirm the theory that something had gone wrong. In this case, they'd have found the confirmation quickly enough, if the government had let them get close.

Renya scrolled through the rest of the pictures. She could do it right now. She could confirm accident status.

She loaded her next set.

In those pictures, the technicians were bent over consoles. Their faces showed hardly any muscular activation at all. That wasn't surprising. They had work to do. The fear that they would have felt would have manifested in tingling fingers and legs, the body readying to run, but their minds would have been engaged and on task. Fear manifests in the in-between times. The program would be primed and waiting for more unusual activity. There was sweat. Renya circled beads of sweat on foreheads. The program might be able to scan for these signals in newer pictures, taken with better cameras. She wrote a note to herself to program for sweat detection and body heat in general, if possible. She could compare these signals to assumed ambient temperature, presumably.

ALGORITHMIC OUTPUT

Target set: April 26, 1986 / Chernobyl unit four / moment of explosion target set three

---

Dominants: fear, terror

Displays discovered: fear; major activity in supercilii muscle group

---

Statistics [fear expressions]:

Qualitative review of what was observed in the target-set material:

Technicians shown in control room.

Subjects display extended and uniform fear expressions.

More information required immediately.

Her program had detected fear where she hadn't. *Huh.*

The next target set was harder to read if anything. Two of the technicians had left the control room. One might have walked up the ladder, to figure out what had happened. One said that he'd surveyed the site of the accident. The others left in the station were facing away from the camera. They'd be showing fear, then, Renya bet. They were just thinking, scanning through possibilities. They had nothing to do, so they would have been feeling their emotions. She couldn't find a shot of their faces. She might not want to see that anyway. That would be incredibly sad.

In the next series of pictures, the two missing technicians were back. When they got inside, they were tanned, she knew. The program wouldn't flag the radioactive tan, but it would find the expressions of the people who were seeing it. The technicians' mouths were stretched open, their teeth bared slightly. Those were expressions of grief and shock. Their colleagues were sitting back, their fingers lightly touching consoles, eerily still. Their friends and colleagues had a radioactive tan. They all knew what that meant, and you could see it on their faces.

ALGORITHMIC OUTPUT

Target set: April 26, 1986 / Chernobyl nuclear power station unit four / post-explosion

---

Dominants: fear expression; zygomaticus; corrugator supercilii; frontalis

---

Displays discovered: fear; sadness; grief

Statistics [fear expressions]:

Qualitative review of what was observed in the target-set material:

Technicians shown in control room.

Subjects display extended and uniform fear expressions.

Fear expressions exceed emergency upper-limit set for location. More information required. Urgent action requested.

Here was the bottom line: there was fear across enough people, across enough time, that her program had figured out that something was wrong and had flagged it. The flurry of unusual activity in the world around them after would sound multiple alarms too, hopefully. She'd see. She'd run those pictures too. If they'd had a program like this, the international community would have known to press for information. They could have known.

First reactions hadn't been what she'd been thinking when she pitched the idea, but that's where the interest lay. She'd figured that out at the initial funding meetings, all those suits asking questions, writing furiously in identical black notebooks. *How do you know if scientists have found something of concern? How quickly can you read the fear?* They were interested in scientists in private places, Renya had figured. How would the suits have access? There were bound to be security cameras in research facilities, yes, but they'd be closed-circuit surely. But who knew. That first funding meeting had happened fast, and she hadn't even been introduced to the men and women in fancy clothes at the table. She still had no idea who they were, from which organization they'd come. But she'd picked up on how they'd leaned forward, how none had even blinked. They must have weird access. Oddly, she found she didn't care.

Scientists would be the people to watch, she realized. Maybe the suits had been right. They'd know more than the news broadcasters. They understood the equipment, and they'd be able to zoom out and understand the broader implications of the problems they were witnessing. Maybe you always needed to find the people who understand the broader context.

The scientists in this facility right now were interesting, but maybe there were other people who would know more. She didn't have permission to spy on the people who worked within the research centre, like the cooking or cleaning staff, but maybe they'd be worth watching because they knew the area better. Maybe she could try to get permission. Maybe she could find a way to talk to them at the very least. She could also look into the security guards. The security guards could be the most interesting. Some had permission to get really close. Some even worked in Prypyat itself. They couldn't stay long, presumably, but they'd have noticed things. Noticing things was their job. Maybe she could find the security guard she'd noticed before. For some reason, she was drawn to seeing him again.

Anyway, the historical case was working. She'd found pictures. She'd run them through her program, and her program had created the appropriate alarm.

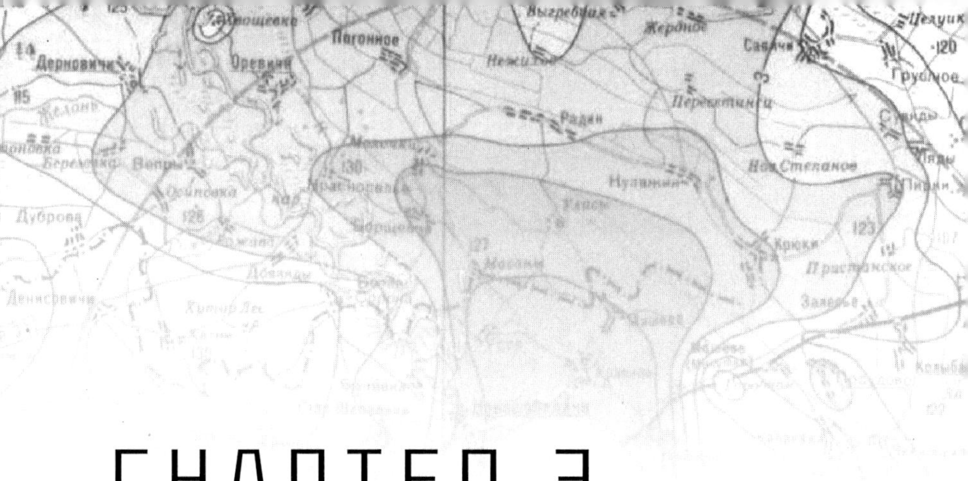

CHAPTER 3

THE NEXT MORNING, RENYA WOKE TOO EARLY AGAIN, SO SHE ignored her grid and walked back to the clearing that she'd found two days before. She found the area quickly, first the downed tree, and then the grove in which the man had stood. She lingered, kicking leaves and listening to the soft shush as they crumpled under her hiking boots. This wasn't like her, isolating a fear and worrying it. The man had been young, she thought now, but she was having trouble remembering details. He might have been handsome. He was different from these scientists anyway. He'd looked kind of feral. She was reminded of her life as a teenager, when she would sneak down the creaky stairs, ease open the front door and slip out of her house to meet up with the wild kids, the ones she'd met in the church basement, among other places.

And just then, Renya did see the person from the other morning. He stepped into the clearing. She hadn't heard him approaching. She had no idea from what direction he'd come. She stumbled back a half-step, her heart suddenly pounding. Fear. She was feeling fear. She hated the immobilizing kind, she thought vaguely, grabbing on to a tree trunk as her muscles locked.

Then she noticed the uniform. He *was* security. She'd nailed it! And he *was* young, her age about, or maybe even younger. He was rugged-looking, lanky and wiry. He had the kind of muscles that hadn't been worked on in a gym. He swept dark-brown hair out of his eyes.

He bowed formally, but when he straightened again, she saw that he was smiling. She nodded, wanting to walk, or move, or fidget at least. She forced her body to be still. Be cool, she told herself. She felt something tug at her stomach. It was an excitement, an attraction, a burning fear. She waved. He turned and walked away, crunching back down the path, deeper into the radioactive forest. She took out her camera and snapped shot after shot of his retreating form.

Then she headed back into the woods to find the large-animal researchers. Inside, still, she was thrumming. She recognized the feeling, but it was an unnameable one. She remembered it from standing in front of the older kids, balanced precariously on washroom windowsills, blowing clouds of cigarette smoke out of cracked windows. She remembered it from standing at the top of the stairs in her house as a teenager, holding her breath and preparing to creep down so she could sneak out. She remembered it from drinking, from dancing, from kissing, hiding, from patrolling adults or headlights or teachers. She remembered it from every time she'd knowingly got herself into trouble.

⊙ ⊙ ⊙

Nick walked closer to the camera. His face suddenly took up the whole screen. "You know why I don't believe you?" he said. "You have more sense than that."

"I guess I don't," said Renya, revelling in the *ha ha* feeling. She had no good judgment. She never had. She'd chased after a security guard today. She used to insinuate herself into crowds of bad kids. She'd blown off school and snuck out at night. And he'd married her. At least she could throw doubt onto *his* good judgment.

"Your father has more sense than that," Nick said.

"Are you joking?" she said. "His kid suddenly interested in physics again, maybe going back to hard science – wanting to go back to the old country – anyhow, why don't you just ask him?" She shifted on her stump, to give him a better view. She'd brought her laptop outside. Somehow, the Wi-Fi worked here.

"I don't want to admit to my boss that –"

"Your father-in-law."

"In any case. He wouldn't have . . . He understands the dangers there." Nick shook his head, impatient. "He wouldn't want you to get hurt."

"He says the risk can be managed."

"That does sound like –"

"Direct quote."

Nick paused. He rubbed his hands together, watching her. That was a tell. Rubbing his hands together was a tell. It was a signal for some emotion, but she'd never figured out which one precisely. "Do you understand the physics of what was happening there?" he said.

Renya turned back to her day bag. She pulled out her old notebook. She didn't want to fight the old fights anymore. That wasn't why she was here.

"If you're so interested –"

"I've been reading," she muttered. "I've been doing my homework. Obviously, I don't understand it the way you do, but I do know the basics."

"If you really wanted to understand," he said, "if you were actually interested in –"

"They were splitting atoms," said Renya.

"Obviously, you're an expert now."

Renya flipped through the book cradled in her lap. Her technical notes weren't in this one though. But he wasn't an expert either, she reminded herself. This wasn't Bose-fucking-Einstein. "They split a uranium atom. It releases neutrons, and radiation." She looked up. There was anger all over his face, she thought, but it was a messy display. It could be frustration, she conceded, or maybe fear. She'd have to take a screenshot. He'd flip if she did that again.

"I've done the research," she said again. "A neutron comes in and hits the uranium-235 atom. The uranium absorbs the neutron. It then becomes uranium-236, and that's unstable. It's not a stable configuration. So it would have to crack in half, approximately, and turn into barium, I think, and maybe krypton? Does that sound right? It's something like that. Anyway, the uranium would turn into smaller particles. And that would release three neutrons, oh and radiation obviously. Anyway, those neutrons would have to go on to hit another uranium-235 and split that apart. But to make it a stable energy source, you need a critical reaction. That means that every neutron released has to split apart another atom, so those three neutrons would have to go on and –"

"That's –" Nick started.

"That's correct," said Renya. "I've done the work. I've been wanting to research this for a while, so I've looked at –"

"The physics?"

"I know some physics."

"I know but –"

"So the reaction has to be self-sustaining."

Nick raised a finger. "Not quite." His smile was infuriating.

"It keeps itself –"

"No. Here. Let me . . ." He grabbed a piece of paper and a pen, another tell. He didn't know what he was talking about. He was thinking it through as he went, or he'd just have launched into the lecture without asking permission, without having to find a fucking pen.

Renya ran her fingers through her hair and yanked as they snagged in tangles. Nick would have to draw a diagram to figure all this out. But she knew it! She understood this part! He was going to talk about the moderator now, and that was even more infuriating. Obviously, she knew about prompt reactions and moderators, what did he take her for?

She looked up. He was scribbling.

Well, she'd already done the work. There was a chance she knew more.

Renya reached behind to her backpack. She dropped her notebook back in and pulled out an oblong machine, a Geiger counter, no, dosimeter, a last-minute purchase as she'd waited for her plane tickets to come through, her first time paying for express post. Nick paused to notice, but pointedly ignored it.

"It's like billiards," said Renya.

That stopped him.

"Like pool," she said. *Ha ha indeed*, she thought darkly.

"Let's not . . ." Nick had blanched. He was playing with his pinky finger, the other tell. This one she knew very well. He'd put his paper down.

"I hit the ball with my cue, and the ball goes on to break a set," said Renya because he just made riling him up too easy sometimes. "Then one of the balls from that set has to break another set. And one of the balls from that set has to break another one. And so on and so on, the world's biggest, never-ending game of pool. But to make it self-sustaining –"

"It's more complicated than that."

"I'm not stupid, don't make me feel like –"

"No! I'm just trying to help. It's just that the reaction needs work. That's all I was . . . It can't be sustained without . . . See, the neutrons emitted are what we call prompt."

Renya buried her head in her hands. "Yes," she said. "I know. They move too fast to split another particle."

"They move too fast to split another particle," Nick said at the same time. "Like if your, uh, your pool cue were to move so quickly that you couldn't aim it anymore, and if the balls moved so fast that you couldn't ever hit them anyway. So now we have to slow down the neutrons. We use what is known as a –"

"Moderator."

"Yes! I'm just – Ren, I'm just trying to –"

"Obviously I know about moderators."

"The moderator slows down the neutrons. Imagine putting the billiard balls in a pool of Jell-O. That would slow them down so you can aim at them. In Chernobyl, they used graphite at the bottom of the control rods, that sort of, that works the same –"

"We needed a moderator," said Renya, "for our marriage."

Nick paused. "Don't," he stammered. "Don't –"

"You were allowed to make up analogies."

"You equate things when you don't understand – You create these metaphors when –"

"You're the one who created the metaphor."

"I was just trying to get your attention."

"And now you're just trying to pin your lack of judgment on me."

There was a silence. "I think that might be true."

"It is true," Renya bellowed. Her fingers tingled. Her feet throbbed. He shouldn't have ceded. He shouldn't have agreed with her, because she was right, dammit. She deserved to be angry. She deserved to yell. She needed to have someone to push back on. She was right. He'd been wrong. He was wrong, still. "Whatever I did," she said. "Whatever I did or didn't do. Whatever I did wrong, it didn't mean that you should fuck another woman."

"I didn't!"

"You did something."

"I acted like a child."

"You went out to play pool with some woman, and you kissed her, and who knows if –"

"You were right when you said . . . I acted like a spoiled child." Nick knelt in front of his computer. "I didn't think you'd leave. I wanted a reaction from you, but you have to believe that I didn't want that."

Renya sat back. She did think just that. She hadn't been there for him when he needed her. She'd made herself unavailable when he'd needed her most, so he in turn pushed her away, and some other woman, some ghostly apparition, had taken her place – that was precisely what she thought.

Nick smiled slightly. "Can we talk about something else?"

"Like what?" What was there left to talk about?

"A lot has been happening while you've been gone. My department is getting a shakeup. Can we talk about that?"

Renya rubbed tears off her cheeks. Despite herself, she was interested.

⊙ ⊙ ⊙

When Nick finally ended the call, the forest felt suddenly very quiet and oddly empty. It had seemed full before, booming even. And suddenly, Renya didn't know how loud she'd been in the beginning of the conversation. She hoped desperately that nobody had heard her yelling.

She paced for a minute. The light was seeping out of the sky. It would be full dark soon. She packed up and trudged back to her room.

⊙ ⊙ ⊙

Once inside, Renya threw her things on the chair that she'd turned into a way station of stuff, and sat on the bed. The sun had fully set now, and the window radiated dark. A breeze whistled through the pane. She felt the chill against her cheek and neck. No air was supposed to get in from the outside. Nothing here worked quite right. She shuffled to the bed and checked on the air purifier. It seemed to be humming contently. At least there was that. She turned on her laptop to scan through the day's results for the video feed by the entrance to the research centre.

ALGORITHMIC OUTPUT

Target set: September 29, 2013 / Zone of alienation, outer ring, research centre interior

Dominants: fear

Displays discovered: fear; happiness

Statistics [fear expressions]: scroll down

Qualitative review of what was observed in the target-set material:
Target set includes video of researchers entering and exiting the centre on September 29.
Fear detected, dominant, short duration / increasing from previous target set.

She scrolled through the raw data. Fear had been detected more often, and the durations were increasing substantially.

She tried to look outside but could only see her reflection in the window. This was still a work in progress, she reminded herself. Everything could change. The scientists could be back to excitement tomorrow.

She could justify working on the historical case. It was a good use of time, maybe, since there wasn't much she could do in the present; she still had to wait for more info. She'd have a better idea of the overall patterns here once she ran more sets.

She'd already run the 1986 accident pictures through her program and generated the red flags, but now she could use the program to look at the reactions in the days that followed, in all the surrounding areas, to confirm that something out of the ordinary had indeed happened. She could zoom out to look at the aftermath of the explosion.

She selected the next target set and ran it through the program.

These pictures had been taken in Prypyat the morning after the accident. Men in massive radiation suits were shown walking through the town, among unprotected people in street clothes, mostly women. There were children in the pictures too. The women displayed fear. She circled their expressions and their diminished postures. She circled the space that they made for the men in haz-mat suits. The women's faces were haunted, sad and drawn, and knowing somehow. They showed a particular kind of fear that she wanted to program for, but didn't know how. It wasn't an emotion that she could easily pinpoint. She didn't know which facial muscles to investigate. The expression wasn't uniform across subjects. It was more a feeling that *she* got from looking at the pictures. Because you know the risks, when your husband works at a place like that. When you marry an older man, you know what that will mean, eventually, too.

She ran the set. It worked. It spat out a warning. It didn't matter if she could describe that feeling or not because her program had caught it and flagged it as fear. She filled out the report, careful to write Prypyat in the Russian way, the way all the scientists and researchers seemed to.

ALGORITHMIC OUTPUT
Target set: April 27, 1986 / Prypyat set one
Dominants: fear
Displays discovered: fear; activity in supercilii muscle group
Statistics [fear expressions]:
Qualitative review of what was observed in the target-set material: Photo set shows bystanders in Prypyat on the morning after the explosion. Subjects display fear expressions.

The window above her shone a blue light, then headlights bobbed and engines hummed. She didn't know who would be going out at night here. She didn't know where they would go. Oh wait, some of the scientists were studying nocturnal creatures. She didn't bother to track them at all because she didn't want to generate extra light, and her pictures would be useless anyway. She let herself be grateful, for just a minute, that her work didn't force her outside here, alone in the dark. She breathed deeply again and the tingling in her limbs ebbed.

She found more pictures of Prypyat bystanders watching the men in the contamination suits. They knew there was an issue, obviously, but they didn't know what had happened, and they didn't know what it would mean for them and their families. *Physicists and technicians are so good at the science, but they never think about the aftermath. They forget about all the people left reeling after the event.* That was an unfair thought. She shook her head as if to clear it. She found another picture of the townspeople, the alien scientists. She found another with normally dressed men and women pausing to watch the scientists wave their instruments around, with children playing at the playground, exposed. The town hadn't yet been evacuated, and the population hadn't been told. Only a few women realized that their husbands hadn't come home from the night shift.

Renya copied the set, shuffled through the target pictures and zoomed in on faces. She circled wide eyes and wrinkled foreheads, stretched mouths, bared teeth, distrust visible despite the graininess. There was some wariness, distress too. Their fear expressions were unmistakable. The program should have no problem finding them.

ALGORITHMIC OUTPUT

Target set: April 27, 1986 / Prypyat set two

Dominants: fear

Displays discovered: fear; activity in supercilii muscle group

Statistics [fear expressions]:

Qualitative review of what was observed in the target-set material:
Target set shows people of Prypyat in the days after the explosion.
Multiple subjects display uniform fear expressions. **More information required.**

Bingo.

The results were great, but bystanders always showed fear. They had nothing to do but watch and wait and see what unfolded. Fear always manifested in moments of stillness, and what could a bystander be but still? The town would soon be evacuated. The people would be told not to take any belongings because they'd be able to re-enter in a few days. Most would never come back. She didn't have any photographs of the people of Prypyat hearing those messages, but she could imagine the terror displayed.

In any case, she'd generated a confirmation.

Maybe this project was possible. Maybe she'd be able to make what she'd promised: an early warning system. "I'll be able to devise a program," she remembered saying, her voice steady but her whole body quaking, "and that program will search all images of scientists, researchers, from the news, from meeting videos, from whatever feeds you can give it." In all her meetings with her supervisor, she'd been bluffing. She'd made herself look confident and unworried, because she hadn't seen the harm, but she hadn't quite believed that she could pull this off. She'd try, certainly. She'd fail most likely. And what would be the damage? There would be some grant money blown, but she wouldn't get much, and those funds had to be spent anyway. And, she figured, this wouldn't actually get off the ground for years. She hadn't been all that interested in the program itself. She'd just wanted the travel grant. Well, now she had both.

Because then her supervisor had called a meeting right away. She'd planned to be blustery and unconcerned as usual, but she'd had the confidence knocked out of her as she'd walked into the room – when she'd seen all the serious, expectant faces, those fancy clothes, those important-looking people she couldn't place. It hadn't been a regular departmental meeting. She hadn't been able to breathe for a moment. She'd had to grab a chair-back and pause to catch her breath. "The program will determine when the scientists are frightened, when they don't agree with the politicians and interpreters, when their expertise doesn't align with the official explanation given. This research doesn't work very well for individual reactions, but it's powerful when you plug in numbers. If you're looking at one person, then a fear reaction could be misinterpreted. It could be surprise, or indigestion, even. But if the computer program flags hundreds of fear reactions, or thousands, then you know there's a pattern. You know that you should look into the matter more deeply." She'd made eye contact with her supervisor, and he'd nodded encouragingly, as the suited men and women stared. She'd had to reteach herself to breathe, she remembered. Somehow, she'd gotten the rhythm of it all wrong when she'd started, but she'd figured it out as she went on. "And it will send out an alarm. It could even potentially flag the words and sentences that triggered the reactions." A woman to her left leaned in. Renya had been making that last part up, more or less, but she went with it, given the clear interest. "The program could suggest questions and warning signs." She wasn't lying, not exactly. She was embellishing to explain emotional truth: this is what she wanted, and these were the concerns she wanted to capture. It was aspirational, perhaps, but she really believed that it was possible. She considered explaining that she was not quite finished that last bit of programming yet but couldn't quite stop the momentum of her speech. "Politicians lie. They spin. They cover the truth, but they can't hide from it completely. They can't hide from their own emotions, nobody can." Now everyone was leaning forward, pens out, taking notes in slick black notebooks. She'd been talking nonsense though. Well, she'd hoped she could tweak the program to do all that. She'd assumed she could teach herself to do it. She'd just gotten excited because they'd gotten excited. "Because at the end of the day, they know, and the scientists, they know too. Nobody can school reactions well enough to hide from scientific truth and the fear that it can cause, even if only in slips."

Renya stood and stretched. She'd just been blustering at first. But her programming skills had definitely improved, and she was scheduled to audit more courses when she got back. Maybe she could actually do this, all of it.

⊙ ⊙ ⊙

Renya crept through her hallway and found the staircase. Instead of running down the stairs like she did every morning, she turned and went up. She climbed and climbed until she came to the top floor. Here, the landing led to a closed door. Renya tried the knob. It was locked. There was a small window though, with a view of the forest. She couldn't see much right now, just some gravel. Maybe she'd come back in the morning. She pressed her forehead against the glass. She'd hoped to find an attic or some hidden view to present to Claire. She'd been hoping to run into cleaning staff.

Renya turned and walked back down the stairs. Instead of stopping at her second-floor landing, she kept walking, down to the first floor and down again. The first basement housed loads of labs, she remembered.

The corridor was small and airless, the ceilings much lower here than in the upper floors. The locked doors and fading yellowish paint gave the place the feeling of a horror-movie setting. At the end of the hall, however, she came upon an open door. She peeked around and found one of the disconcertingly modern lab rooms. It sparkled with bright-white linoleum and shining silver equipment and cages. The inner wall was inlaid with computers and computer equipment. The outer-facing wall was set with cages and containment units. Gleaming metal island tables held machinery, and there, huddled over open notebooks, stood Claire and three other scientists.

Renya knocked lightly on the door. Claire and the others turned.

"I don't want to bother you," she said.

One man pointed questioningly at the top of the door, where her camera, pointed out into the hallway, blinked contentedly.

"The cameras are working," said Renya, "thanks. I just kind of wanted to see other people's research."

His eyebrows raised ever further.

"Out of interest," she quickly added. "Your work looks fascinating. I'd love to understand it more."

All four welcomed her in. It was aggressively clean inside, but it still smelled like a zoo. As she entered, the odour became oppressive. The air was hot, and humid somehow, and it smelled of wet wood shavings. Then Renya saw the nests being examined on the lab tables.

"I always feel like we need to defend ourselves," Claire said, noticing her attention, "but we're not monsters. Birds don't actually live in nests. I promise! They lay their eggs in nests, then abandon them when the babies are grown. We're not running around stealing birds' homes."

"Nests are more like nurseries," said one colleague.

"The idea they live in them is kind of comforting," said the other, "but it's a fiction."

Then Claire made the introductions and showed her around the lab. Her colleagues explained the equipment.

When the others had gone upstairs for a snack and to call their respective homes, Claire and Renya leaned against the island side by side. "I went up to the attic," said Renya.

"Find anything?"

"Just a locked door. I was hoping to find some discovery to tell you about."

"Like a hostess gift," said Claire, reaching out to touch her arm. "My family taught me that too. We're both well-trained. But I was hoping you'd come."

"This is interesting," said Renya. "It's so different from what I do. It's easier for me because I can ask my subjects questions."

"The birds have a lot to say," said Claire. "But they're certainly hard to understand sometimes."

"It's also trickier for me because I'm not allowed to take my research subjects apart."

Claire laughed. "I probably shouldn't be allowed to either."

Renya ran her fingers along the cool metal counter. "I've noticed some trends in your lab, I think, I mean among people's emotions."

"What are you seeing?"

"What would you expect?"

"A sense of creeping dread."

"Your findings are that bad?"

Claire banged her feet against some inlaid drawers, shutting them. The sound echoed hollowly. "It's strange because we didn't know what to expect," she said. "Some earlier groups said the birds are adapting to the ionizing radiation. Some reports showed that they're thriving since there are so few people."

"What are you seeing?"

Claire shrugged. "I'm waiting on results." She turned toward the nests. "I'm unsettled today, and not for a reason I ever would have expected. We've just found microplastics in the nests."

"Here?"

"I know, right? I wasn't looking for that. I was looking at nest construction, to compare to city birds and country birds, and, well, I just started noticing weird things in the nests themselves. It's strange. These birds are territorial. They really don't go far. They live their whole lives in a very tight radius. But microplastics are *here*. I've found them inside the birds too. Maybe that physicist was right. Maybe the radiation is the least of our problems."

"How would there be microplastics here?" said Renya. "Nobody lives here."

Claire nodded. "You've seen fear?" she said.

"Some," said Renya. "Not a huge amount so far. I was expecting fear when we got here, and then excitement when we got used to the place. I'm finding the opposite."

"But you like fear," Claire said lightly.

"I do."

"Why?" said Claire. "I'm a romance person, I'll admit. I could never handle horror movies."

"Fear is a very useful emotion," said Renya. "You experience fear, and your body takes over. Your nervous system gets you ready to react with a speed and force that you couldn't access in your regular life. It's not just adrenaline either. You get extra glucose. You get extra oxygen to muscles and calcium, and, of course, there's the dopamine. That's my clinical answer."

"Do you have a personal answer?"

"I swear, it all goes back to when I was a little kid, reading Stephen King novels under the blankets with a flashlight. I lived for terrorizing myself. I loved imagining the absolute worst and coming back to my real life. The relief of taking a break from a horror book, looking up and seeing my pillows and bookshelves, it's incomparable. Stephen King is still my favourite."

"Mine is *All Creatures Great and Small*," whispered Claire. "Also, it's the only reason to study."

Renya looked up. Claire was nodding. "I study birds because of my pet parakeet who died when I was eleven. And of course, that old paperback copy of *All Creatures Great and Small* that my grandmother gave me. We read it together. It was our thing."

Renya watched Claire closely, but she couldn't make out any pulled-up lip muscles or tightened lower eyelids. There were no ironic muscles activated on her face at all. "Really?" she whispered.

"The bird was Pookie. She was a gift from my grandmother too."

"Pookie."

"The pet store named her."

"Right."

"We never talk about it," said Claire. "But there's always a strange reason we do what we do. Well, our reasons are strange or kind of ridiculous. Mine is ridiculous. It's always something like that though. Unless you're following the money, and then you're kind of just ridiculous. Some people follow the praise, I guess, but that never gets you anywhere good."

"I didn't know other people had things."

"There's always something," said Claire. "With great passion comes great weirdness."

"I think that's true," whispered Renya.

"We all have supervillain origin stories," said Claire, "except for science, of course, not for villainy."

"Yes!" said Renya. She felt something that she couldn't readily describe, like a tingling that started in her solar plexus and radiated down through her whole body, a deep resonance that she wouldn't have admitted to any other person. Sometimes she did feel like she was a supervillain, well, of the academic variety. She was on a set path, and something had started it. What had been her origin? What was her origin story?

"Honestly, I'm just so happy that I've found someone who I can talk to about this," Claire was saying, eyeing her suspiciously, it seemed to Renya, her corrugators activated to draw her eyebrows together and down, and to wrinkle the skin on her forehead. Her depressor anguli oris might be activated too, pulling down on her mouth. Was she frowning? "But I still want to be taken seriously, obviously."

"Oh," said Renya, understanding, "you don't have to worry about that. I will absolutely still take you seriously."

"Thank you."

They packed up to go for a walk in the forest.

"With great passion comes great weirdness," Renya whispered to herself. The phrase echoed hollowly in Renya's mind, throughout the hike, and as she worked into the night. In her dreams, people from her life took turns saying it to her, and she woke up remembering paging through Chornobyl books with her dad and her grandmother. *My subconscious*, she thought, *has no subtlety*.

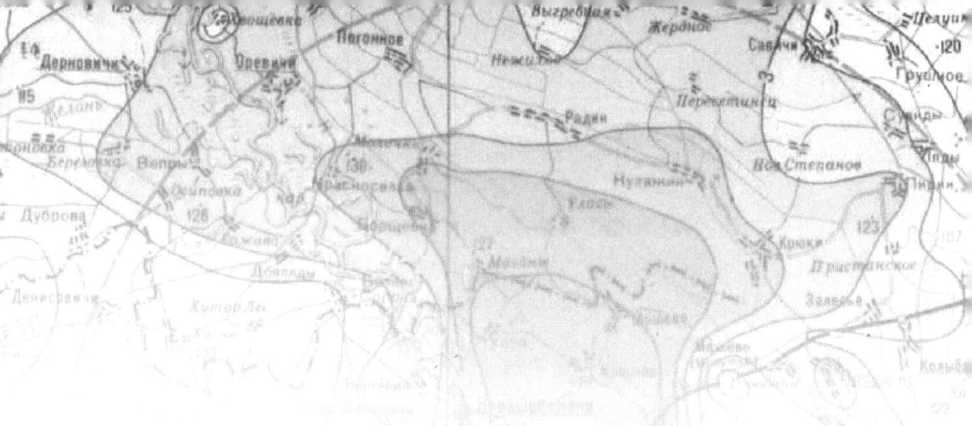

CHAPTER 4

THE NEXT MORNING, RENYA WOKE STILL THINKING ABOUT weirdness. She took extra time in her suite bathroom making herself look presentable. As she walked through the great hall to the dining area, she checked herself for visible oddities in the entrance mirror. She didn't see anything obvious. She smoothed her hair back, tightened her ponytail and crept across the worn carpet. She'd set her alarm even earlier than normal, hoping to eat breakfast alone and to look through her notes. As she neared the dining room, she paused just outside of the door.

"Well, if it isn't Mrs. Dr. Nick Trotter." Telerson crept up behind her. Renya started. She hadn't heard him. The floorboards were creaky here. He must have made an effort.

"I was hoping to get a cup of coffee," Renya stuttered. "I'm just going to get some coffee and run." Also, she was a doctor too, well, she had a PhD, they both had PhDs, obviously, or she probably wouldn't be here.

"You're up early. But you've been having trouble staying awake. I haven't seen you in the nightly gatherings. Have you considered just sticking to the time zone you're in? It takes some discipline, but it works."

Renya wasn't jet-lagged. She was just avoiding the parties. "Well, yes, I'll try. I'm trying."

"I just want to help. Your research is wild, I've been told. You need your beauty sleep to think outside the box all day."

And then a large group creaked down the stairs, through the main hall.

"Hey, Renya," said the man she recognized from the earlier meet and greets, and from the way over. Tiv. "The emotions expert!" He stopped as others filed past. Then Charlie appeared. Renya stepped aside so he could walk past. He didn't.

"I've been hoping that I'd see you again." Tiv seemed kind. They'd sat together in the airport waiting for one of the connecting flights. They'd talked, and she'd genuinely liked him. He liked to talk about his kids, she remembered. Renya softened. "I want to know more about your research," he was saying.

"I focus on fear," she stammered. "But I think we talked about it a few days ago, forgive me." They'd exchanged CVs in that airport lounge, but then they'd mostly talked about other things.

Telerson and now Charlie were standing beside her, hovering. She was having trouble concentrating with them so near.

"I'd love to hear more about *your* work," she said. "Wolves, right?"

"My wife was really into it when I told her about you on the phone. She knew all about your stuff."

Renya smiled. Tiv hadn't made any demands on her. He'd let her get all passionate about emotions and stats.

"Renya started studying physics like her dad, like her husband, Nick," said Charlie.

Renya straightened. Tiv's expression darkened slightly, his ocular muscles tightening and his mouth pulling down. She sighed. Tiv's wife was in science too. He'd probably understand at least a little bit.

"You've probably heard of Max Eidelman and Nick Trotter," Charlie was saying. "But you quit physics after undergrad? Is that right, Renya?"

"I just didn't have the staying power, I guess," she said. "Anyway, it was just a minor. I've always focused on psychobiology."

"My wife has read your papers," Tiv said, stepping away from Charlie. "I think you're much more powerful where you are."

"Feelings can be fun too," said Charlie.

"She's changing the way we think," said Tiv. "You can't say that often."

"That's kind of you," Renya stuttered.

"Admit it, Tiv," said Charlie. "She's also changing the way you think about your wife. Look at that shirt. And pants don't have to be that tight, but I appreciate when they are."

Renya felt her cheeks burning, her whole body radiating heat. She forced a shrug that could pass, she hoped, for nonchalance. Then she turned and started to walk away. She was just following the recommendations. She'd chosen her clothes based on the research centre guidelines.

"I'm happily married," Tiv called after her. "Don't listen to this please."

Renya forced herself to turn around and smile at him. She'd been going for cool and unbothered, but had probably only managed seething and unsettled. But she was leaving, so there was that.

⊙⊙⊙

As Renya stumbled out of the conference centre, she was thinking about the experience of being unsettled: it was less an emotion than a doorway, a transition between emotions. She jogged out into the woods, her usual track now a well-worn neural pathway.

Being unsettled transported you from one feeling to another. Sometimes it took you from excitement to fear. She'd seen that recently in the pictures of the unit four technicians, as they saw the experiment go wrong, as they felt the ground move. Sometimes it took you from happiness to anger. She didn't want to be angry at Telerson. She didn't want to think about him at all. She'd rather think about handsome strangers in the woods.

Renya jogged out to her downed log again, and leaned her hip against it. He'd come back. She knew he would. And this time, she would talk to him.

Sure enough, the security guard emerged from a thicket almost immediately. He might have been there for a while. He nodded. She nodded back. He leaned against a tree slightly, but still, his posture was confident: his back was straight and his chest was open. He probably had strong trapezius muscles. That was a ridiculous thought. He might be showing increased corrugator activity, but he might not. He looked vaguely interested, but that wasn't very scientific. His dark hair caught the breeze and fanned out boyishly.

"You look like you're planning a revolution," the security guard said in heavily accented English.

"Yes," said Renya. "That's exactly what I'm doing." She still spoke a bit of Ukrainian and a small bit of Russian. She thought of telling him that, but she couldn't decide how to say it, and so she continued in English. "I'm thinking of changing the focus of my research."

"Studying a new kind of soil," he said.

"What?"

"I've worked this area before. You're all digging in the mud."

"Not me," Renya whispered. She looked up. He was handsome, sure, but he didn't look quite as she remembered. His uniform was faded. A loose thread dangled from his sleeve. "I'm studying scientists." She narrowed her eyes. The cool kids, she remembered, had always responded well to a tensing of subocular muscles. It showed a hint of disbelief if you overthought the gesture, but they would never overthink. They were too busy with other cool concerns for that.

"That's a revolution?" he said.

"I'm studying the scientists themselves," she said, giving up on the posturing. "I'm looking at them like they're exhibits in a zoo."

"I would visit a zoo of scientists. I do, frequently, I feel. Why would you call this a revolution?"

"They don't like it when you study them."

"Naturally."

"Also, it might not be scientific enough. I mean. Maybe it's not important enough. Some people think it's not real science."

"You don't think it's real and, however, you wish to study it."

"There's something there. I know I can . . . My colleagues, the men here . . . My father doesn't think it's real. My husband doesn't either."

The guard looked down at her hands.

"Soon-to-be ex, maybe," she stuttered. "I don't know. I took off my ring."

He nodded and shook a cigarette out of a small brown-and-white package that he'd been carrying crumpled in his palm. He held it delicately, and cupped long, tapered fingers around it. His cuffs were dirty, she saw, the shirt underneath so threadbare as to be almost translucent, certainly not made of tightly woven fabric like all the preparation documents had suggested.

"Are you a real security guard?" she whispered. He couldn't reasonably be a ghost, but there were other options. "Or are you a freedom fighter?" She'd heard rumours. The other technicians gossiped sometimes at dinner. They thought that maybe Ukrainians were pretending to secure this area from looters, but were really plotting against the Russian government amid talks of invasions and coups.

He took a long drag of his cigarette, and made it seem thrilling, almost indecent. "What the fuck is freedom?" And oh God, why could she never say things like that? "Do you believe in freedom?" The men in the dining hall would never bother her if she could just say intense things like that.

She opened her mouth to answer, but then closed it again.

"What *do* you believe?" he said.

"I don't know."

"You must believe some things."

"Sure," she said. "Love is good. Cigarettes are bad."

"Well." He took a drag, watching her. "Believe this," he finished after a long moment. "This place isn't as safe as they tell you. Nobody survives being here, not for long."

"What do you mean?"

He winked, cupping his lit cigarette against the breeze. What was he referring to? Did he mean political violence? Or was he talking about the cancer risk? That was more likely. The place was radioactive. There was more to worry about than being teased in the common areas and at social gatherings. She would do well to remember that, he was right.

The man turned to exhale out into the breeze, and his hair ruffled around his ears. His jacket, she noticed for the first time, was torn on the side, a break yawning out through the seam.

"*Are* you really security?" she said.

"I'm working, yes."

"I see you all the time."

He nodded to the camera. "And you just take pictures."

He flicked the cigarette to the ground and stepped onto it lightly, already turning away, his mind already processing other matters, she saw. He crunched off into the woods, on a patrol, sure, but how legitimate? But these were ridiculous thoughts. What reason would he have to come here, if he wasn't paid to watch over the grounds? Nobody would be fighting over the exclusion zone. It wouldn't be safe to resettle for hundreds of years. Some people thought it wouldn't be safe for thousands. And how could he have got through the checkpoint anyway? Everything was in some form of disrepair here. Surely nobody cared that much about a uniform jacket.

"Hey!" she called out. For a moment, he kept walking, but then he stopped. He turned around wordlessly.

"Would you show me around?" she called out.

"Where?"

"Prypyat. Everywhere. I want to see the damage. I want to see what's been done to this place."

He moved closer. "You want to see Prypyat?"

"Yes."

"You want to be a witness." He seemed to hesitate. "Why would you want to be more dangerous?"

"I'll pay you."

He paused, then nodded once. "Fine. Find me here."

"When?"

He shrugged, then slunk off into the trees.

Renya crunched off in the woods in the opposite direction, one step, then one step farther. Then she turned back. He'd been lying about something, surely. She'd felt it, but she couldn't pinpoint why or what about, and she didn't have any pictures of his face to prove it, not that she'd feel equal to finding evidence of lies even if she did have pictures. Maybe he was just trying to capture her interest. Some people flirt by throwing others off balance. Maybe that's all it was.

Anyway, it couldn't be so dangerous. Her administration had signed off on her being here. Ditto for her country. Ditto for her dad. She had to be at least baseline-safe. City air was polluted to almost unbreathable. Unofficially, they all said you're probably more likely to be hit by a car in Toronto than get diagnosed with something after a short trip here.

She spent the rest of the afternoon photographing researchers, taking picture after picture of group after group, as the security guard's voice echoed in her head.

⊙ ⊙ ⊙

When Renya got back to the research station, she found Claire in the dining room with a woman. She was beautiful, this interloper, in designer clothes, with brightly painted nails. She looked like all the fancy women Renya had left behind in Toronto. She was smart too. They both had something that Renya didn't have. They weren't just academically brilliant, but they were socially aware too. They'd fled that party before finding themselves alone with the men. It's not everyone who knew to pick up on cues, clearly.

Renya swerved. She pretended not to notice either of them, but Claire jumped up and pulled her over.

"This is Shantoo," said Claire, forcing Renya into a seat. "She's good. Disregard the nail polish. It's not what you think."

Shantoo was nodding. "Yes," she said. "And my sister dresses me. You should see me back at home. Usually, she does my makeup too. Inside, I look quite different."

"I do my own makeup," said Renya. "I do it to blend in. I'm like a wild animal that way, so maybe you should study me."

"The rumour is that you're studying us," said Shantoo.

Renya watched them. Claire seemed unconcerned. Shantoo was leaning away from her, squinting, upper eyebrows pulled down and lower ones activated, mouth corners tensed too. It could be distrust or anger. It was slight, but it was there.

"I study fear, mainly," Renya said after a moment. "I study emotional displays and short-duration expressions, among other things. I do studies based on large numbers. I rarely look at individuals." She'd disclosed all this in the proposal. Nobody had objected, but who knew how carefully they'd read it? She'd figured it would be an issue when she had the idea, but she hadn't pictured eating lunch with her test subjects at the time. She'd hadn't imagined wanting to be friends.

"We were all hoping that you're secretly from *National Geographic*," said Claire. "That's why we all signed the release for the pictures."

"So you can tell if we're lying?" Shantoo interrupted. "Can you see from our faces what we're thinking? Can you tell right now?"

"If I took a series of high-speed pictures and videos and slowed down the frames, I'd get clues as to how you're feeling."

"What about lying?"

"I can't get my head around lying. There are just too many variables. Just talking to laypeople is ninety-nine percent lying, if you overthink it, and I do tend to overthink. Even emotions are tricky, especially when you're targeting the fleeting ones. I run pictures through a program looking for fear and I worry that a lot of the positives are just gas. That's why I need large numbers."

"That's just what I'd say if I was studying a subject," said Shantoo.

"Really though, I'm not concerned about individual emotions. I'm looking for patterns, like when lots of people have the same emotion all at once. Think, watching a movie, all together, or learning about an explosion at a nuclear power plant. That would trigger some emotional responses, and they'd be the same, roughly the same, across subjects."

"But wouldn't you use the same methods when interacting with individuals?" Shantoo turned to Claire. "I don't have anything to hide. At least,

I don't think I have anything to hide. You always worry. What if I *do* have something to hide? What if I'm hiding it from myself? What if she uncovers something that I've been hiding even from me? *What if my family and my colleagues find out?*"

"Find out what?" said Claire.

"I don't even know!" said Shantoo. "That's the scariest aspect!"

"My husband had an affair," said Renya. Finally that information was useful. "So clearly, I'm not that good in real-time. I don't think you have to worry that I'll uncover anything."

Shantoo twisted the ring on her finger. "Your husband slept with someone else," she breathed. She relaxed, leaning in, putting her elbows on the table. Her sympathetic expression seemed genuine. It reached her eyes anyway.

"He said it was just an emotional affair," Renya found herself saying. "They were only starting to fall in love, he said. Only. He got sick too, I should mention. He had a mild heart attack. He's fine now. I didn't pick up on any of that as it was happening though."

She had left and someone else had come. She couldn't keep him company, so another woman had. Renya didn't know her name. She didn't know what she looked like. She was a ghost, of sorts, haunting her erstwhile marriage.

Claire was watching her carefully. Shantoo's posture, however, had loosened, her expression now relaxed and warm. It was because of the disclosure! All the books said that's how to make friends. Well, now she finally had something to disclose. Academic lives were boring. Apparently, you had to blow them open to finally be worthy of social contact. She leaned forward. Shantoo and Claire, she noticed, mirrored the behaviour and leaned forward too. And she told them everything, about the heart attack, the affair, asking Nick to leave but not really wanting him to go, about wanting to be with him but finding reasons to be absent all the time, because she was afraid. She told them about how she was feeling now, waiting to see what came next. And then they told her about their lives at home, their relationships with their partners, the times they'd asked them to leave.

As they talked, Renya felt a lightening or unburdening. It was 40 percent happiness, 40 percent relief and 20 percent some other emotion that she couldn't quite place. They stayed into the evening, until she felt, she was quite sure, only happiness and nothing else.

⊙⊙⊙

Back in her room, Renya plugged in her camera and downloaded the day's shots. She checked the program for the pictures she'd already uploaded and the video feeds from the entrance. Some alarms had gone off from last night's feed. There had been extended fear expressions in the lab corridors again. That could mean anything, however. Everyone was fighting with people at home. Nobody was sleeping well. Everyone was out pacing in the corridors at all hours, lately. She had photographic evidence. Maybe she was catching some strange side effect of jet lag.

The lamplight made the room look aquatic, and the muffled voice next door heightened the effect. The voice seemed mad, or under stress or constraint. It had that pinched quality, although she still couldn't make out any words. She wondered whether she should look up the effects of stress on vocal cords. She wondered whether Claire might know who was staying in the room next door. She or Shantoo might know his story. They seemed plugged-in.

Renya scanned through the photos she'd taken that day. She flipped through picture after picture of scientists. Some were checking traps. Many were crouched in the dirt. Their faces were generally broadly visible. Obviously, nobody's masks had worked any better than hers. She'd run the pictures through her programs, but she stopped and checked some faces, just to see. There was no fear here. Their expressions were mostly neutral. She found one smile. She saved the picture to her early report folder and circled the skin around the eyes. She showed the muscles working, pulling down eye corners. In general, the scientists here were happily engaged, she'd hazard, maybe so happily engaged as to have forgotten where they were, and the hidden dangers of their environment. At the moment, there was nothing much to show her supervisor and all those people in suits. At first glance anyway, these researchers could be anywhere. So far, fear was really only found in doorways. She considered running the entranceway videos. Maybe in a second.

She'd work on the historical data first.

She opened the next folder of historical pictures. She found a group shot of firefighters. These must be the ones who'd been called to unit four accidentally. She scrolled further and found more pictures of the teams and the nearby stations.

After the explosion, the core was on fire and melting down, its chain reaction ongoing. It was too hot and radioactive to go near. They needed to find a way to put out the fire and contain the reaction. But the fire had triggered an automatic response from local fire units, so teams of firefighters showed up. They shouldn't have gone, of course. There was nothing they could do. They couldn't pour water on a reactor fire. Water is a moderator and slows down neutrons. The reaction was still ongoing, and more slow neutrons would make it worse. That could cause chain reactions, a nuclear explosion in other words, and blow up the entire region. It could have created an explosion much bigger than the one that razed Hiroshima. Now all the fire trucks were still there, apparently, parked beside reactor four, too radioactive to go near. Many of the firefighters died soon after. She scrolled through the file and found shots of them in hospital beds. She could run the shots, but it probably wouldn't yield much: not enough faces were visible. In any case, fear was expected in a hospital setting. She'd set a high bar on the program for places like that.

She kept scrolling. She knew from looking into the history that the pilots had come shortly after. You couldn't use water to put out the fire, but you could use other things. They'd loaded up planes with bags of sand to smother the fire, boron to absorb neutrons and to stop the reaction, and lead to protect from the radiation. And there they were. She found a whole folder just for the pilots.

She clicked through. She found a video of helicopters circling around the ruined reactor. The reactor was still on fire at that point, and producing plumes of smoke, spewing high-velocity particles just everywhere. If Renya squinted, she could see the bags of sand and boron that were being dropped into the hole. The pilots were flying blind, she knew from interviews conducted later on. The co-pilots were trying their best. It was so hot that everyone's eyes were filled with sweat. The heat and the smoke wouldn't allow anyone to aim with any precision so that few of the bags, tiny looking in the presence of the massive fire, made their mark. The fire raged out of control. She ran the video, but the program spat out an "inconclusive." That wasn't surprising. There were no close-ups on their expressions while they were in flight. Their faces would likely have just shown concentration, anyhow. The images themselves were grainy as a result of massive amounts of radiation, and old technology, obviously. The video seemed to crackle.

She scrolled on. There were pictures of the pilots sitting and waiting for their turns to fly. The program detected some sadness and some fear, but it must have been subtle because Renya didn't see it. It looked to her like their expressions were mostly flat. She looked through the detailed report and saw that the muscle activation hit the lowest threshold for emotional display identification. That made sense to her as well. At a certain point, fear becomes overwhelming. The body drains of adrenaline, previous surges having already used up too much energy. People's minds and bodies shut down. There's only so much a person can take. Even if the expression didn't begin as the paralyzing type of fear, it could get there eventually by that mechanism.

By then, the pilots might also have already been too sick to express much. They only flew short attempts before being replaced with other crews, but still illness caught up with some of them quickly. She found a series of shots of pilots resting between shifts. She ran them. The program found some fear, but mostly sadness and grief. She'd have to think about that.

Renya scrolled back to the folder of the day's entrance and exit videos. She should process them at least. She uploaded the day's field pictures into the program and ran them. It wasn't a perfect program. She'd written it fast, over the course of a weekend in which she'd hardly slept and drank far too much coffee. Still though, it worked. The program generated the appropriate red flags. Fear was found. The detection numbers and display durations were increasing quickly now. All other emotions were being detected with less frequency. *Well great.* She was stuck here though. There was nothing she could do about it.

Much later, after having paced for much of the evening, prickling at spending any more time alone, Renya decided to explore the building once again, well, to look for people. She walked slowly down the basement hallway, listening to the crush of her footsteps bounce against the walls. She peeked around into Claire's lab to find her friend alone, leaning against the island, staring at a notebook. Claire looked up. Renya wasn't a body-language expert, but she could see the tension clearly. She hesitated in the doorway. "This seems like a bad time," she said.

"I would love company," said Claire. "I was thinking of going out to mark a few nests. Do you want to go for a walk?"

"I'd love to." Renya had wanted company so badly, but this seemed fraught all of a sudden. She searched Claire's face. She was on high alert. She had been since Renya had come. The calm of her demeanour was a ruse. Renya could clearly see the stress in Claire's jaw, in the masseter and temporalis muscles, in the medial pterygoid for all that.

"Tell me about your project here," said Claire, as she packed a camera and some other gear into a backpack. "Oh wait." She opened a drawer. She passed Renya a mask and put one on herself.

"Yours don't snap?" But Renya tried it, and it fit her face tightly.

"I borrowed some." Claire turned to leave, and Renya followed. "Oh! I'm not trying to hide anything from you. I can take it off if you're uncomfortable."

"Not at all," said Renya. "They don't interfere with my project either. My programming is mainly based around eye muscles and foreheads, for this particular project. I put a mask on every morning, but they always break." She sighed. "I should have brought some from home too."

"I got these from the large-animal guys," said Claire. "They'd heard that there were quality-assurance issues, so they sourced good ones before they came. They have extras, they assured me. I can introduce you if you'd like to ask for some."

"I'd appreciate that," said Renya.

"Do you ever ask yourself about where your lab gets its funding?" Claire said abruptly.

"What do you mean?"

"How much do you know about your funding stream?"

"Some NSERC, some fellowships," said Renya. Some people bragged about funding, she knew, but she'd been turned down enough times that she wouldn't want to do that. This all felt like a lotto win, or, more honestly, like a mistake. In any case, everyone here likely had similar successes and similar sources.

Claire didn't respond. She gestured toward the door, noisily fishing her keys from her pocket.

"I don't get asked about the little details of my work that often," Renya said as she moved toward the exit. They were all busy here. They were all excited, itching to talk about their own research. Rarely did people make time for others. So why the interest? But she didn't know how to ask. "Usually, people are so bored that they change the subject before I answer any questions about my research at all."

"The challenges of academic life," Claire said quickly. She was smiling under the mask, Renya could tell, but her smile didn't reach the muscles around the eyes. Her orbicularis oculi weren't activated at all. Her eyes looked sad.

They took the stairs at a run, then pushed out of the research station and walked quickly down the gravel road. "I've never thought about it that much myself, but now I'm looking into it for my own lab," said Claire.

"I apply for anything I see. Funding can be really hard to get where I am so I go for just about anything."

"I'm really interested in this case. You weren't on the list, then suddenly you were, then suddenly there were all those new forms to fill out."

Renya nodded. She'd been wondering when she'd be called on that. "I had an idea last-minute," she said. "I'd been doing a pretty boring postdoc. I was measuring the angles and tension of facial muscles, comparing the degree of emotional display across cultures, et cetera, et cetera."

"Cultures?"

"But then I had this idea for a practical application of the work that I've already done. I didn't think they'd jump. They jumped. I got more money than I asked for. There might be funds for a student when I get home."

Claire stopped walking. Renya almost walked into her. She backed away quickly.

"You're doing race things?"

"My cultural specialty is the scientific community, if you can believe it."

Claire guffawed, but then quickly shushed herself. "Scientists as a race," she whispered. "I love it. I think I read you were doing that. I should have remembered."

"They have pretty unique display rules. It's actually really interesting. Scientists are really strange animals, as individuals *and* as groups."

"I can see that," she said. "I'm just a bit concerned about the money, and not just for you of course, but all of us. I'm not concerned. I'm interested. You said you got more than you expected?"

"I'm not following the money," Renya said quickly.

"No," said Claire. "That's clear enough. Where did the funds come from though? How did it all come through so fast? I've looked a bit, and I can't figure out who's pulling the strings."

"I only applied to get a travel grant, and to get into the residence, obviously. The project idea was secondary. My family is from here, from close, from Ukraine anyway. I used to read about the accident and the exclusion zone. This was just an excuse to come. In fact, I originally applied for residency in the next calendar year."

Claire slowed. Her frontalis muscles were pulling so hard that her eyes were huge and the skin of her forehead wrinkled. Surprise. Shock, even. "You applied for next year?"

"Then I got a meeting within a week. They sped up the timeline."

Claire started forward again.

"I mean, the project wasn't completely secondary," Renya continued, hurrying to catch up. "I think about this a lot, about devising projects that harness emotion. I thought about anger first, and about a program that disables cars when the driver exhibits too much anger or frustration. I'm still working on that one. There are a lot of technical issues, obviously. Cars would have to be jacked to make the whole thing work for one thing, and how much anger is too much because some people are always baseline a little bit angry, but, I'm still trying with that one. Anyway, then I thought about fear. Then I thought about the evolutionary uses of fear, how it's used to warn us of danger. So when I thought of this project, I had to find an environment in which there would be a background fear that I could measure, to see if I could catch displays or seepage as scientists were working. This placed just worked."

"The exclusion zone is certainly conducive to fear."

"I didn't cheat," said Renya. "I don't even know how I would cheat. I had a fellowship already. Then I proposed this system to monitor for fear displays. All of a sudden, I got a huge meeting with important people who never even introduced themselves. I even had to pull an all-nighter to get the programming at least sort-of done. Then more funds came through, and I got a travel grant and money for a PhD student, possibly. I'm as baffled as anyone by the amount and the speed. I mean, my dad is important in the university, but I don't think he helped. I don't think he particularly likes what I do. Honestly, if I did know how to cheat the system, I probably would have done it already quite a while ago."

"I didn't think that," said Claire. "And you're certainly no nepotism hire."

"What *are* you worried about?"

"What are *they* really worried about?" said Claire. "You're studying fear. How worried do they think we're going to get?"

"Oh," said Renya. That concern hadn't occurred to her. "I mean, I'd assumed, I wrote in my application, that I'd find fear in the beginning, and then there would be a levelling off as we all got used to the location."

"But that's not what you found."

"We were all excited when we got here," said Renya. "The fear came later."

"With results."

"I guess so," said Renya.

"Could they have predicted that?" pressed Claire.

"Who?"

"It's not that I'm complaining," Claire said quickly. "I'm glad that I got to meet you here. And it's not that I'm worried about you or your work at all."

"You think that some other people might have predicted that our results would make us nervous?"

"It sounds implausible, I know."

"I think it sounds very possible," Renya said lightly. "I mean, we're in Chernobyl, near the site of one of the most dangerous accidents in human history."

"But I'm not unsettled because of the usual Chernobyl reasons," said Claire. "I mean, it's not the radiation, although it is the radiation, although it's not." She sighed.

Renya stumbled. Claire grabbed her arm and righted her. Renya was reminded, quite uncomfortably, of dinners with Nick and his colleagues, when they'd all talk about their work in granular detail and she'd twirl her cutlery like a child accidentally seated at the adults' table. "I'm trying to understand your concerns."

Claire nodded. "My administration told me it would be safe to be here," she said. "Well, safe enough."

"Baseline safe," Renya recited from the pamplets she'd received, from the conversations with supervisors and organizers, "as long as we stay in the outer ring and we don't eat local vegetables."

"Right," said Claire. "No foraging. No river-bathing."

"You wonder if they believed it?"

"I wonder if they have evidence to the contrary."

"My funding committee seemed happy enough with the 'fear at the beginning of the trip hypothesis,'" Renya said after a minute. "In fact," she went on, remembering later conversations at the conference table, "they were concerned that I wouldn't find *enough* fear. They were concerned enough that they gave me documents from the time of the accident to run through my program as proof of concept." Or they wanted her to compare sudden, paralyzing terror to the slow-dawning variety, but she wouldn't want to voice that concern to Claire.

Soon, Claire stopped at a tree and took out her camera. She focused carefully and snapped pictures. She seemed to know what she was looking for. Renya couldn't identify it. It looked like a regular treetop to her.

"There are nests here?" said Renya.

"We scoped them out earlier." Claire pointed. Renya nodded, pretending to see. Claire capped her camera and kept walking. "I'm glad that you ended up in my research group," she said. "I've made some actual friends. That, at least, is comforting."

Renya crunched over dry leaves. There were so many here. She had the impression, again, of bouncing on a mini trampoline. "I was so mad at my husband," she said. "I'd thought, for some reason, that my supervisor was helping me get away, but that's absurd. He didn't even know about the heart attack, or, I mean, about the affair. I mean, I never told him. I don't think he'd particularly care if I did."

"I'm sorry." Claire paused, her eyes sad again. "I usually don't care about this sort of thing, about funding, about how people are chosen."

"But you do now?" Renya considered this. "I probably should have cared more, when the money was available so fast, and certainly when I got help with the applications. Nobody ever helps with the paperwork. But I didn't question it. I wanted to go, so I went."

Claire nodded. "I would have done the same." And they walked deeper into the woods. Their footsteps crunched. The forest seemed to crackle in answer. "In fact, I did do the same. I don't know who holds the purse strings in my group, either. And there were questions before I left. Some people from an earlier group complained about feeling unsettled by some results."

"Radiation?"

"It was a creeping baseline of radiation," Claire said after a moment, "from what I remember. And some chemicals they found that are starting to be seen in cities, or maybe they were recorded in cities first, I can't quite recall. I'll have to look it up properly when I get home. I should have listened more carefully. I'm like you. I just really wanted to come."

Soon, they found themselves in a thicket, and Claire paused to take more pictures. Again, she pointed out the nests. At first, Renya saw only the treetops streaking the purple evening sky like so many veins. But then she saw little circlets of leaves, sticks and mud tucked into corners. Those birds were good at camouflage. Renya would never have noticed them. But, then again, she wasn't used to looking up.

"I've started looking into where my funding is coming from," Claire said after a long silence.

"Isn't it mostly just the government?"

Claire shrugged, looking through her camera again. "I'm afraid," she started. She put down the camera. "I have some industry sources too, I think. At least, my lab has extra sources. And I'm afraid that they wouldn't like what I'm finding. I'm asking myself, for the first time, what is their motive for funding us."

"More than just to figure out what's happening here?"

"Do they want the information exposed?" said Claire, still looking up at the treetops. "Or do they want it covered up? Or do they want to control the narrative when the story eventually emerges?"

⊙ ⊙ ⊙

Eventually, after what felt like hours of exploring, Claire put her camera away. She took Renya's arm and squeezed it.

"It's the first time I haven't been looking for people here," Renya said after a minute.

"I come out alone all the time," whispered Claire. "When I'm here by myself, I can imagine what the world would be like without any people at all. But the more research I do, the more I realize that just might not be possible anymore." She sighed. "Maybe my fear isn't very Chernobyl-related at all."

After, they walked a long way in the woods, mostly in silence.

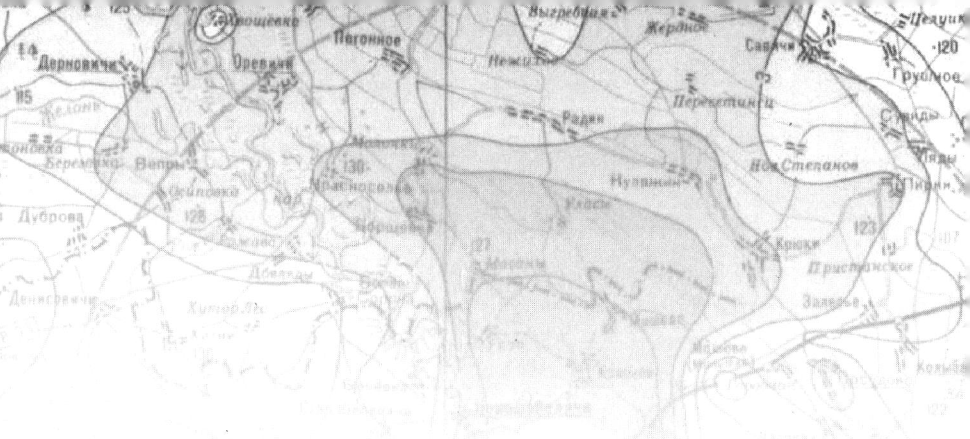

CHAPTER 5

THE NEXT MORNING, RENYA VENTURED OFF THE PATH TO skirt the edge of the fauna specialists' territory. She crunched out into the middle of the woods, her map tucked under her arm, rubbing her hands together for warmth. Then she sped up to a jog. She ducked under branches, zigzagging to narrowly escape twigs and tree limbs. She loved everything here, the ozone smell of the woods, the whirring insects, the crunching-paper sound of her footsteps. This was a more physical existence than any she'd previously known. It was exhilarating. She liked moving, it seemed. It was so much better than marking, or plotting numbers on graphs, or thinking all the time. Her desk life before seemed not like living, in comparison.

She turned a corner and skidded to a stop at the crest of a small hill. Below her was a small field. She saw two men she recognized vaguely from the cafeteria. She ducked behind a cluster of bushes. They showed no signs of having seen her.

Renya crouched, focused the camera on the two men and snapped picture after picture. They were crouched down too, facing each other and angled slightly away. They weren't making eye contact. Suddenly, her dosimeter popped quickly. She noted the readout on her map. She looked at her watch and wrote the date and time. She reached into her pocket for her mask, then remembered that it, like the others, had broken when she'd tried to put it on that morning. She'd hung Claire's in the window. She'd wipe it down later, and use it again. Reusing a good one was probably better than not wearing a mask at all.

She turned back to the fauna guys. She focused on the first of the faces. This man was frowning. Renya zoomed in. There were worry lines visible on his forehead, the procerus and corrugators clearly activated and working. She zoomed in on the other man. He had wrinkled skin above the bridge of his nose, right in the middle of the forehead too. Fear. These were the first overt signs of it she'd seen in the field. This wasn't seepage even, but real, extended fear tells. Then, as quickly as it had come, the fear disappeared. The men started talking again. Renya captured that too.

Then the men stood. They stomped their feet, flexed and unflexed their fingers, and looked all around them. They were talking, it seemed, but still not making eye contact. Renya zoomed out and snapped shot after shot.

It could be that they'd simply remembered where they were. It could be that she'd just captured the moment.

The men turned. They walked back to the path, heads down, pace quickening.

The fear could also have nothing to do with the work at hand. You never knew what caused the emotion, even when you did find it. They could have just received distressing news from home. They could be arguing about personal stuff. The subjects themselves sometimes didn't know what had triggered an emotion.

The men paused again. Renya steadied her camera. She shot more photo bursts.

Fear. She'd found fear, as a real emotional display. It could be nothing. But it could mean that her project had merit. It could also mean that she was in more danger than she realized.

The men were talking. One held his heart. The other man touched his shoulder. Renya zoomed in on them. Their cheeks were ruddy, if anything. Neither looked pale. They didn't look like they were in distress. Nick had held his chest like that. But when Nick had had his incident, there had been other signs too: he'd looked colourless and his face had been beaded with sweat. These men looked fine. They looked upset, sure, but otherwise healthy.

It could just be the toll of the research mission itself: they were under tons of stress here. Stress could alter your physiology.

Renya waited until they'd walked out of sight, and then she walked back to the path too, warming her fingers with her breath. She took out her grid to find the next group of researchers. But then she put the map away. Suddenly, she thought of Nick, and she remembered Nick on the day of the incident. She'd looked up, and he was holding the door frame, one hand on his heart, just like that guy in the clearing. She remembered, for some reason, the feeling of his cold hand in her warm ones, as they rode the ambulance. Until that moment, her hands had always been the cold ones. His hands had been pale. His nail beds had shone like blue-tinged moons. Nick would be under stress right now too. That was yet another thing that Claire had noted before she had: they were putting their families under stress, just by being here. She wanted to talk to Nick. She shouldn't, she knew, but she needed to hear his voice. She shouldn't put him under strain, no matter what he'd done to her. She found herself running back to the research station.

⊙ ⊙ ⊙

Nick's face seemed to float on the screen when she finally got him to accept the call. His background moved around him. Clearly, he'd picked up the laptop and was walking. "I was looking at the Weather Network earlier," he said.

Renya leaned closer to the computer and looked searchingly at the screen. He looked fine and now she felt foolish for running back, and for insisting, via messenger, that he click accept. "There are cold spells in Europe . . . The Black Forest, Freiburg. Thuringia . . ."

"You're probably very warm, where you are." The good weather wouldn't hold forever. People were talking about political instability. She should have taken more pictures. Nick was fine. He was healthier than when she'd left, she'd bet. The thrill of new relationships could do that.

Nick had moved the computer again, to the dining room this time. There were multiple wineglasses on the table. Had he ever specifically said that the relationship was over, he and that other woman? She couldn't remember. She felt her eyes, the upper and lower lids, tense. Concern had turned back to anger again, dizzyingly fast.

"You could always come back," said Nick, his smile tentative.

"You're probably very warm, sitting on your armchair – wait – what's on that other wineglass?" There was a smudge for sure. It couldn't be lipstick. Surely that only happened on TV.

"I'd open a bottle of wine, we could talk this through, we could –"

"You probably don't want me to see that she's in the bedroom."

"It wasn't anything!"

"*She's* probably warm in –"

"It was nothing. A fling, you would call it, we never even –"

"What would you call it then?"

"An indiscretion."

Renya reared back. "Fucking –"

"We never . . . We kissed, we only –"

"You have fucking terminology for everything."

"It wasn't appropriate. I regret that it happened." Nick raised his hands. "She's not in the bedroom. There's nobody in the bedroom. I don't even sleep there. I can't even *be* there without you. I sleep on the couch now and my back is wrecked."

"I have something to show you." Renya unzipped her backpack as wide as it would go and pulled out the dosimeter. "I wasn't going to show you this," she started.

Nick seemed to pull the computer closer. His face filled the screen. His upper eyelids were raised, his forehead creased. She had his attention anyway.

"But I've been hearing it clicking," she finished.

"A Geiger counter."

"Dosimeter."

"Right," said Nick. "Dosimeter."

"Sixty bucks! On the Internet."

"What does it read?"

"I knew there are hot spots in the woods, but I didn't think they'd be in the outer ring."

"Tell me!"

"Point-five microroentgens."

"Renya!"

"Now do you believe me?"

"I don't even . . . Microroentgens? I thought we used sieverts now. Anyway, I said that you can have an affair."

"And I told you that you should leave." Renya reached for her computer.

"Do you really want me to?"

She froze. *Obviously not.* Renya felt her body fill with heat. Anger was the worst emotion to experience. She always got overwhelmed by it. She'd never figured out how to experience it with any maturity or dignity.

She was angry now though, frustrated that he'd offered so foolish a response, infuriated that he'd said so boneheaded a thing as *she could have an affair*. But no. She didn't. She didn't want him to leave. She didn't want her marriage to be over either. She didn't mean it any more now than when she'd originally said it. And that was infuriating too.

Renya looked down at her fingers. *Find a way to end this nicely,* she told herself. Nothing good would come of this. *Find a way to channel the anger productively. Find a way to make this emotion ebb.* Renya pictured her favourite room in the library at home. She took a deep breath, closed her eyes and counted.

"I've got to go," she said through clenched teeth.

She wouldn't be able to manage this here, without extricating herself. She knew herself well enough to know that she'd just escalate this ridiculous situation.

⊙ ⊙ ⊙

A few minutes later, Renya found herself outside again and as she jogged out into the woods, she felt her breath in her throat, acidic and hard. She was angry. She let herself be angry. But as she jogged, the feelings ebbed. The trick was knowing that they did that. Emotions tended not to last. You could even trick them into dissipating faster.

As she turned to jog back to the station, she was in love with everything again, including the world and her place in it, including this eerie spot. As she rounded the final bend toward the research station, she saw the security guard leaning against a tree. He cocked his head. She slowed and mopped her forehead self-consciously. She hadn't expected to see him here.

"So this is what you do instead of cigarettes," he said.

She didn't know what to say, so she held up her hands and held his gaze. She didn't know what she meant by this gesture, but she wouldn't admit it to him if he asked. And it worked, it seemed. He seemed put off a bit, his smile now uncertain.

"What's your name?" she asked, riding the victory.

"Yuri."

"That's like all the Ukrainian names I heard in church."

"You are churchgoing? Religious type?"

"No."

"Then why were you in a church?"

"I don't know. It was the place to go."

"I don't think so."

Renya wished she had something clever to say. He was right, of course. Plus, she was Jewish, at least nominally. They'd only gone because of her stepmom.

"What is your scientist revolution?" said Yuri.

"I'm writing a program to detect fear displays." He looked at her blankly. "I look at scientists and government officials. I study their faces on the news, and try to figure out the emotions they're having but trying to hide. It's to catch emergencies as they're happening. First, I have to prove that I can catch fear as people work, even in scientific communities, or in repressive states, I guess."

"Your America is a repressive state," he said.

"I'm Canadian."

"Is there a difference?"

She wished she knew something about politics, that she wasn't so focused, so myopic. "Honestly, I don't know." Researching other things always felt like wasting time. There were things she wanted to know, things she needed to do, and balance had always seemed like a project better taken on later.

Yuri flicked his cigarette. "You don't know your own politics?"

"I don't know . . . I know about the university. That's repressive, depending who you are."

"And who are you?"

She was a woman in academia, in historically male-dominated fields, but she didn't want to point that out to Yuri. She didn't know why, but it didn't feel particularly safe. "I'm not used to being listened to," she said after a moment.

"*Should* anyone listen?"

"Suddenly, I think so."

Yuri nodded, the gesture quick and tight, his expression closed off. She couldn't interpret it, but she felt she'd seen it before.

He'd made her nervous before, so she hadn't looked hard at him. But now she really watched him. He was slouched, telegraphing uncaring more than showing it. His facial muscles were hardly activated at all. She'd seen this flattening before: in repressive regimes, all over Eastern Europe after the Wall fell, in abuse victims, in compulsive liars, in certain types of mental illness. But she'd seen it before all that too, long before, in that church basement and in the ravine where all the dangerous kids smoked. It could also be a symptom of a person trying to seem cool and unaffected. They were hard to read on purpose. There were many reasons to not want to be easily understood.

"For the first time," she said, "I think maybe I deserve to be listened to."

They heard footsteps, and both backed against the trees. More men were walking through the grove. There weren't any groups scheduled to be in this quadrant. Then Renya saw the uniforms. She nodded toward them. "Security also?" she whispered.

"Another shift is starting," he said.

They turned, and Renya saw that they were both wearing masks. They didn't acknowledge Yuri. They disappeared into the trees.

"Why aren't you wearing a mask like them?" she asked.

"Why aren't you?"

"I put them on every morning, but the elastics snap."

Yuri nodded. "Government masks," he said. "Mine too. Smart people buy from America."

"Nobody told me to," she said. "They gave specific packing instructions. There were official guidelines and unofficial guidelines. I even bought an old dosimeter from the Internet. Nobody said anything about masks."

"Scientists," said Yuri, shrugging. "They think they're better than anybody. They think they have superpowers and nothing bad could ever happen to them. Doctors are the same."

"What could never happen to them?"

Yuri dropped his cigarette and stepped on it, hard. "Health isn't part of your character," he said, lighting a new one. "It's not, what would you call it, a character trait. It is brief. It is a thing that passes. You have it one day, and then the next day, you don't. They're so smart and yet they don't understand that." He looked up, his face flashing. "Do you believe that?"

"Sure," she said. "I mean, no. I mean, I understand that good health comes and goes." She used to feel invulnerable. So had Nick. Then Nick had had that heart event, and they'd realized that they weren't superheroes and that everyone was vulnerable, all the time, because you never knew what was happening inside you. Oh God. She shouldn't have come here. She knew she shouldn't have come.

"Do you consider health a character trait?"

"No."

Yuri turned away.

"I thought it was fairly safe," Renya whispered, "for short stays at least. That's what they told us."

"And you believe your government?"

Renya said nothing.

"You really trust everything they say to you?" Yuri pressed.

She didn't know if she trusted the government. She didn't know if she'd believed what her administration had said. She didn't know if she believed it now. But Yuri was right. She had been exposed. And she was here.

When Yuri was called back to work, Renya walked back slowly.

"We'll explore soon," Yuri called over his shoulder.

⊙ ⊙ ⊙

Back in her room in the research centre, Renya couldn't shake the unsettled feeling. She couldn't get comfortable. Finally, she wrapped herself in Nick's sweater, oversized on her and cozy, and she lay down on her stomach on the floor. She turned on her laptop.

ALGORITHMIC OUTPUT

Target set: October 4, 2013 / Zone of alienation, outer ring, research centre interior

Dominants: fear; disgust

Displays discovered: fear; disgust; excitement

Statistics [fear expressions]:

Qualitative review of what was observed in the target-set material:
Target set includes video of researchers entering and exiting the centre on October 4.
Fear detected, subdominant, short duration / increasing from previous target set. More information required. Follow-up suggested.

Her program running the current set, from the current damn time period, had sent out a red flag. It was requesting immediate follow-up action on the research mission right now. *Huh.* She hadn't expected that.

Renya scrolled through raw data. The fear displays were increasing in number and duration, and the intervals between fear displays were diminishing. Why had she even programmed for that? That wasn't a metric that mattered. Maybe it mattered. Maybe it was a bad sign. She'd been generous when she'd programmed in the fear tolerances here too. She'd figured that it wouldn't really matter.

Renya sat up. The man next door was having an argument again, heated this time. His voice was constricted with anger, but sometimes the rage bubbled out. At intervals, it boomed through the walls. She stopped to listen, but she still couldn't make out any words.

She didn't want to think about what follow-up action she should perform on the research mission she was currently stuck on. She could find more confirmation for the historical case instead.

Renya heard the man's voice boom again, the argument back in full swing. There was a crack against the wall, something thrown in the other room, and Renya startled. Maybe she could find audio of the calls for help, the calls to decision makers, from after the accident. Those would have been explosive. It was the nineteen eighties, so they must have telephoned. Would the calls have been recorded? Would they have been saved? Politicians recorded and kept conversations, certainly, although on tape, or something similarly sticky and ridiculous, at that time, and would that have even survived everything that happened after? It was a moot point anyway. The suits hadn't given her any audio files.

Renya flipped through the images they *had* provided. She found picture after picture of firefighters, pilots and miners, liquidators, biorobots. Okay. She'd already run the firefighters and pilots. She'd move on to miners.

The explosion caused fires to rage above, and the reactor to melt down below. The core was melting down, literally melting everything around it as it dripped down through the reactor floor first, and then through the earth and rock. If it hit the groundwater, it could poison the Black Sea. It could kill everything around it, and everything that depended on it. Water was a moderator too, so it could also cause the fuel to go critical. So they sent miners to shore up the site from below. They had to dig underneath and then build something to protect and isolate the reactor, well, what was left. They had to install a liquid-nitrogen refrigerator all the way down there to cool down the core, and they had to do it *fast*. It was hot. At the time, the reaction was still unprotected and generating heat. The miners had to strip down or they couldn't move. They had to take off their masks or they couldn't breathe. They dug tunnels. Some of them died as they worked, of heat, of stress, of radiation poisoning maybe. It's speculated that some had ingested poisonous dust. The pictures seemed to show them getting ready for shifts, then cooling off after. In the images, the miners held shovels and other tools. They looked straight ahead. To Renya, their expressions looked flat. She couldn't detect any muscle activation at all.

ALGORITHMIC OUTPUT

Target set: April 28, 1986 / exclusion zone surrounding / miners

---

Dominants: fear

Displays discovered: fear; disgust; zygomatic and levator labii activity detected

---

Statistics [fear expressions]: scroll down

Qualitative review of what was observed in the target-set material:

Target set includes photographs of miners resting after shifts digging under the crippled reactor four.

Fear detected across many subjects. Emotional displays are uniform and consistent, and surpass the fear threshold programmed for this location. More information required.

Again, the program had found what she hadn't. The subjects were displaying fear. It was at the lowest threshold amount, but it was still there. The displays were uniform and consistent.

Renya took a deep breath and loaded the pictures she'd taken outside in the field.

ALGORITHMIC OUTPUT

Target set: October 4, 2013 / zone of alienation, outer ring, research quadrant eleven

---

Dominants: happiness; fear

Displays discovered: fear; excitement; disgust; activity in supercilii muscle group

---

Statistics [fear expressions]: scroll down

Qualitative review of what was observed in the target-set material:

Target set includes photographs of large-animal researchers on location in quadrant eleven of the outer zone of alienation.

Fear detected, subdominant, short duration / increasing from previous target set.

Renya sat back. Her fingers and toes tingled. She was experiencing fear right now. Maybe it wasn't real fear. Maybe it was apprehension, or nerves. Maybe those emotions were close enough to fear to count.

She'd generated a red flag in her program. She'd caught real fear too. She'd seen unhidden fear responses while taking pictures outside. Maybe those guys had been working too hard, and she'd caught them as they were taking a break, as they'd broken themselves out of the spell. Or maybe fear was fear. Maybe it could break through. Maybe some findings were just scary, no matter how busy you were. Renya wondered what the people out there had found. Claire had said she was concerned about early results too. Just about all the researchers were affected now. They'd been excited but were becoming afraid now. The emotional displays were consistent across fields of research. That had to be meaningful.

⊙ ⊙ ⊙

Renya sat down on the bed. She turned off the bedside lamp and lay down. She turned over. She told herself to sleep. Somehow that didn't work. She waited.

So she might be in a bit of danger here. At least she'd made friends.

She turned the lamp back on. She stood, then walked circles around the room, then stared out the window a while. Finally, she grabbed her computer and flung herself back onto the bed. It creaked satisfyingly under her weight.

She settled in and started the search: Claire first, then Shantoo. Renya didn't have to work hard. Claire's name came up everywhere. She was a Rhodes Scholar. She had endowment after endowment. Her articles were cited all over the place. For all that Charlie and Telerson were touted as the hotshots here, Claire had lapped them, and she was young too.

Renya looked up Shantoo and found the same, her name cited in every major publication, mentioned on all the forums. She was a prodigy.

She was interesting too: she'd come up in a gentrifying city in a rapidly building country, and had somehow convinced builders to let her piggyback on soil sampling, so she had one of the most comprehensive soil-analysis programs ever. Renya found article after article after article in all the big publications.

They were the stars here. You wouldn't know it from how they acted. Charlie was the one who was always talking about accomplishments, but he'd done nothing compared to these two.

Renya grinned. She was proud of them. She liked them too.

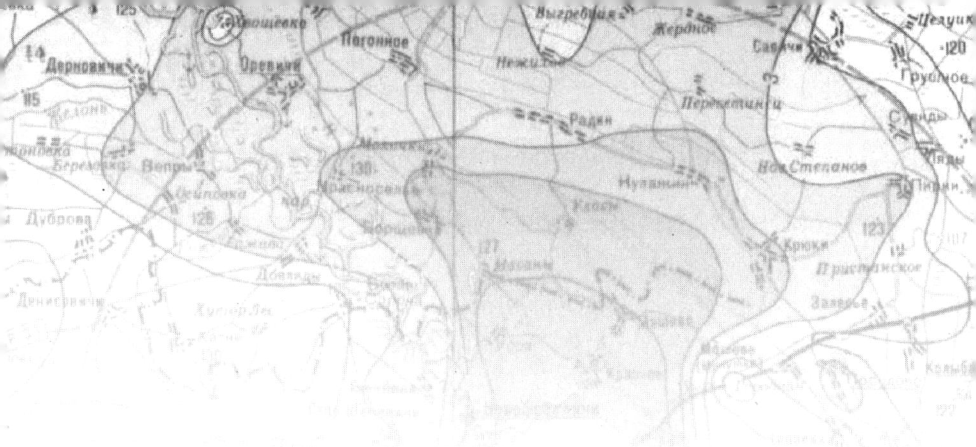

CHAPTER 6

RENYA WOKE AND IMMEDIATELY GRABBED FOR HER COMPUTER. She checked Skype, but it was just habit now. She hadn't expected Nick to be around, but there he was.

Nick's face popped into view, suddenly taking up the whole screen. He was holding the computer close, or kneeling right in front of it, she couldn't tell. She blinked and blinked, still not completely awake. "Why are you up?" she asked.

She'd hoped to see him. She'd been lonely when she'd reached for his hand this morning and come up with nothing, just an aggressively flat pillow. She was certainly not going to tell him that.

"What do you mean why am I awake?" he rasped.

Renya leaned in toward the computer. "Are you okay?" She scrutinized the screen. "Are you short of breath?"

"I'm fine."

"Do you feel any tightness in your chest?"

"No."

"Anything in your jaw or arm?"

"Stop it, Renya."

Nick's brows were knit together, his upper eyebrows raised. He was feeling anger, or frustration, more like. "I'm worried about my wife."

"You don't have to worry about me. I'm working. I'm fine. There's nothing wrong with me."

"Renya, we've been through this. I'm fine. It was nothing."

"Right."

"You didn't have to go."

Renya watched his image on her computer screen. He had bags under his eyes. His face was sallow. His hair was greying too, but it had been since they met. He was still handsome, but in a very different way from Yuri. There was nothing fragile about Yuri. But then, there hadn't been anything fragile about Nick either.

⊙ ⊙ ⊙

Renya didn't bother to dry her hair, or even to get coffee from the cafeteria. She just jogged out into the woods. She huffed up a small incline, past scratchy little trees and scrubs. Her dosimeter popped contentedly from her day pack. She ignored it and ran faster.

She was angry. Of course she was angry. Nick had had an affair. It didn't matter if it was just an emotional affair. It didn't matter if it was just a kiss. It didn't matter. None of it mattered. He'd cheated. She'd been faithful, and he'd cheated. They'd promised each other, what, something, and he hadn't kept up his side of things.

Renya slowed. She touched the side of a tree. She'd been faithful, technically. But she'd arranged to be gone a lot. It could be said that she'd left by other means. You could probably make the argument that she'd left before he had.

She picked off a scroll of bark. These were the mechanics by which she lied to herself, she knew. She experienced an emotion, anger say, and she attributed it to a cause in which she was in the right.

She leaned against the tree. She wasn't angry about the other woman. The indiscretion, or whatever he wanted to call it, made her feel bad, but maybe it wouldn't have gone any further than a kiss. It was a fine thing to focus on when she was angry, but she shouldn't do that anymore. She wasn't some grad-school wife anymore, some young academic. She should grow up. Before the affair, the indiscretion or whatever, he'd gotten sick. She shouldn't be mad at a person for getting sick, for having an event or an episode, for whatever they'd decided to call it in the end. A good person wouldn't be angry about that.

She marched forward.

⊙⊙⊙

Renya found one of the large-animal groups huddled around some traps. They were wearing masks, but she could easily work around that. She hid behind some trees and took the requisite pictures. There was Robert, that guy who'd wanted her to read his work. She would not be reading his work. She watched the rest of them vaguely. She picked up mostly contentment and focus. Maybe there were some short displays. Maybe, in the case of the men in the back, some muscles had been pulling up the skin of the foreheads, but it had been quick and she'd have to look at the pictures later to be sure. She squinted, then refocused her camera. Their traps were empty. There were some smudges around the front though. Was that fur? Could there be blood? There were dark red stains on the leaves. The men were gesturing toward whatever it was as they talked. She'd ask them about it later, in the exit interviews and all that.

Renya turned. She heard something from deeper in the woods. Quietly, she skirted past the bushes and farther into the trees. Somehow, she knew that she'd find Yuri. And there he was, leaning against a log, fiddling with the delicate papers of a cigarette. He was immersed in rolling it between his fingers, but she knew that he was acutely aware of her presence. He was forcing her to make the first move.

She skidded to a stop. For a moment, they just stared at each other, and Renya was that shy little girl in the church basement again. But then she realized that *he'd* found *her*. This wasn't their usual spot. He must have been looking for her. "Are you following me?" she said.

Yuri lit the cigarette. He inhaled deeply. If it wasn't for the constant smoking, she'd wonder if he was a ghost like the ones her grandmother had talked about. But that smell was real enough. She reached out and touched his arm, then dropped her hand again. He was solid. He was watching her quizzically now.

"Do you want a ride?" he said finally. He motioned to a motorcycle. It looked like it had been cobbled together out of parts of kitchen gear.

"Does that even run?" said Renya.

"You can't live here and not know how to fix anything that could break."

The kickstand seemed to yaw. "Is it broken now?"

"Anyway, I have my handy," he said.

"Handy?"

Yuri took a clunky old cellphone out of his pocket. Renya hadn't seen anything like it in a decade.

"Oh." She crept toward the motorcycle. "A cellphone," she said. "A cell."

"Cell cell cell," said Yuri. "You will come? I have something to show you. It's better than your scientists. I finished my shift and I can take you."

Renya touched the handlebars delicately. At home, she would never have even considered the offer. She wasn't a person who took those kinds of risks. But she'd asked *him*. She'd even offered to pay. "Yes," she said. "I want to come."

Yuri swung himself onto the bike, and Renya sat clumsily behind him, resting her knees against him, feeling his legs, ropey and muscular. She hesitated for a second, then put her arms around his waist. He smelled smoky. She'd expected the stench of cigarettes, but he smelled more like outdoor leaf fires. He was remarkably solid. She leaned in.

Yuri struggled with the bike. She felt his muscles pulling. His movements were getting brusque, frustrated, but then the ignition took and they were moving surprisingly quickly and she forgot about her fear, about his mood, about the sensation of being pressed to him. She forgot everything. The woods turned into a stream of sickly yellows and greens. Finding air was hard. When Yuri finally slowed, she was relieved.

⊙ ⊙ ⊙

Yuri gestured Renya toward a clearing as she extricated herself from the bike and smoothed her tangled hair. She looked up to the battered remains of a house.

"This was from before the accident?" she said.

Yuri nodded. He shook out another cigarette.

Renya stumbled on tree roots. She fell to her knees. There were tire tracks in the dirt, thick imprints pressed into the mud around the root systems.

"Men in uniforms came here once." Yuri knelt. He offered her a hand and pulled her up remarkably gently, his other hand holding her back lightly. "They were making all the houses fall apart. I wasn't here then, but I heard."

"I heard that too," said Renya. His hand was warm. His fingers were long and delicate. He didn't let go. Neither did she. Yuri moved closer, so that their shoulders were touching, and Renya felt her breath quicken. She studied the house's support beams and foundations, and didn't look up at his face. She didn't know whether he was watching her. She couldn't control her breathing.

But then she looked around again. The house was fascinating. The walls were crumbling. A part of the roof had fallen right in. She let go and walked closer. "They were going to raze all the surrounding towns," she said, "but realized that they were creating even more radiation when the dust from the houses hit the air and blew away. It was more dangerous to knock them down than just to leave them."

Yuri curled his fingers around his cigarette, protecting it against the wind. He lit it, with a spark first, then a glow, then a quick movement of the hand. "And now," he said, "it gives the people someplace to go."

"Sure," said Renya, "but nobody could possibly live here."

"Where else do they have to go to?"

"This is the exclusion zone."

"So?" He turned away from her to inhale deeply. He seemed to shiver.

Renya shivered too. Maybe it was a sympathetic response. There was probably still dust in the air. It was probably still radioactive. She walked closer to the house. Nobody seemed to know for sure what the radiation was like here. There were camps, and those camps all had things to gain. There were farmers nearby, still growing produce. There were competing manufacturers. There were multiple governments. But nobody supposed that prolonged exposure was safe. This was the outer ring of the zone of alienation, sure, but it was still closer to the inner ring than even where she was staying. You could stay a matter of days, a couple weeks max, no more.

Renya breathed carefully, hoping she didn't ingest anything bad. She wished she'd remembered Claire's mask. She wished she'd remembered to ask for more. She heard Yuri walk up beside her again, and they watched the house in silence. There was still glass in the windows. It was cracked, but it seemed more or less intact. This was safe enough as long as they didn't go inside any untreated structures.

Finally, and with more courage than she thought she even possessed, she reached out and touched the doorknob gingerly. Yuri pushed past her. He opened the door with his shoulder and walked right inside. Was that safe? Renya crept in after. Maybe it was safe. It would be safe enough as long as they left the door open. The interior of the house was airless, dark, and smelled like mildew and rot. Long streamers of light from the windows illuminated squares of floor, dust mites, and mounds of dust and sand. There was still furniture here. There was a big room right at the front with a heavy old wooden table and three dining-room chairs. On the table was a silver spoon that caught the light. In the corner, by a window, was an armchair with an old woollen blanket thrown across it. Farther still were three closed doors, leading to bedrooms, presumably, where people used to sleep. The people who had lived here had all left. They'd been forced to leave all their stuff. They'd abandoned their whole lives. A hole of sadness yawned open inside her. It seemed to rip from her solar plexus down through her stomach. She swallowed. She was facing a big move too.

A flash of motion caught Renya's attention, and she wheeled around to face the fireplace. There were ashes inside it, some glowing a dull blue. An ember danced. That's what must have caught her attention. Beside the fireplace was a child's doll. It was muddy, but the colours of the fabric dress looked bright. She crouched beside it. The plastic face shone coolly. There was no dust on it at all. She leaned closer to inspect it, and she swore she could see fingerprints.

Renya's breath caught in her throat.

"Come." Yuri motioned farther into the house. He gently opened one of the doors, and they crept into a gloomy bedroom. Sunlight struggled into the room through drawn wooden shades, and Renya could see the dust in the air. She held her breath. She opened a creaking dresser. Inside were clothes folded neatly. She slammed it shut again.

Renya stumbled out, through the hall and out of the house. After a few minutes, Yuri reappeared.

"Come," he said, touching her fingers again, motioning around the side of the house, up an incline.

Nobody could be living there now. What must your life be, if this was your safest option, if you would bring a child here? Those embers must have been a trick of the light. That doll must have been long abandoned. No children could be here.

Once they reached the top of the hill, Yuri pointed. Far in the distance was a grey tower.

"That's a cooling tower," said Yuri.

Renya stopped. She felt fingers of fear creep up her spine, then tingle down again. Fear. That was fear. It was thrilling.

"That's it?" she whispered. She stepped close to Yuri again. She felt the fabric of his pants with her fingers.

"Reactor one," he said. "Still running. The sarcophagus is behind."

The skies threatened. She turned back and noticed that all the trees here were barren, skeletal almost. There was hardly any colour at all. But it was fall. That could be normal. She drew in a breath. "I hadn't realized we were so close," she breathed. But she'd wanted to come closer, hadn't she? Every morning, she'd lain in bed and psyched herself up. Every afternoon, she'd ventured nearer. Again, she'd asked him to take her.

"There's something else I want to show you." Yuri gestured toward the motorcycle. He jumped on, and Renya climbed on behind him and they sped farther into the woods, in which direction Renya couldn't guess. The trip passed in another blur. This time, Renya hardly noticed the rushing air. She was going to have to move, she reminded herself. She was going to have to reinvent her life. She was going to leave everything in her old life behind. She had options. She wouldn't end up in the exclusion zone.

⊙ ⊙ ⊙

"There." Yuri quickly dismounted, and Renya followed him up another small hill. At the top, he stopped abruptly and pointed. "There," he said again. "Do you see them?"

Renya crested the hill and saw many little red rectangles at the bottom, some distance off. She squinted, struggling to make sense of what she was seeing. Then she understood.

"Those are the original ones?" she whispered. "Those are the fire trucks?"

They were so far away as to look tiny, like little toys left out in a park for too long. Could they really be the originals? She knew they'd been left. She knew they were still there. She'd seen pictures. She'd seen videos. Her fingers tingled. She felt her face flush.

"They came to put out the fire in the reactor," said Yuri. "Nobody can move them now."

"They're still radioactive," she breathed. She'd pored over pictures of them in books. And now she was here. She was looking right at them. This was living history. She was part of it now. She was seeing it. She was living this history too.

"Even I don't go close to there." He stroked the small of her back, then motioned for her to follow. Renya tingled all over. "Now. I'll take you back to our place. I can show you more tomorrow. I can take you to the settlements. Where people live now. Or maybe I'll take you to Prypyat. We'll see tomorrow." And Renya's skin prickled, with fear, with anticipation, with the unanticipated pleasure of hearing this strange man say *our place,* and *we.*

⊙ ⊙ ⊙

Yuri dropped Renya close to the centre, at the bottom of a hill just before it would come into view, Renya knew. Renya watched Yuri wheel the motorcycle around and disappear into the trees. She hesitated. She should go back inside. She didn't want to. She still wanted to explore. She wanted to run in the woods. She wanted to ride this high. Instead, she stomped around the worn shrubs for a minute, then forced herself to be quiet. She still had work to do. She fished her topographical map from her pocket and looked up her next scheduled photography session. It was the bird team. That was fortuitous. She turned and jogged through the woods until she found Claire and her team.

She took out her camera. She focused on Claire, then started to take pictures. The camera made a satisfying snap in the quiet of the woods. Then she looked through the shots in the display. In the first pictures, Claire's eyebrows were wrinkled, the space above the bridge of her nose contracted. That signalled fear, maybe, or it could be grief or sadness. The overall picture presented was complicated. Above all, Claire looked lost in thought. She could be thinking about something sad.

Renya crept around the trees to get another angle. She took more pictures. Claire's eyebrows suddenly smoothed. Then she frowned. Then she grinned. Then she stuck out her tongue. *Oh no.* Had she been so excited that she hadn't remembered to be quiet? Had she come too close?

Renya stepped out of the trees and put her hands up. "You caught me," she called out, walking toward her briskly. The wind had picked up. The cold air snapped past her neck.

"Sorry," said Claire, rubbing her hands together, distancing herself from her team.

"I don't mean to be intrusive," said Renya. "I certainly don't want to interrupt."

"I was just going to go back in," Claire said, signalling to the mask around her wrist. One elastic had snapped and was waving in the wind. "I must have forgotten to take the good ones."

Maybe that was the source of the anxiety she'd seen? She should ask, she knew. She didn't.

Claire was distracted anyway. She pointed to Renya's backpack. "Clicking," she said.

"Oh yeah." Renya wrestled her day pack off her back and pulled out the dosimeter. "It doesn't really do much," she said.

"You came prepared," said Claire.

"Not really," said Renya. "I didn't even think about masks. Anyway, this is a relic. It was left over from the fifties' scares, I'm guessing. They scan us as we leave anyway."

"I don't know what I think about the final scans," said Claire.

"Why?"

Claire nodded to the dosimeter. "Have you been recording?"

"I'm not very good about it," said Renya. "I just jot down the readings and times on my daily map printouts as I think about it, or as the machine freaks out. I transfer numbers to a notebook but not religiously."

"Can I review the numbers?"

"Sure," said Renya, as Claire took her by the arm and steered her back to the path. "It's not very scientific though. It's not structured at all. I've marked down the time and location of the measurement, but I haven't organized a scheduled study or anything like that. It's pretty random."

"I'd be interested to see what you have," Claire said and walked her back to the centre.

⊙⊙⊙

Renya and Claire found Shantoo sitting by herself in the cafeteria, playing with the frayed ends of the table's off-white tablecloth. Everything was dreary here. Even that was thrilling today.

As Renya sat down, Shantoo looked up. Her eyes were wide and sad, but she was smiling, bravely, it seemed to Renya. The skin around Shantoo's eyes was smooth. There were no orbicularis muscles activated. There was barely any zygomaticus major involvement either.

"You'll have to forgive me," Shantoo said, as if noticing her professional interest. "I've been staying up late at night, and I shouldn't."

"You've been talking to the climate team," Claire said softly.

"I definitely shouldn't do that," said Shantoo.

"Not if you want to sleep," said Claire. "Not if you want peace of mind."

"Some of them are measuring albedo like me," she said, "albedo and carbon capture. Others are worried about the effects of here on other places. I'm concerned that problems from other places are showing up here. I'd say we're all ruining each other's sleep."

Claire perked up. "Did you find something new?"

"Microplastics."

Claire nodded grimly and started fidgeting with the tablecloth as well. "We've been finding that too," she said. "Inside the nests. It's inside the birds too. I've run tests to see if it's even crossed the blood-brain barrier. I'm waiting to see."

"I've found it much deeper than I would have imagined possible."

"I don't even think we're the first groups to find it. I've heard people talking, but I haven't seen anything published yet."

"Have you looked for chemicals?" said Shantoo. "PFAS?"

"Waiting on results."

"I have a list of specific compounds you could perhaps search for."

"I'd love to see it."

Shantoo turned to Renya. "You can perhaps settle the argument."

"What argument?" said Renya.

"What we're supposed to be most afraid of." Shantoo stroked the tablecloth's frayed edges. "Claire told me about your conversation the other night. You wanted to create a program to detect fear. Important people got excited. They sent you here."

"I asked to come, in fact," said Renya. It was part of her scientist origin story. She didn't know how to tell them that. She wanted to.

"You knew they were important people because they were wearing fancy clothes," said Claire.

"Fancy clothes in large numbers," muttered Renya, "that's significant."

"What fear do they want to monitor?" said Shantoo. "What should we be afraid of? There are possibilities, you see."

"I don't know," Renya said. "I don't know that they cared about the location at all."

"You think they just cared about the programming."

"They were interested in international news and private feeds," said Renya. "*I* just wanted a life change. Nick told me about his affair. I'd just heard about a grad student going on a research trip, she's one of the plant people, you might know her, she was on the last cycle, and then I googled it and wanted in too. I proposed this idea. Really, even before the problems with Nick, I'd wanted a change." They were staring, Renya saw.

"What I do is so small," Renya explained. "I was measuring degree differences in muscular movements, eyebrow-raises in emotional displays, that kind of thing, comparing hundredths of degree of differences between scientists and non-scientists. At the same time, I was watching all these documentaries about Chernobyl. The scientists then, they were living big lives. They'd invented a new way to create energy. They created whole new fields. And in the midst of all that, they were working and networking and trying to avert wars. Then I watched all these news clips from back when the accident happened, and I couldn't stop watching the scientists' faces, the newscasters' expressions. They kept saying that they weren't scared at all, but they were so clearly in the midst of terror. They were lying and I could prove it. Well, I couldn't prove they were lying, but I could prove they were afraid. I knew I could write a program to catch it. So I made the pitch. I didn't expect my supervisor to jump, but he jumped, and got me this strange meeting three days later. I still don't know the funding bodies."

"People were interested," Claire said softly. "They're interested in your work in general anyway, the scientists, the Eastern German thing, reading expressions in repressive places, the road rage ideas. I looked you up. You're important."

"I'm not important," said Renya. "I'm not particularly listened to at all. But then, at that meeting, I asked, 'What if I could identify signs of fear in scientists?' And suddenly, everyone was listening." She looked down at her fingers. She was so obvious in her preoccupations. Scientist husband has a heart attack, find an early warning system for physicists. "I asked, 'What if I can find out when scientists are experiencing distress? What if I could program software to flag it?'"

"Scientists?" said Shantoo.

"I've made myself an expert on scientists as a population," said Renya. "Finally, that might work for me."

"So here's why it's important," said Shantoo. "I'm finding some deeply strange results, some chemicals and other traces in the soil here that you wouldn't expect in depopulated areas. I've heard chatter about other scientists seeing similar things, here and in some other locations, the Amazon basin, for one. I have seen no published articles about that either."

"They want us to come," said Claire. "But do they want to monitor our results just to quash them?"

"Universities are very dependent on industry sponsorship," said Shantoo. "Some of those industries like plastics very much."

"I thought at first that the government didn't want us delving too deeply into climate change," said Claire.

"Maybe my administration doesn't want me looking into earth degradation," said Shantoo, "at least not-*industry*-caused earth degradation."

"Or maybe, I thought, they didn't want us upsetting the larger populations." Claire turned to Renya. "Who is worried if *scientists* are distressed?"

"Me, obviously," Renya said slowly. "My husband had a heart attack. I didn't see it coming."

Shantoo and Claire looked up. "I'm sorry," they said at once. But then they turned to each other once again.

"Are our governments worried about what we'll find?" said Shantoo. "Do they know already what's out there? Or are they worried about who we're going to tell?"

"Why bother monitoring a population's emotions unless you plan to control them?" said Claire.

"Researchers are already dependent on funding," said Shantoo.

"When I mentioned the location," said Renya, "when I said the word Chornobyl, sorry, Chernobyl, they, the funding committee that is, didn't show any obvious reaction. I got the distinct impression they didn't particularly care." She didn't want to control. She wanted to harness. Maybe harnessing emotions and controlling people were distressingly similar as concepts. That was a worrying thought. Too late now though. She'd think about it later. She'd add it to the list.

"So *you* proposed the location," said Shantoo.

"I told you," said Claire. "There are wider benefits to monitoring fear, obviously."

"For who?" said Shantoo.

"Governments," said Claire. "Universities too, I guess."

"Who would they be concerned about?" said Shantoo. "What are they looking for?"

"Outbreaks for sure," said Renya. "Weapons research too, I would guess."

"Wait," said Shantoo. "What?"

"They're scared of weapons?" said Claire.

"I don't really know what they want," said Renya. "All I know is that suddenly all these well-dressed people were listening to me, so I had to figure out something to say, and fast. So I made a bunch of stuff up. I said I'd use the program as a way to check whether countries are telling the truth about arms research and manufacturing. I also talked about outbreaks, accidents, nuclear of course, but chemical too. Also, I said we could check in on virologists and doctors, all the people studying flight paths of infectious agents. Governments tend to placate. They tend not to allow the whole truth to be told, even as they're broadcasting images of scientists at work. But you can find the truth if you zoom in on the scientists, you know? Sometimes they show shots of triage and hospitals on the news. Often, there are scientists next to politicians in press conferences, but doctors can't act as well, and emotional reactions creep up on you. Fear is a powerful emotion. There are compelling reasons for it to make itself seen. Sometimes the newscasters themselves understand that the information they're relaying is false or falsely reassuring, and they can't repress their emotions all the time. Repressive governments can withhold telling the truth, but nobody can repress fear completely. Anyway, that's what I was envisioning. That's what I talked about, with all those people turned toward me, in the midst of all that silence."

"How would governments have access to working scientists?" said Claire.

"On the news, I was assuming. I pitched it as a way of studying foreign news broadcasts, but I got the impression the people in the meeting had other ideas too. I don't know. They didn't say anything directly, but I got the impression they had some access somewhere."

Claire and Shantoo were watching each other with measured expressions.

"They must have credible worries," said Claire.

"Not the ones I thought," said Shantoo.

"Hard to tell," said Claire. "Same programming regardless."

Shantoo was nodding, pressing the tablecloth between her index finger and thumb. "Maybe there are multiple concerns." She paused. "There are labs shared among governments, for studying viruses, among other things. I've heard rumours about gain-of-function research. I hear sometimes that the government handlers get concerned about what the scientists get up to."

"What they do?" said Claire. "Not what they see?"

"Officials don't always understand," said Shantoo. "They can sometimes not enforce appropriate boundaries, when they don't properly understand the research being carried out."

Renya watched their faces. They displayed raised upper eyebrows, slightly open mouths. They were breathing quickly and shallowly. The fear was evident and unhidden now. She should ask about it, she knew. She should ask for clarification about what was making them this alarmed. She couldn't. She didn't. She didn't know that much about international labs, except for this one, of course.

"I doubt that I can actually pull this off," Renya said slowly. Claire and Shantoo weren't listening. She knew that they weren't worried about that. There was something else, something bigger, that was bothering them. Only Renya herself had been worried about whether she could actually do this. But she *was* doing it. Her program had raised the alarm. Scientists were scared. Claire and Shantoo were all but confirming it. Whole teams seemed to be unsettled. They hadn't been outwardly scared, and now they were, and she'd captured exactly the moment when the mood of the research trip had changed. This, she knew, was precisely what an early warning system was for. This was proof that her idea had merit and might even be working, although these were not the circumstances she'd foreseen, not exactly; she'd expected some general seepage, a few emotional slips every once in a while, not a complete sea change, a total turnaround in atmosphere and opinion.

That was important information. These were people whose worries should be heeded. But she didn't want to heed the warning, not yet. She wanted to see Yuri again. She wanted to see Prypyat.

"The labs out there are a problem," Claire was saying, although Renya had missed what she'd said earlier, "there's no denying it. That doesn't change the fact that we might not be as safe as we'd hoped here."

Shantoo turned back to her. "And are you finding lots of fear? You must be."

"No," said Renya. "Well, yes. To be honest, my program sent out red flags earlier this week, and the signals have been getting stronger. Now, I've seen some instances of unhidden fear. There have been some pretty big displays. That's all very unusual in the science community. It breaks display rules. It's not at all what I was expecting."

"That makes sense," said Claire.

Why? Renya didn't ask. "Usually everyone is happy," she said, "or engaged at the very least, and I can't read anything. It's just recently that I've found some other emotions, that fear that I mentioned. But, like I said, you can never tell what caused it."

"You're looking for large numbers," said Shantoo.

"Yes," said Renya.

"And you're starting to see the large numbers."

"I guess."

Shantoo and Claire looked at each other, and the silence stretched uncomfortably. The skin above their foreheads was wrinkled, but she didn't want to look too long. She wanted to think about Yuri, her adventure, going to Prypyat, finally seeing the city she'd obsessed over for so long. She quickly packed up her things.

She should pack up completely and leave this place. She did know that, even though she worked hard not to acknowledge it. But she couldn't, she realized with a jolt. She was stuck here. They were all stuck here, in all this radiation, safe or not. The transports back to civilization wouldn't come for another five days.

"Can we see your Geiger recordings?" said Claire. "Dosimeter readings, rather."

Renya smiled weakly at her companion. She pulled out her notebook. The annotated maps were all tucked inside. "How about I just leave them with you?" she whispered. "I need to grab some things from my room. I need to pack for my excursions tomorrow."

"Are you going back out again?" said Claire.

"Are you sure you don't want to focus on work here?" said Shantoo. "On things you can do from inside?"

"There are just a few things I still need to see," said Renya. "I have a bit more information to collect." She'd promised to meet Yuri again the next day.

"I suppose we all still have data to collect," said Shantoo.

Renya stood. As she retreated to her room, she thought about sitting on the couch in the days after Nick's illness, watching the flickering TV screen, poring over the documentaries that she already knew by heart. She'd brought some with her, downloaded to her laptop. She'd put one on so she could listen to it while she worked. She'd watched them before, plenty of times. She used to pore over this accident with her grandmother, with her father. She was just a kid when they'd started. She didn't know why they did that, but they always did, just the three of them. When faced with difficult circumstances, they'd always retreated to stories about Chornobyl.

⊙ ⊙ ⊙

Renya found herself pacing her small room, watching the lights across the worn carpet. She turned off the documentary. She paced more. She wanted to go outside again. She wanted to explore. She understood that she should stay inside. Someone was also pacing, just outside her window, it sounded like. She could hear footfalls crunching through gravel, and an angry muted voice, speaking in Mandarin.

She sat back on the bed and pulled out her computer. As she opened it, she heard the familiar trill, and she clicked on the jiggling phone icon. Instantly, Nick's face appeared on the screen. He was in his office now. There were papers and clothes scattered on the floor. That wasn't like him. His office was sacrosanct. He dusted. He even dusted his books. There was a suitcase leaning on his chair, its giant mouth yawning open.

Nick leaned in instantly. "What's the reading now?"

"No hello?"

"Renya!"

She should tell him the project is working. She should tell him that she'd found fear. There were danger signals and her program had identified them before she had. "I saw two microroentgens on the road today," she said instead. "It was higher in the grass."

"It's cumulative, you know. That's above the legal limit, even for nuclear workers!"

"It was like a hundred in this moss I found."

"That would kill you in two hours."

"People *live* here." But she remembered Claire's hesitance, the strange drifts and pauses in conversation, Shantoo's pallor as she looked through her notebook. The readings were high, she knew. She hadn't looked for patterns. She hadn't estimated daily absorption amounts. They were supposed to be safe in the forest and in the compound. They were outside the outer ring of the exclusion zone. Sure, there were hot spots around, but it was supposed to be safer here.

"I just want you to be safe," Nick was saying.

"The government says –"

"You can kiss someone else! I gave you permission to . . . Look, it's a logical – I don't see why you're getting angry, I sincerely –"

"Who wouldn't want to hear something like that," said Renya.

"I want to fix this," he said. "Listen, I'm trying something. I don't want to say too much in case I can't pull it off, but –"

"There's a graveyard here, just for fire trucks," Renya interrupted. "They're right beside reactor four, dozens of them. Right where they were when the firemen started dying. And nobody can move them anymore! You can't get near them because they're so radioactive. They'd kill you. They'd irradiate you. After the explosion in the nuclear plant, a fire broke out and that triggered an automatic response and lured firefighters to their death."

"Don't touch anything. Don't stand under trees or branches."

"That wouldn't pose much of a concern now that so much time has passed." Maybe he understood the physics behind this even less than she thought. Maybe he didn't know everything, but why had she assumed he would, since she knew how focused physics was. Nuclear was not his specialization.

"Don't go off the roadway at all," Nick was saying. His eyes were wide and pleading, his upper eyelids raised. She still loved that face. She'd loved him for so long though. Maybe this emotion flooding her now was just habit. It could be the result of electrons running down well-worn neural pathways and nothing more.

Had anyone ever studied if feelings calcified? That might have to do with neural paths or plasticity or something similar. She could look into that next. But probably she shouldn't. She knew what she was feeling, but she didn't want to feel it. She loved him, and she was baiting him. She'd prefer to be the type of person who acted differently, who felt something else. She didn't want to be mean. She didn't want to love him still, if he was just leaving anyway.

He was leaving because she'd made him leave. She didn't want to admit that to herself either. He was leaving because she'd pushed him away. She'd been gone all the time, and another woman had taken her place. She tried to imagine Nick and the other woman kissing on the rain-slicked sidewalk outside of the bar that night. She couldn't picture her. She had the mental image of a ghost, but that wasn't right.

"None of the firemen understood what was happening," she said. "They didn't know it was the *reactor* on fire. They died within the week, many of them. It was acute radiation poisoning. They had to be buried in lead coffins. The coffins had to be welded shut."

"Ren!"

"What?"

"Please."

"Okay." She searched his face for anger or impatience. She found nothing. Just tenderness. "Yeah, okay." But that could be habit too. Feelings were hard to pinpoint. People got passionate about plants.

"Please," he said. "Please, this is important."

"I'm listening."

"I need you to be careful. Don't ingest any radioactive particles. Try not to swallow too much. Something that's okay on the outside could kill you if you swallow it. Even if it isn't that radioactive, even if it's only emitting a few alpha particles, when you swallow it, it continues to emit, and no doctor can get to it because it's just dust, it's impossible to find."

"That was more common then, Nick," she said softly. "There are different dangers now." It was the accumulation you worried about now. Different particles, different emitted radiations and energies. It was still dangerous, but not what he was imagining.

"For God's sake, don't go inside any buildings."

"Stop!" She held up a hand, and it worked. "Listen now. Listen to me." Nick shut up. He stopped the weird broadcast mode he was in anyway. "The government of Canada has okayed this trip. Top physicists, your buddies, have reviewed the information and concluded that we can be here safely for short periods. As long as we're careful, as long as we don't eat the local vegetables, as long as we don't forage the local fruit, as long as –"

"Do you believe them?"

She didn't. Maybe she had at the beginning, maybe she hadn't, but she certainly didn't believe the party line now. "Yes," she said. Her voice was hard. It boomed in her ears.

Nick knelt in front of the computer. "Do you understand what's happening there? Please. Please at least let me tell you what I understand, what I know of –"

"Okay yeah."

"I just want to –"

"No, I'm serious this time." Renya let out a breath. He'd studied up on it, the history, the physics behind the event. She knew him. "Tell me what you've figured out." He wouldn't stop. He'd just talk and talk and interrupt and interrupt until she let him get this out of his system. "Just say what you need to say."

"Radiation means high-velocity particles," Nick said. "We're made up of particles, but they're spread out. On a molecular level, we're mostly just air."

"I'm not some first-year."

"I know but –"

That's how he started his first lectures. "I do like that thought though." She used to sit in for the first class. She'd thought it was such a poetic way to begin. "I've always liked that thought."

"So if these high-velocity particles hit one of our component parts, it will knock out one of the pieces. And the cell that it's part of will never regenerate. It could either trigger a mutation, or the cell could just die. Mutations are bad, obviously, but if enough cells die . . ."

"How do you know if the particles will hit you?" said Renya. "It's so unlikely that they will. We run the same risk everywhere. It's just heightened here."

"It's not just a hit. They have to hit you in the right way."

"Like a pinball game."

"Yes. Exactly."

"Pinball games, billiards . . . Anyway, those high-velocity particles occur naturally, from the sun. When I rode that motorcycle, I felt like I was mostly air."

"When were you were on a motorcycle?"

Renya didn't answer.

Nick ran his hands through his hair. "Okay," he said, shaking his head. "Okay. Anyway, most of the sun's particles are blocked by the ozone layer. And since we're mostly empty space –"

"It was a really crappy bike," said Renya. "Everything you find here is shitty."

"But when you're near a radioactive source, it's like a wall of high-velocity particles, coming right at you. There wouldn't be that much gamma radiation anymore. You're right about that. It's probably all alpha and beta now –"

"It's alarmingly beautiful though."

"Ren?"

"It's all grown in with these brown grasses and straggly trees, and no people, well, no visible people, and so few houses. And you can feel that it's not right somehow. But it's all . . . everything here . . . it's damaged and weird and unbearably beautiful."

"Ren, sweetheart."

Nick was kneeling by the computer again. For a moment, Renya was disconcerted. "Yes?"

"This is important. Everything there is a radioactive source."

"Right."

"Everything. I know they've told you that you're safe. But remember that everything there could be radioactive, and so high-velocity particles could fall from them like rain, or more like a brick wall, because there could be that many of them. They could be coming at you like a brick wall. Make sure that you're never standing too close to anything."

"Nick," she said softly. That wasn't right, not exactly anyway. He must know that he didn't understand. "I don't know why it took me until today to realize this. But I know more about this than you do."

"I know you do," he said softly. Nick reached to touch the screen. "I don't know why I needed to say all that. I just needed to do something. Even if I just make sure that you're paying attention, that you're remembering the risks. I can't let you get caught up in the adventure part of it, especially since I should have been there. I should have joined you for the adventure." His hand fell away, and Renya wondered what he'd just seen from his end. Did he feel like he'd just touched her cheek? He hadn't. "I've been playing catch-up. I'm always playing catch-up with you. I even had to borrow your old textbooks."

Renya nodded. Nick reached out a hand to the screen again.

Renya reached out to her computer screen too. She dropped her hand. She hadn't consciously decided to do that. Maybe it was just habit. Maybe it was just an automatic empathy thing, like how you mirror the facial expressions of young children. But she remembered the feeling of his hand holding hers. She'd always liked that feeling.

CHAPTER 7

RENYA'S ALARM BLEATED PLAINTIVELY INTO HER EAR. SHE rolled over, half-expecting to find Nick's arm beside her, wanting to curl into him. But she was alone. Of course she was alone. And she was cold. Her blanket must have fallen away in the night.

She quickly showered, dressed and packed. What day was it, even? Saturday, she thought vaguely. During her childhood, she'd mostly spent Saturdays outside, in the park or the ravine, to give her father and stepmother space. In the first years of their marriage, she and Nick had mostly worked through Saturdays, but then they'd had lazy Sundays, always together. They'd had park strolls, pancakes, coffee. They had an apartment with a small balcony where they'd do the crosswords together, or sit in silence watching clouds. She wasn't missing it. She was just missing familiar things. She was tired too. She'd been so excited since she got here. She hadn't wanted to miss any opportunities. So she'd slept only a few hours at a time. It was just catching up with her, that was all.

As Renya struggled to get her sneakers on, she felt a cramp in her foot. She froze and sat down heavily on the dirty carpet. She tore off her sock. But her foot was still her foot. It was a bit red maybe, but otherwise the same as it had always been. She massaged it, pressing hard into the arch. She didn't feel anything out of the ordinary.

A bit of redness was fine. This was fine. She was being ridiculous.

She'd been walking tons. It probably meant nothing.

She put her head on her knees. There was something empowering about being here, about being one of the only people who was brave enough to come. But then there was also that background fear, starting again, evidently. Just like before, just like after Nick's illness, she didn't trust the feelings in her body. After the event, she'd felt that same panic, distrust of his body, sometimes distrust of her own. She'd scrutinize every look and every gesture. They could have been communicating some other meaning. She'd slept with one hand pressed against his back to feel his breathing.

Renya crammed her feet into her shoes. She pushed out the door and froze. The man next door was creeping out of his room too. She'd been so distracted that she hadn't heard the creaks in the floorboards. The man was frozen too. His face was wide open and young-looking, but his hair was peppered with grey.

Renya nodded to him. He nodded back and walked quickly down the hall.

Renya gave him a moment's lead, then walked quickly to the front door.

⊙ ⊙ ⊙

Renya hadn't realized just how closely she'd studied the pictures of Prypyat until she stumbled off Yuri's bike and stepped onto the cracked concrete. Even the tufts of brown grasses growing through the town's roads seemed oddly familiar. She felt like she was stepping into a dream.

Yuri wheeled the motorcycle to a nearby building and leaned it against the wall. He walked back to her, his hands in his pockets, seemingly unaffected. He gave the impression that he'd been here many times before. But that would make sense. It was his job, after all.

Renya looked down. The sidewalks were cracked and breaking, with plants and grasses growing in and around them, right into the streets. She looked up, at building after building, surrounded by trees, once carefully planted along avenues but now growing wildly everywhere. And the buildings themselves were being overtaken by plants and vines. And most disconcertingly, all were deserted. There was no major movement in the entire city. There was just the swaying of branches on spindly trees. There was hardly any sound. The silence weighed on her. It felt like it was pressing down on her. This was exactly as she'd imagined.

"You come here often?" she whispered, unwilling to disturb the stillness, the silence that felt almost sacred.

"We come all the time."

"For work?"

"Sometimes," said Yuri. "Sometimes with friends."

"Oh." Renya looked around again. He was joking, she was sure. "Okay." She worried briefly that Yuri might be mistaking her intentions. But what could he expect? They were in one of the most dangerous places on earth. She had a professional interest.

Yuri took her elbow and they walked farther into the city. After a moment, he stopped. He nodded to a tall building.

"This," he said, with some circumstance.

"It's the Palace of Culture," breathed Renya.

Yuri nodded. "You've seen the photographs," he said, mouthing a cigarette.

He steered her down another street, then another and quickly another, then pointed at another building. "Do you know this place?"

"No," she said. He'd moved so quickly that she was disoriented now. "Maybe. Is this the residential area? I'm trying to get my bearings."

But Yuri was already running, onto another street and toward another building. "Do you want to climb in the window?" he called over his shoulder.

"Is it safe?"

Yuri hopped through an empty window frame. Renya paused, holding her breath. Nick had said, everyone at home said, above all, don't go inside any buildings. She'd read that too, but it had only been true in the early days, really. It should be fine now, well, fine considering, no worse than anything else. Yuri and his colleagues went all the time, he said.

"Well?" Yuri appeared again in the window. He was watching her, not entirely kindly.

She found that she didn't want him to know that she was frightened.

"Coming," she said.

Yuri had made it look easy, but Renya didn't see a clear way inside. She carefully picked her way over, across the sidewalk, through the brambles and over the wreckage of broken things piled up beside the building's outer wall. The empty window frame had jagged glass stuck inside. It looked too high to just jump in as Yuri had. She imagined how she would get inside: hold side of frame, place one foot high, swing the other leg up. She reached for the window frame and held it gingerly, careful not to touch the jagged glass. She felt for the ledge with her foot and swung her first leg inside. Suddenly Yuri grabbed her other hand, pulled violently, and she was stumbling. She reeled, now inside the dimly lit room. She felt a searing pain in her leg. She grabbed the first thing she could, a jumble of timber, the remains of a table, a chair maybe, and reached down. Her hiking pants were torn, and blood was already dotting the fabric. Yuri noticed, she saw, but said nothing. So she didn't say anything either. She rubbed her bloody fingers on her thigh and surveyed the room. There was rubble everywhere. As her eyes adjusted to the gloom, she found herself surrounded by old furniture and dirt. The walls themselves were full of holes, everything streaked with dust in a coating heavy like paint. It was like a bomb had gone off. "Was this the blast?" she asked. "Did this happen when the reactor exploded?" She hadn't thought the city had been affected.

"Looters," Yuri said simply.

He turned and walked out of the room. Renya hesitated in the doorway, then followed deeper into the building, through dark corridors and an even heavier silence. She focused on keeping her breathing steady. What did Yuri mean by looters? That wasn't in any of the books. There were rumours on Internet forums, but Renya had assumed those were just scary stories. Everyone had left this place. Nobody had been allowed back. They certainly hadn't been allowed to take their things. This stuff was radioactive, all of it, not in high doses anymore, but constantly emitting. You were allowed to be around it for short intervals, but you wouldn't want to bring into your home. Who would want that? Who would want to be slowly poisoned?

She walked farther inside the structure. She hadn't planned to go inside at all. For all her bluster, this was a risk that she hadn't planned to take. So she'd keep this visit short. It was a risk, sure, not 100 percent safe, but nothing was completely safe, here or anywhere. It had been more dangerous in the early days. She'd try not to touch anything. She wouldn't take anything home, obviously. Low doses should be fine as long as she kept it to relatively short durations.

She was inside anyway, so she might as well explore a bit.

Yuri walked faster still, and she followed. She was a bit afraid of him, she realized. But she was more afraid to be alone. He reached the landing and sped down a hallway, so she sprinted after him, trying not to breathe too deeply.

Renya followed Yuri into a cavernous room. There were giant windows on two sides, and the streaming daylight illuminated slanted ribbons of dust. This space was empty now except for a flimsy arch of some sort, that might have been a goalpost of some sort once. Could this room have been a gym?

Yuri was kicking at the floor with the toes of one boot. He knelt, then picked something up. He put it in his pocket.

Renya looked away. She walked away from him, toward the far wall. Through the mostly glassless window, she could see down into a courtyard where fragile green-tipped trees swayed in the breeze. Yuri had put something in his pocket. That couldn't be safe. If that thing, whatever it was, had been here since the accident, then it would be radioactive, a constant source of high-velocity particles, beta waves at the very least, and he was walking around with it next to his body? Did he do that a lot? If so, there'd be no kids for him, she hazarded. Incongruously, she wanted to laugh and she had to put her hand to her mouth to stop herself. That was a weird stress response, she guessed. Yuri must have left something of his own here during his last patrol. That must have been something he'd brought from his home. Or maybe he just wanted to study it and bring it back.

Renya looked out the window again, careful not to touch the railing. A sound startled her and she jumped back. Suddenly Yuri was beside her. He clutched her arm protectively, although she'd been in no risk of falling.

"You're very brave, coming here," he said, his voice husky.

Renya breathed. Talk of bravery made her think about the risks, and she didn't want to think about the dangers right now.

"Not many women come here," he went on.

She shook her arm out of his grasp. "Not many men, either, I imagine."

"You're brave like a man."

Renya looked behind her, back into the room, at the warped and bending boards and joists, the buckling ceiling, the dust streaming in the unfiltered sunlight. This was unsafe for many reasons. It was also an avoidable risk.

"Nobody should be here," she mumbled. "Nobody was supposed to come back for hundreds of years."

He reached to touch her arm again.

Renya turned away, suddenly disgusted. Had she wanted him to touch her? She didn't think so, exactly, especially not here, not like this.

"You needed to see this?" Yuri said.

"I did," she whispered.

"You're taking pictures," he said gruffly. "You're a witness." He edged nearer. "I understand. I'm a witness too. We're the same, I think. We're being witnesses, for this place, for them." He took her arm, squeezing. "I knew that you were like me, that first day I saw you with your camera. You won't let this place be forgotten."

Renya shook herself free. "Please take me back to the research station," she said.

"But on our way, do you want to get close to reactor four?"

She paused. "How close?"

"It would be safe enough," he said. "I'll slow down the motorcycle. I won't even stop. Just to see."

"Not too close?"

"You'll go?"

"I'll go."

"Okay." Yuri was grinning, rocking back and forth on his feet. "We'll see it from a distance. Then one more stop on the way back."

"Where?"

"This place isn't dead, like people say. That's what people don't understand. That's what Dima doesn't understand."

"Dima?"

"I'll show you. There is so much to see here. I can help you see it. I can help you take your pictures. This is how I can be helpful. I can show you. This isn't a dead place, and we can be witnesses. We can help in that way at least."

⊙ ⊙ ⊙

That evening, back in the research centre, when Renya opened the computer, it was already buzzing. She opened the dialogue screen, unthinking. Nick's torso appeared immediately. He was holding a calculator. After a few seconds, his face came into view.

"I'm trying to figure out how to convert from roentgens to sieverts," he said.

He looked frantic, messy and moving, and he had piles of papers on his desk. There was that suitcase beside him, and there were even more clothes and supplies all around him. Already Renya could feel the tingling fingers, the buzzing feet, anger in all her limbs. Was he moving in to that woman's place? Were they going off for a weekend together? They could be camping. Nick hated camping. He'd go for her, Renya had no doubt.

"Ren?" said Nick. He knelt by the computer.

"We got close today."

"What do you mean, close?" Nick said. "Close to where?"

He knew what she meant, and she knew how to get his attention.

"Close to the reactor." She was in the midst of anger, she knew. She wouldn't see anything except that which would confirm her emotions. Bias bias bias. She didn't care. She also didn't care that now she had things to hide too. He'd kissed someone. She'd held some lunatic's hand at Chornobyl. "Before I wasn't going too far from the hotel, but today I went out into the inner zone. You need a special visa to go there. There are ecotours, but I went. We went right into the city."

"We?"

"We." Renya felt defiant. She should pinpoint the source of the emotion, she knew, but she didn't want to. She wanted to twist the knife. "I made a friend. Yuri. He's a security guard."

"What are the readings?"

"On the way back from Prypyat, we stopped at a house." She wanted to tell him about the threadbare carpets and the walls that were rain-streaked on the inside. She wanted to tell him that there were still cups on the table, and that she'd seen Yuri steal things, like spoons and napkin holders. Again, she'd pretended not to notice. He'd picked up a lot of things though. What were the odds that he was planning to bring them all back?

"I need to know the background radiation there," Nick was saying.

"One of the houses, it looked like the husk of a whale. The roof was partly gone and the structure was exposed."

"Ren, I need to know your exposure."

"It looked like a rib cage. And it felt like – I thought I saw someone moving out behind it, but it must have been a trick of the light."

"What does the Geiger counter say?"

"Dosimeter."

"Right," said Nick. "Dosimeter."

"It felt like nobody had been inside it for a century. I was born the week it happened, you know. I feel like I'm a century old too. Whenever something bad happens to me I feel like that. I feel like I've been alive forever, like it's never going to end."

"You're going to be fine, Renya," Nick said softly. "We're going to be fine." And then his voice was hard again. "What are the readings?" His upper eyebrows were lowered and his lips were pressed together. His depressor anguli oris were depressing the angles of the corners of his mouth. He was getting angry.

Anger usually just wrought more anger, but Renya didn't feel it now. Suddenly all the anger she'd felt earlier drained out of her. She just felt tired. Anger, she thought again, was not her favourite emotion. "You can hear it," she said. "That's enough."

"Renya . . ."

"In the house, the numbers were through the roof. Get it?"

"Jesus, you didn't –"

"You should have seen that house. It's falling apart, just disintegrating. The paint's all peeled and bubbled, and the walls are seeping inside too. You don't see that level of disrepair very often."

"I want you to come home now. Please, Renya, it's enough." Nick watched her, his eyes wide. "Are you surprised? How could you be surprised? Obviously, I want –"

"You haven't *said* it."

"I love you, Renya."

"You haven't said that either." Renya was surprised to believe it, and to feel a swell of love herself. "Anyway, it's too late for that, I can't. Even if I wanted to come home, the transports aren't for days."

"Renya. Please."

"I feel like there's something I need to see. You know, I've been obsessed with this place."

"I'll help you, we can –"

"I'm obsessed. Ever since you had the affair."

"I didn't sleep with her!"

"Ever since you kissed her."

"I said that I'm sorry!"

"Ever since you had your emotional event, or existential occasion." Renya didn't know how to finish. She didn't know what she wanted to say anymore. After he'd had the affair, she'd isolated herself. She'd sat alone in the living room rewatching all those documentaries. Then, he'd even tried to watch with her, but she'd leave the room as soon as he walked into it. She'd forgotten that reversal.

But now she wasn't dreaming about coming to Chornobyl, planning a trip that she sort of assumed she'd never take. She'd come. She was here. "I'd better go." Even to her own ears, her voice sounded flat. "I have work to do."

⊙⊙⊙

Renya scrolled through the reports from the day's video feeds and pictures. There were many red flags now. Her program was asking for more information and threatening to send emails to appropriate authorities, although it didn't know how to do that yet: she'd programmed in the threat but not the action.

She stared at her screen. She didn't know what to do with these results. Instead, she scrolled through the historical pictures again.

The next target set showed biorobots.

The explosion had made a mess. The core was fractured and exposed, and pieces of the core and lid were everywhere. Tons of metal and other debris imbued with unimaginable amounts of radiation had been blown just everywhere. The reactor fire was creating highly radioactive dust and ash. All those things were still emitting. If the dust was blown away, it could irradiate cities far away. If it got into populated areas, it could kill thousands, hundreds of thousands. If anyone ingests radioactive dust, it keeps emitting high-velocity particles until the person who swallowed it gets sick, until they die. You get bombarded, from the inside. No doctor can get it out. It's tiny. It's dust. And dust travels. It travels far. A little bit of wind, and it can fly clear out of the country. They had to clean up.

First, they had to get the debris of the reactor lid off the roof. That debris was intensely radioactive, and it was hard to deal with other problems while it was still there. And, of course, the other reactors were still producing energy, and still tied to the grid. They were needed.

In the defense of all the authorities in charge, they did try to use remote-controlled robots first. They sent them onto the roof to push the debris down, but the robots all malfunctioned. They even borrowed lunar landers that should have been used in space missions. But nobody could control any of the robots. They tried and tried, but the radioactivity messed up the radio controls. The area was so radioactive, the environment so full of high-energy radiation, that the robots all went haywire and threw themselves off the roof. So they used people in the end. They had no choice. They rounded up soldiers and offered them the choice of four years in Afghanistan or four minutes on the roof, or something ridiculous like that. They nicknamed them biorobots. They suited them up, and each one had to go for a few minutes at a time. The first pictures showed these biorobots putting on spacesuits and masks. Further in the set, she saw pictures of them at work. Finally, there were pictures of them sitting on benches between shifts, sweating and visibly exhausted.

ALGORITHMIC OUTPUT

Target set: April, 1986 / exclusion zone surrounding / biorobots

---

Dominants: fear

Displays discovered: fear

Statistics [fear expressions]: scroll down

Qualitative review of what was observed in the target-set material:

Target set includes photographs of workers nicknamed biorobots suiting up in preparation for outdoor manual-labour shifts, and completing said labour.

Uniform fear expressions detected. More information required.

Fear. The program found fear. Again, it had noticed something that she hadn't seen.

The next picture set showed the liquidators. That was the nickname chosen for the people who dealt with the situation on the ground. They put men in massive radiation suits and marched them through the exclusion zone, the whole surrounding area. First, the biorobots threw the reactor pieces and bits of graphite off the roof. Then the liquidators buried them. Then the dust was toxic, so they had to spray foam and tacky stuff on all the roads and lanes, to glue it all down, to keep radioactive dust from flying off into the big cities. They shovelled soil over the irradiated earth, razed the buildings, killed the animals, to keep the surrounding populations safe, or safer anyway.

The liquidators had to bury a whole forest. They had to kill all the animals, including all the pets. The animal fur could have been irradiated. If someone breathed in radioactive fur or dander, it would kill them.

There were dozens of pictures of these guys, at the feet of the reactor, on the road carrying hoses, holding shovels piercing damaged earth. In some pictures, their eyes were visible. Renya couldn't make out muscle activation. She couldn't make out much at all.

ALGORITHMIC OUTPUT

Target set: Date unknown, 1986 / exclusion zone surrounding / liquidators

---

Dominants: fear

Displays discovered: fear, sadness

Statistics [fear expressions]: scroll down

Qualitative review of what was observed in the target-set material:

Target set includes photographs of workers nicknamed liquidators, working on the grounds, preparing for shifts and resting after shifts.

Fear detected across all subjects documented. More information required.

Again, the program found fear.

She moved on. The next folders had videos from news broadcasts, scanned newspaper articles from around Europe.

Somewhere in the midst of all this, the world found out about the unfolding situation. Scientists and technicians who worked at the nuclear plant in Sweden started setting off the radiation alarms. There was a general panic about what must be happening inside *their* facilities, but then they realized that they were setting off the alarms on the way *in* and not on the way *out*. They tracked the source. The radiation was on their shoes. It was a rainy day, and the radiation had come from the water they'd tracked in. The alarming dose of radiation had come from outside, and it was everywhere, everything was contaminated, because it came in through the rain and the rain went everywhere just by definition. She had no pictures of this event. She wanted pictures. She'd ask around when she got back. She'd bet the suits could find them. In any case, the information had travelled.

The scientists informed their governments, and the governments informed their militaries. They called other European governments. They turned to satellites to collect information. The suits could probably grab pictures of this too, but they'd never admit it to her.

At that point in history, the news picked it up. She hadn't needed the suits for this. She had ample videos and screenshots. Newscasters around the world informed the populations. But they lied. All of the newscasters, in all these free countries, lied. The European news was especially laughable. They were so close to Chornobyl. Everyone knew they were all contaminated and a ton of damage had already been done. Very dangerous ionizing radiation had come in with the rain. Everyone knew it was a mess. But that's not what they reported. They talked about circle cyclones, wind anomalies, strange weather events that acted to keep the radiation away from them and their families. The weather events weren't happening. They were verifiably unreal. Swedish nuclear workers had *just* confirmed general radiation contamination in *a parking lot*. You just had to look out your window to know it was all a lie, but, apparently, everyone bought it. They believed it and they were comforted. They went outside despite it all, instead of protecting themselves. They let their kids play. They opened their windows.

Renya sighed. She ran videos from European news through her program, and they generated red flag after red flag. Despite the comforting information, despite the push to placate, the broadcasters were scared and she could prove it.

So her program worked.

Here was how she could help. She couldn't pinpoint exact lies. That was too difficult and too diffuse, but she could find fear. And she did. She'd found it. She would have known there was a problem. She could have done something. They could have sent help a little bit earlier. They could have suggested that people stay indoors for a few days, that they close their windows, run air purifiers, wash their hair. They could have told people to wear masks, shower, clean their outdoor clothes. It wouldn't have taken much, but nobody did even that. Instead, they told everyone to go about their lives as if nothing was happening. There were May Day festivals. They went on as planned. People celebrated outside. They partied in radioactive contamination. People got sick because of it.

A breeze blew in from a crack in the window. Renya looked outside. It didn't have to work like that anymore. She could help. She could do something.

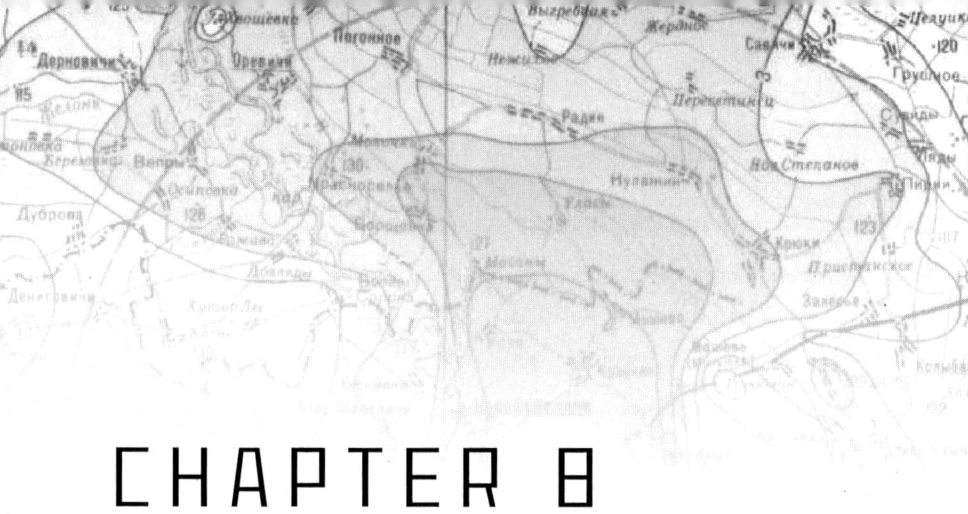

CHAPTER 8

RENYA WOKE DISORIENTED. THE LIGHT SEEPING IN THROUGH the window was sluggish and yellow-green. It had a contaminated quality, as if even the light here could kill. She shivered and wrapped herself in her blanket. Usually, she was quick to get out of bed, and rushed to get her day started. But this morning, she was stalled.

She cowered under her blanket. She felt a stirring in her stomach and a tingling in her fingers. That usually signalled fear, but what was she afraid of? There were so many plausible causes. In any case, anger was easier to handle. Righteous anger was the best of all. She sat up and grabbed the laptop from her bedside table. She was such a child. This thought didn't stop her from making the video call.

When Nick accepted the call request, Renya bent as close as she could to the screen. His usually spotless office was in disarray. There were clothes on the desk and on the floor, although they were meticulously folded now. They looked like his clothes though. "What happened to that woman?" she demanded.

"She's not here," Nick stammered. "Of course, she's not here." He stopped. He scratched his face. "You can kiss someone else. Would that make it better?"

Renya kicked at the computer. It slid farther down the bed.

Nick raised his arms. "I don't know what else to say."

"Well, that was the wrong thing."

"Why did you go there?" said Nick.

"Your indiscretion freed me," she said. "I was afraid to, before."

"That's a good fear. I mean, you should be afraid. There are risks. There are dangers. That's not baseless. Just like you should be afraid of touching downed live wires, because if you do, you could die."

"I'm still afraid."

"You're supposed to be! There are some things you're supposed to be afraid of, like lightning, fire, radiation. If you're smart, you're definitely going to be afraid of radiation. And you are smart. This means that you're smart."

"But every minute I survive this, the radiation, everything, I feel better. I feel more like I'm surviving. I feel like I might survive this."

"By 'this' . . ." Nick trailed off. He scratched the beginnings of a beard. His eyes were wide, his mouth pulled shut. This wasn't an expression she recognized. "By 'this' you mean . . ."

Renya stared at the computer. She didn't know what she meant.

"I've been doing the math," said Nick. "Proposals tend to be very detailed. You would have had to have started this months ago."

"The timeline was sped up. My supervisor got me in early."

"Still," said Nick. "It would take some time just to book a room for a meeting, never mind to write up your ideas."

Renya felt herself blink and blink. He was right. She had started the proposal months ago, long before the affair. She'd started when he'd had a heart attack, after the doctor's appointments and follow-ups, after all that fear. She'd started after living in days and days of existential terror. She didn't want to admit it though. And his health had all worked out just fine. He'd had to get a stent. Many people got those. He was okay now and there looked to be no lasting damage. "I write fast," she said, and she wondered whether she was lying to herself or to him.

"Look," Nick started.

"You could always just call that other woman."

"I would never call her," said Nick. "I don't even like her. I don't seem to like anyone anymore. I haven't even gone in to work in days. I teach my classes and then just leave."

And that's when she saw the suitcase again. Nick was packing. Packing meant leaving. That meant he was closing down the life they'd had. When she got home, the apartment would be empty, well, half-empty.

Renya didn't know what that particular emotion was, but she felt it like a weighted ball landing in her stomach. "Do you know how the world found out?" she said vaguely.

"You mean about the –"

"Swedish nuclear workers tried to get into their power plant."

"Oh, you mean –"

"The one in Sweden, I mean, but they couldn't! They were setting off alarms."

"This was back then, you mean, in 1986."

"They'd been contaminated! They assumed it was just an instrument malfunction at first because it was as they were going *into* the building, not coming out. The sensors kept pointing to their feet. Their shoes were radioactive."

"I keep thinking about this idea you had," said Nick.

"It was raining that day," said Renya, "and the puddles outside in the parking lot were full of radioactive water."

"Renya, I think this fascination started before. Could it have been before my . . . indiscretion?"

"Fuck you. Fuck your fucking indiscretion."

"It's because . . ." Nick paused. "You're studying fear."

"Yes."

"Fear specifically."

"Fear specifically," said Renya. "I had a breakthrough. I can't identify lies in the news. I can identify fear though. What if I primed my targets for fear?"

"And you thought about this while you were watching the Chernobyl documentaries."

"There are all those news reports from the time of the explosion."

"You started watching those again that night."

Renya froze. She remembered Nick holding his arm, clutching at his chest, struggling for breath. She remembered time stopping, her own breath catching. Her breath caught again, now, months and months later. That wasn't emotion. That was memory, emotion's shadow. "No. Nothing happened that night."

"The day after it, I mean. When we got home."

"No," Renya said again. "No. Nothing happened after that night."

"It makes sense though," Nick whispered. "You were thinking about fear. I was afraid too."

Renya stared. They never really talked about it. They discussed appointment dates, dietary changes, exercise schedules, but nothing other than the practical.

⊙ ⊙ ⊙

Renya crunched outside. She stalled on the footpath, disoriented, unable to decide on a direction to jog. Instead, she paced, shoes crackling on the gravel in the still, silent outdoors.

Don't think about Nick, she thought. And then she pictured his face, paper-white and sweating as he held the doorpost, as he fell to his knees. Enough. She'd been sitting at her desk, but she stood then. He held his chest, his arm, then he toppled to the white carpet. He didn't move after that. She could hear him panting, his breathing strange and laboured, and fast, he was breathing so quickly. A second passed. She struggled to interpret what she was seeing, although she felt so foolish after, it was so obvious. Then she grabbed the phone and ran to him, dialing 911 as she crashed to the floor beside him. Enough, stop. There had been light streaming through the window. The shades must have been partly drawn because she'd noticed the geometrical pattern on the floor as the phone rang, the sun a strange yellowish orange, and the air had felt thick like syrup. Stop! Enough. Enough of that. So then she pictured the suitcase from this morning instead. He was packing. Nick was packing. She could be mad. She could choose anger again. She'd been doing that a lot. Despite not liking the emotion very much, Renya had been gravitating toward it often, it seemed, and with an intensity so intentional as to be unhinged. Despite what Nick was saying, he might be going off with another woman. She'd asked him to leave, sure, but he was using the suitcase from their honeymoon.

But Renya didn't want to think about that anymore either. She didn't want to think about any of it.

She took off at a run. She stumbled on a branch and it took her three steps to right herself again, to redirect the veering momentum, but she kept running.

She needed to think this project through. It had a lot of potential, but she wasn't as far along as she'd hinted to her supervisor. Her breath boomed in her ears. Good.

She tried to stop and instead skidded in the dirt.

Directly in front of her was a tree whose branches were twisted and gnarled and unnatural. There were strange-looking twigs growing through each other, sick-looking leaves waving eerily in the breeze. It was damaged, really damaged. Renya felt a shudder tickle down her back. She stepped away. It was dangerous here. She'd known that. But this was the first time that she really felt scared. She turned and ran back down the path, to the usual meeting place. Would Yuri be there? She didn't really want to go back to Prypyat, if she was honest with herself. She'd forgotten to ask for masks again. She was even less prepared than before. But she felt pulled onward, hopefully for better reasons than to have something provocative to say to Nick when she talked to him later.

When she found Yuri, she climbed on the motorcycle before he could explain where he wanted to take her.

⊙ ⊙ ⊙

Renya found herself in another abandoned building, in another giant room, that had once been a gym according to Yuri. Yuri liked broken gyms, it seemed. Windows showed a plaza outside, more broken sidewalk and plants. It smelled of still, unused air. She shuffled forward, her steps echoing dully. Renya had never experienced the level of silence that she felt in Prypyat. It was oppressive, like pillows pressed to her head and face, pushed down. It was more intense than the forest with its constant background of scurry and crunch. It was surprising every time.

"There is Dima." Yuri's voice echoed in the silent room, and startled her. Renya forced herself to breathe.

"Do you see?" Yuri was saying.

It took seconds and seconds for Renya to find the other person, but she finally spotted him, a still form crouched inside the old empty swimming pool in the middle of the room.

"Show the girl what you found," Yuri called out.

Renya stood straighter. She was as old as these two, at least. She might be older. She wasn't used to being called a girl. Nick's friends thought it, she had no doubt, but even they would never say it.

"Come," Yuri said, his beckoning look juxtaposed strangely with the force behind the words. Again, Renya hesitated. Maybe she should think of their attitudes as refreshing. They didn't hide behind politeness. They didn't leave room for plausible deniability and gaslighting. They were upfront with their foolish beliefs. Maybe she should also admit that they scared her. She shook her head. She didn't need to be scared.

"Come on in," Dima called out from inside the empty pool. He stood, and she could see him clearly for the first time. He was taller than Yuri. He was sturdier too. "Come on. Don't be shy." And his accent was different. It was more refined, his English more practised. He was from a different background from Yuri, clearly. They wore similar clothing, but this one was born to money, quite obviously, even if he pretended otherwise.

Renya picked her way around the deck. There were large picture windows. Maybe it was safer to be close to the outdoors. If she was determined to take risks, maybe she could still minimize them.

Dima scrambled out of the pool, hauling his finds. She tried not to breathe the cloud of dust that billowed out around him. Renya glanced at Yuri. They'd be photographing those things surely. Surely, they'd be bringing them back. Yuri talked about documenting all the time. This must be their unofficial documentation. "Why do you say nothing?" said Dima. His smile didn't belie that his every utterance was a demand.

"Why do you explore in here?" she said.

"I want to know what it was like."

"Life before the explosion?"

"Life lived in fear," he said.

"Fear?" breathed Renya.

"Everything stopped here, and it stopped in terror. These people, they weren't uneducated. They were nuclear workers, nuclear-worker families, and they knew what explosions in the containment unit meant. They knew the stakes when they moved here, and yet they came."

Renya couldn't look away. "You're interested in fear?"

"They lived in fear before this," Dima replied. "They knew that there were risks. Then it happened, the thing they were afraid of most. You can feel it in the air, can you not?" He took a deep breath. Renya watched him, astonished, impressed despite herself. This Dima loved fear. He was resistant to it too, it seemed. He breathed freely here, in this place where the dust could kill you.

"I'm studying fear," said Renya. "That's the focus of my project."

Yuri laughed from somewhere else in the room. Renya couldn't see him. She felt frozen in place. "Dima isn't just interested in fear," said Yuri. "He creates it."

"That's interesting," muttered Renya.

"That he creates terrors?" Yuri's voice had an edge to it.

"That this is a world that stopped in fear," said Renya.

Time had indeed stopped in terror and loss, but for the landscape only, not for the people. The city was frozen in time, but the people weren't. The people had moved on, propelled by terror, maybe, but their lives had changed and progressed. Fear had made these people move. It had made them go. It had made them pack up and leave and face whatever came next. It had forced them to make unbearable decisions that wouldn't have been possible in any other context. Because who would just pick up and leave their life, and abandon all their things? People always said they're just things, like worrying about stuff makes people small and petty, but these were the small but very necessary objects that people couldn't live without in this world, like clothes and plates and blankets and cutlery. And she'd seen pictures. You weren't petty if you didn't want to leave your family photo albums behind. And now people were perhaps making impossible decisions again, moving back into a forest, cut off and radioactive and uninhabitable, and they weren't doing it because they were happy or content. Dima reached up a hand and Renya took it. Dima smiled, his eyes flashing like emergency lights in the gloom. Renya stepped into the dust-and-debris-strewn pool.

"The people who lived here," Dima said, "they knew fear."

Renya touched the old tiles. There were broken tiles. There was dust. There were mounds of desiccated insects. She'd faced fear. It had been big. It had caused her whole life to fracture. And it had made her more than what she'd been.

⊙ ⊙ ⊙

"Yuri, he has to take you home early," said Dima, suddenly clutching the back of Renya's neck. Renya jumped. She shrugged out of his grip. She hadn't seen him walk toward her. She looked at the watch on her wrist, but she couldn't remember when she'd entered the building. She didn't know how long she'd stayed. She didn't know how long she'd been lost in thought.

Dima looked meaningfully at Yuri. "We have a meeting to go to. We'll show you more later."

"Sure." Renya climbed out of the pool, still thinking about how fear had changed this whole world, how it had changed hers too.

⊙ ⊙ ⊙

After that, Renya's visit to Prypyat had ended quickly. Yuri had ushered her right to the bike, and now she was speeding through the forest once again. As the trees whirred past her, she realized that Dima was right. This *was* a place suffused in fear.

Renya squeezed Yuri's torso as soon as the path came into view. Fear had infused this landscape. Fear was informing everyone's lives here. Fear was informing all their work. Fear was forcing progress.

Yuri slowed his motorcycle. He put out his legs to stop. Renya extricated herself and stumbled off. Yuri bowed slightly. "I will see you soon," he said.

He winked. Then, as he swung the motorcycle around and sped off again, Renya took off.

She listened to the squeak and whisper of her sneakers on the hard-pressed dirt, and watched as the forest flew by. She felt the adrenaline and endorphins pump to her every extremity. Happiness was for suckers. It was a waste of time. It led nowhere. Contentment meant decay. Satisfaction was complacency. Nobody invented vaccines because they were content. Nobody invented new technologies because they were into the status quo. Fear was motivating. Fear made you think, made you search, made you seek and find and move and work. In terror, you found power. This was progress. This was living.

Renya crested a hill, then found herself skidding down the other side. She lost her balance and wheeled, and suddenly she was on her knees in the dirt. Dust flew up all around her. She watched the particles dance. She held her breath. Any of these dirt molecules could be radioactive. Any single one could kill her slowly, if ingested, if breathed into her body. She stood and brushed herself off. Wait, she shouldn't do that. She stopped. She looked at her hands. That just made the dust airborne. But she didn't want to take it home with her either. She brushed at her legs.

There was a stunted pine tree growing beside the path. Its branches looked like fingers. She touched one, then another, then another, enjoying the feeling of rough bark against her fingers. Anything here could lead to death. If the radiation didn't get her, the freedom fighters might, or the looters, apparently.

This was how you found your life.

⊙ ⊙ ⊙

Back in her little room in the research centre, Renya couldn't shake thoughts of fear imbued in place. It was a wild thought. There was something to it, and it wasn't only for this location.

She ran more pictures through her program. She looked at the reports generated but she couldn't focus. She couldn't remember which target set she'd just run. For hours, she'd been doing this: flipping through the reports, realizing that she hadn't been paying attention and starting again. *Focus*, she told herself. But she couldn't. *Sit still*, she said, but her body rebelled, and she found herself up and pacing. Her mind was rattling with excitement, with thoughts about fear and the world, fear in the woods, terror and landscape. She couldn't sit still. But she didn't have to.

Just then, Claire knocked at the door and asked her to go for a walk.

"I'm going to visit Tiv and the wolf researchers," she said, resting her head against the door frame. "They work farther out than I've ever been. They're closer to the inner zone. Do you want to come?" She ducked her head. "I admit," she said, "I'm scared to go alone."

Renya was already grabbing for her day pack. "I'm in," she said. She pushed into her sneakers.

Claire unfolded the map to show her Tiv's spots. The one they'd visit this evening was far, beyond where Renya had walked to before, though it was close to Prypyat. She should tell Claire that she'd been in that vicinity. She didn't.

"The wolves are near the city," Renya said instead.

"I hear they howl around the abandoned buildings at night."

"Did they always live so close?"

"I don't know." Claire pointed to several spots on the map. "That's where Tiv's team set up some of their traps."

"I wasn't allowed to go that far when I was taking pictures," Renya said as she turned to lock her door. "They didn't want me scaring the wolves or changing their behaviours. I was only allowed at the very edge of their territory."

"Apparently, they're wrapping up in the next few nights," said Claire, motioning into the forest, "getting ready for the hand-off to the next team. That's why I got the okay to visit. I was so excited to see the territory at first, but then I got nervous."

"Is there something specific you want to see?"

"You were talking about having wider perspective," said Claire, "and I like that idea. You've inspired me to reach out to other teams. I talk to

Shantoo all the time, obviously, and I've checked in with the plant people. I've been talking with the climate people, maybe too often. These guys have a different schedule and a wildly different territory though, so I haven't checked in with them much at all. They sleep in too, so there's been almost no overlap. Maybe it is a good idea to get some wider perspective. It's like you said, exactly like you were talking about."

"Have you found any patterns?"

"I'm afraid of the outside world," said Claire. "I mean, I'm afraid *for* the outside world, the world at large, I mean, more than just here. I wasn't expecting that. I'm finding things here that I wouldn't expect in a place without modern habitation. I'm struggling to explain it."

As they approached the door, Claire reached into her backpack. She pulled out two masks, wrapped in plastic. "I'm still afraid of Chernobyl though."

⊙ ⊙ ⊙

They crunched into the woods in amiable silence. They passed a lake first, and then a marsh, and then a snaking stream that trickled lazily. Renya had read that nature was reclaiming this area, and she could see it clearly here. It was still and beautiful, but made eerie by Renya's dosimeter, which crackled louder and louder, faster and faster. Claire asked to see it, and Renya let her carry it with her. Renya had become used to the sounds, but Claire, she saw, checked the readings every few steps. She stopped, every once in a while, to jot down readings on a map of her own.

They passed under a thicket of trees, the branches winding together above them, and the dosimeter crackled like a popcorn maker, then stopped abruptly. Claire slowed. She looked at Renya, who nodded reassuringly, though she didn't know why. They moved quickly onward once again.

Dusk was settling onto the sky from above, the clouds streaking with muted purples and pinks, and a new kind of stillness seemed to greet it from the ground up. Insects hummed, then quieted. The sparse forest floor stilled. Smells wafted up. Renya recognized wet plants and still water. Under that, weak but distinct, was a sulphurous note she associated with marshes and mud flats. She didn't know where any of it was coming from. The air was cooling noticeably, and Renya shivered.

They passed by a thicket of trees. Water dropped on them from above. Claire shrieked, grabbing for Renya. Renya held her arm until she got her breathing under control, until they both started laughing. "When Tiv told me where he'd be tonight, I said, 'Sure I'll meet you, no problem! Sure I'll trek through an irradiated wilderness with howling wolves.'"

"Imagine nighttime here," said Renya. "Imagine being here in the dark. It's terrifying in the dusk."

"Thanks for coming with me," said Claire. "I knew that I wouldn't be able to face it alone."

"I don't think I could walk here alone either. I love fear, but in theory, not in practice."

"You like studying it, but not experiencing it?"

"I like to experience it in controlled situations only," said Renya. "Think teacup rides, but not roller coasters, or Stephen King, but not true crime. I like to jog at night, and I scare myself with ghost sightings, but ignore possible muggers."

"I like that," said Claire. "I picture you living a very whimsical life."

They trudged forward once again.

"I've always loved fear," said Renya after a moment. "I mean, the idea of fear." She put her hands in her pockets to warm them. "Fear slows down time. It makes you look more closely, physiologically, even. Your heart beats faster. You get more oxygen to your brain. You have better ocular efficiency. You can practically see in the dark. I used to love going to horror movies and walking home alone after. I noticed everything, I felt. I saw crickets. I found lost jewelry on the sidewalk. I finally learned the star patterns even."

"Do you still scare yourself like that?"

"Of course." But her relationship to fear had been changing. She still liked it in theory, she loved its physiological effects and likely evolutionary provenance, but she didn't actively court it anymore. She hadn't read anything scary in ages. She hadn't been able to watch a horror movie either. She'd been watching only rom-coms for a while.

Claire consulted her map, then steered them around another marsh. The light was fading out of the sky. It was draining away quickly now. Stronger smells were rising up from the soil too, the sweet decay of marshland, the sting of ozone. They plodded forward.

"Wait," said Renya. "No. I don't like to be scared anymore. It's strange. I hadn't even noticed." She looked up at stars just starting to blink in the bruise-purple sky. "I think that I overdosed on fear when my husband had a heart event," she whispered.

"That makes sense," said Claire. "I used to be into tear-jerkers myself. I liked my books and movies sad, the more crushing the better. I lost my taste for that too, after my grandmother died. I can't devastate myself in the same way anymore."

"Maybe everything we did was practice," whispered Renya.

"Getting ourselves ready," Claire said, nodding.

As they crested another hill, they heard a scratching sound. Renya paused.

Claire motioned her forward. "There are caves around here," she whispered. "Tiv and his team should be close."

Renya walked hesitantly until they crested the hill and found a marsh spotted with algae and winking with insects dancing in the gloom. A bit farther, they found rock formations, and, indeed, caves.

"The city must be close too," Renya whispered.

Claire pointed. "That way," she said. "Not far."

Renya squinted. She could see nothing. There was just pooling darkness like an abyss. She wasn't used to so much dark. She was used to winking building lights, the hum of electricity, the shuffle of shifting bodies, and talking, and phones, and cars, and streetlights. She couldn't imagine being in Prypyat now. The stillness would be too much. Were Yuri and Dima there? Were they working? They'd never told her where they patrolled, or when their shifts were scheduled. They never told her what they did in the dark.

"I think we must be getting close," whispered Claire.

Did Dima and Yuri sneak into Prypyat at night? Dima might. What if Dima brought people with him, like they brought her during the day? What if he brought dates? Was that who he was meeting just now? She imagined Dima running through the little alleyway with a woman. She pictured him kissing her there, pressing her back against the cool bricks of abandoned buildings. She imagined Nick and his other woman. They'd kissed in the dark, lit only by streetlights, on a rainy night, on an empty street outside of a bar.

"There's Tiv," said Claire abruptly. Renya blinked, startled.

She turned. She could just make out a form bent over a large cage. That must be Tiv. She looked around and found more colleagues, conferring nearby. Their white masks shone dully in the gloom. Renya and Claire trudged toward them.

⊙⊙⊙

Claire raised a hand to Tiv. "We're not too early, I hope?"

"Just planning the teardown," he said. "We're coming back with trucks tomorrow. Well, it'll take us a few days. We'll be here off and on until we leave. We've tagged a number of wolves and we'll come back to check on them, but not until next year." He turned to Renya. "Our projects are longer term," he explained.

"We have rotating teams that work together too," murmured Claire.

"Time has gone fast," said Renya.

"Honestly, I can't wait for this to be over," said Tiv. "I can't wait to see my kids." On the plane, he'd shown her pictures of three smiling, joyous girls.

"Anything you can share?" Claire asked.

Tiv eyed his colleagues. "We don't know much yet," he said. "We don't do much processing here. We've packed up most of the samples to send to the lab. In the next cycles, we'll get to the more meaty stuff, if you'll forgive the expression."

"Any preliminary surprises?" said Claire.

"Well, the wolves here don't glow in the dark," said Tiv.

"That's a relief," said Claire.

"It is because they seem to be mating all over Europe," said Tiv.

"Right," said Renya. "They don't just stay here. I always imagined they just stay put."

"Animals are terrible at applying for visas," said one of the wolf researchers.

"In fact, it's not even the animals I worry about most," said Tiv. "I shouldn't admit that. I should be worried about animals. I've devoted my career to wolves."

"Who do you worry about?" whispered Claire.

"I worry about us," said Tiv. "Wolves aren't city animals, typically. I've found some issues that you see more in urban animals. I don't know. I'll have to wait to see more."

Claire was nodding. "I've found some things I didn't expect outside of built-up places," she said, "like microplastics and PFAS chemicals."

"I expect we'll see the same," said Tiv. "If I were to be honest, I expect those chemical exposures will be more impactful than the radiation. I don't know what I'm going to see in terms of radiation though."

Renya took a deep breath. "Really?" She'd been exposing herself so much. She'd been venturing nearer and nearer to the accident site, taking more and more risks. This wasn't like her. She should have stayed inside more. But how could she come all the way here and not experience it fully?

"There are some lists of chemical compounds making the rounds," Claire was saying. "Other teams have been reaching out with suggestions of new issues to look out for."

"I'd like to see," said Tiv. "I'd be interested."

"We can compare notes."

"Let's get a move on," said one of the researchers.

Renya walked up front with the colleagues, and Tiv and Claire trailed behind. She could hear them talking in low voices. The trip back was much quicker than the trip out. The large-animal team knew all the shortcuts.

⊙⊙⊙

When they got back to the research centre, they all retreated to their individual labs and rooms.

The room was warm, but Renya felt cold. She felt her fingers and toes and legs tingling. Classic fear. It was an evolutionary response, everyone believed. It prepped the body for running. She could go jogging. She'd just come inside though, and maybe the point was that she should stay in more. She crossed the room and checked the air purifier. It was turned on anyway. It was humming gently.

She should work. She eyed her computer.

She had no *real* reason to be afraid. There was no machete-wielding attacker after her after all. She was under no immediate threat. There was nothing concrete to be afraid of at all. The nuclear accident had been horrific. It had melted concrete. It had made gross distortions of human progress. But that had been years ago, decades in fact. The accident was over now. It was all over. There were the after-effects and long-term consequences of the accident to be afraid of. But a lot of people had signed off on this trip. Her administration thought it was safe. Her government assured her that she'd be okay. She'd signed a barrage of forms and had been assured that it was safe enough, safe within reason. She was experiencing fear, and fear was just a feeling after all, an emotion caused by threat, real or imagined, credible or baseless, immediate, impending, fight, flight, anger, anger was a common reaction too, she shouldn't forget that. She paced. She touched the windowsill lightly. She'd be happier if she had a test to study for, an experiment to design, even a report to plan. She'd write a report right now. Or she could run. She sped and ran from one side of the room to the other, then from the window to the washroom. Where would she run to? The research station was probably marginally safer than outdoors.

⊙⊙⊙

Renya opened her laptop. She clicked her online calling icon, and Nick's face appeared instantly.

"Where are you?" he said. "Where have you been?" He was in the bedroom. It was neat again. He was wearing the greatcoat, readying to leave. That was the coat he wore for long trips. Was he going with the other woman? Did she have a greatcoat too? Was she elegant like Nick? Was she more elegant than Renya? That wouldn't be hard to pull off. Renya aimed for yoga-chic, in her personal life. Really, she didn't pay as much attention to her appearance as she should.

"The disaster started with an experiment," said Renya. Again, she couldn't stand still. So she circled the small room. She must be going in and out of the frame. Did they look alike, she and the woman? *Did Nick have a type?* Renya didn't know how she'd feel if he did.

"Stay there," said Nick, taking off his coat. "Don't go anywhere."

"Do you know what the experiment was? Do you know what they were trying to figure out?"

Nick was staring at her. He touched his silver necklace. It looked nice. She'd gotten him that. It had been a birthday present. *Bastard.* "I don't know," he said.

"They wanted to know whether they could power the cooling system with the regular wind-down of the turbine. That's why the plant wasn't connected to the power grid."

"What?"

"When they stop a nuclear reactor, the reactor doesn't just immediately stop."

"Of course."

"There's still a reaction for a little while. There are still extra neutrons around. The uranium atoms still absorb the neutrons. The unstable uranium still splits apart. It takes some time for it all to stop completely. And in that time, the reaction is still producing energy, and that energy creates heat, and that heat needs to be controlled. They wanted to know if they could use the energy the reactor still produced to power its own cooling system."

Was the woman prettier? Was she more feminine, whatever that meant?

"Why did they need that?" said Nick.

"In case of attack." *Did that other woman wear dresses?* Nick always complimented Renya when she did, so he must like that. Renya rarely wore dresses however. "It was the Cold War," she found herself saying. "If the Americans took out the power grid, would the plant explode, I assume that's what they needed to know. They had backup generators but those take a couple of minutes to spin up, so they had to make sure that the leftover reaction could power the cooling systems in the meantime. They thought it could. It was pretty clear that it could. They just wanted to see."

"What went wrong?" said Nick.

Renya stared hard at the screen. "You want to know?"

"Maybe not."

Did Renya really want to know about the other woman? Maybe she didn't. Maybe she did. She was thrumming with a strange sort of energy, that she knew for sure, and she had learned from being *here* that energy needs to be released.

"Why not?" Renya asked. "Why don't you want to know?"

Nick raked his hand through his hair. "I'm scared of you making analogies," he said softly.

"It was a bad day," she said.

"You mean when I went out to play pool?" he whispered.

"The reaction had been generating by-products that day," Renya went on. "It had been creating extra particles that had been slowing down the nuclear reaction. They didn't know it though."

"Oh," said Nick. "Right. These reactions are still not that well understood. The science is still in its infancy."

"Don't tell me that physicists don't understand every single thing."

"I knew this was a trap," Nick muttered.

Renya reared back.

"Wait, no," said Nick. "Go on. So the generator wasn't producing that much energy earlier that day. To get it to produce more heat, I assume that they took away some of the coolant?" He was rubbing his hands together. He was averting his eyes and fidgeting. So he was feeling fear too. His was of a different kind.

"That's right," said Renya. "Except that was the day shift. The night crew didn't know that, or they didn't take it seriously enough, on the night of the experiment. So they turned off the reactor, disconnected from the power grid, and all of a sudden, all the extra particles burned away and the generator started creating intense amounts of heat. It spiked. It got out of control. This was when the experiment was just starting."

"Oh," said Nick. "So the core must have gotten so hot that the coolant had voids."

"What are voids?" Renya said flatly.

"What?"

"Explain your terminology."

"Oh . . . Places where it suddenly didn't . . ." He looked up at the computer camera, eyes wide, forehead wrinkled.

"Air bubbles," she yelled. "For fuck's sake. You mean that the coolant had air bubbles."

He raised his hands. "That's what I meant."

"You meant steam. Say steam. The coolant was water, and the water was boiling. So it couldn't properly cool down the uranium because there were air bubbles and steam."

"Then what happened?"

"Nobody really knows," said Renya. "Most people think the technicians panicked. It was the night shift. They probably saw there was too much heat and pressed SCRAM."

"SCRAM."

"That pushes the control rods into the reactor."

"That cools down the core."

"It's supposed to stop the reaction," said Renya. "The control rods absorb neutrons. They take neutrons away so that uranium can't absorb them and split apart. And the reaction can't be critical without enough uranium atoms splitting apart."

"But it didn't work."

"No."

"Why didn't it work?"

"That's the question, right?" said Renya. "If it's supposed to work that way, then why didn't it work?"

"It was already too hot?"

"That's what they think. The reaction was already too hot. The tips of the coolant rods were made of graphite, the moderator, and that went in first, so for a moment the neutrons were allowed to do anything they wanted –"

"So they reacted."

"They caused a chain reaction that went out of control," said Renya. "It went critical, first."

Nick was nodding. "Then it must have gone supercritical. Every reaction caused more than one other reaction."

Renya raised her hand. Nick stopped. "It shouldn't work that way," she said.

"Graphite tips on the moderators was a terrible idea," said Nick. "It was a bad design."

"It was designed for failure," said Renya.

"We don't make reactors that way anymore."

"So then there was a meltdown," she said. "The core got so hot that the coolant boiled away. No. It's more than that. First the coolant was boiling, then the water separated into hydrogen and oxygen. And then there was a hydrogen explosion."

"Oh," said Nick. "So that's when the reactor blew up."

"Reactor four," said Renya.

"And then it was burning," said Nick.

"Graphite is flammable," said Renya. "So the coolant rods themselves were burning."

"That was another design problem, clearly," said Nick.

Renya raised her hand.

"They should have thought of that," said Nick.

Nick should have thought of that.

If he preferred women who wore dresses, he should have told her. She shouldn't have to guess about it. She shouldn't be sitting here, kicking herself for not wearing skirts more, after the fact. If he preferred blonds, then he never should have asked her to marry him in the first place. Renya didn't want to talk about faulty designs anymore, about physicists who knew less than they pretended, less than they told the world they knew. "Tell me about *her*," she heard herself saying.

Nick blanched. "What?"

"Is she blond?"

"No."

"She has brown hair?"

"Yes." He stood. He started pacing. Renya stopped moving to watch him carefully. "Wait. It's dark, I think. I think it's brown."

"Is she prettier than me?"

"No. What? No."

"Is she more feminine?"

"What are you talking about?"

If he wanted to marry a physicist, he should have married a physicist.

"Is she smarter than I am?"

Nick paused.

Renya felt her face warm, her body heat. "Fucking –"

"These things are difficult to measure."

"Measure it."

"You're more creative. You see patterns and big pictures. She knows more about physics though, that's all I was saying."

"She knows more about physics?" Renya's voice boomed in her head.

"I meant –"

"She's from your department?"

"She's –"

"Ashley?"

"No! Of course not. She was a –"

Renya felt the world shift. She grabbed the windowsill for support. "She was a student?"

"No!" said Nick. "No. I wouldn't. I would never. She was visiting faculty."

"Visiting faculty," said Renya.

"You never ended up meeting her."

"Does my dad know her?"

"Well –"

"Did he know?"

"I assume not." Nick scratched his beard. "Of course he saw –"

Renya tightened her fingers. "What did my father see?"

"Nothing happened, Ren. Nothing happened in the end. Your dad probably . . . Nothing happened. And I'm sure he didn't know. Renya, why are you doing this? I thought you said you didn't want to know. God, why are you doing this?"

"You're the one who did this."

"We can discuss," said Nick. "We can –"

"I want to see it now."

"What?" said Nick. "Her? She's gone now, she's – Obviously, I don't have pictures. Obviously, we didn't keep in touch. I didn't. I wouldn't have – it was just a bad night at the pub and nothing ended up happening. We played pool. She came on to me. Then I left. I made a bigger deal about it than I should have because I wanted to get a reaction out of you."

"I want to see the reactor," said Renya. "I want to go all the way to the sarcophagus."

"No!"

"People do that."

"I know."

"I want to do that."

"Look –"

But Renya wasn't listening anymore. She was pacing, she found. She was walking *fast*. Should she ask Yuri to take her to the sarcophagus? Would he do it? Would he actually drive there and stop and walk around? When they went before, he'd hardly slowed, and Renya didn't see much at all. Nick was still talking, but Renya was looking out the window, into the shifting, quiet forest. It was like a void. This trip was like an air bubble somehow. Her old life seemed different in her memory. She could still picture it, but it was murky and shifting and full of strange lights, like she was under water and looking up at the sky. She had an opportunity here. She could go all the way, all the way you're allowed to go without protective gear and equipment anyway. She'd take precautions. She could see everything. If Yuri stopped the motorcycle, she could really look at it this time. If she hitched a ride with cleaning staff or on-site security, she could really enjoy it.

She walked out onto the balcony. She looked in what she thought was the direction of reactor four. Then she heard the voices. That would be another gathering outside. She'd go.

⊙ ⊙ ⊙

Renya pushed out onto the main balcony. The door squeak was out of a bad horror movie, but nobody seemed to notice. Renya pushed her way into the crowd and looked for friends, for Claire, Shantoo, Tiv. It was dark though. She could only see faces in outline, and only when the security lights flared and faded. There were some women here. She could hear their voices. There was a laugh that she recognized vaguely. It must be safe enough.

Then she saw Claire. Charlie had cornered her. He was flirting, that much was clear. Claire wasn't into it, that was equally clear. Claire was stuck in the corner between the outer wall and the railing. She couldn't move. And his stance was aggressive. He was getting right in her face. They were right out in the open, right in front of everyone. Renya turned. She turned back. Charlie's hand was on Claire's arm now, tight it looked like. Claire had a partner. She wouldn't want this. There couldn't be consent here. And look at that body language. You didn't need to be an expert to see the fear, the thinly veiled disgust. Claire was pressed right against the wall, and Charlie's fingers were creeping now, up her arm.

Renya's legs screamed to run, to get away, because no good could come of this. If she stepped in, then Charlie would know that she'd seen him touching Claire. He'd know that she'd seen him do something wrong. What would Claire even want? She'd get the brunt of this. Maybe Charlie wouldn't go that much further. Renya usually just rode these things out. They never progressed too far. Sometimes they progressed too far.

Renya's head and neck throbbed. She stepped backward, but then tripped on someone's foot, nearly falling to the ground. When she turned back, Charlie's hand was on Claire's neck, his fingers brushing under her blouse. That was a line though. Certainly, Charlie had to know he was crossing a line, and in the middle of a crowd, what was he doing? Usually they waited to get you alone. The alcohol and semi-darkness were making him reckless. Claire turned and saw her. She opened her eyes wide. They shone in a sudden burst of security lights.

Renya had seen this before. How many times had she seen this, boundaries crossed as if they meant nothing? And the women expected it too. They knew there would be no saving them and that there would be no comeuppance for the monsters who did it. Renya couldn't figure out any clever way to get her out. Well, she'd resort to brute force then. No, she'd make herself ridiculous. That's what she would do.

Renya stumbled over. She pushed three big-animal people out of the way, then elbowed in between Claire and Charlie.

"Can I help you?" Charlie's eyes were narrowed, his teeth bared. Renya shivered. She felt like she'd been doused in cold water. When people talk about bystanders not doing anything, they never talk about the crippling fear.

"I'm sorry," she said. She reached for Claire. "Can I borrow her? Maybe I drank too much. Maybe it's heatstroke. From earlier, obviously. Not from right now." She turned to Charlie. "I ran. I've been running. I've been jogging every day but I haven't been drinking water because I've been afraid of the radiation."

"That isn't very clever," Charlie said coldly.

"Claire's better at making reasonable health decisions," said Renya. "I mean, she's less overwhelmed by the location." She turned back to Claire. "You told me to come and get you if I felt woozy."

Claire took her arm. "If you'll excuse us," she said, smiling tightly. "We can continue our conversation later."

"Sorry for interrupting," Renya said weakly. But already Claire was steering her back inside. They retreated quickly to the corridor with the vending machine.

⊙ ⊙ ⊙

Renya held out a can of Fanta to Claire. "Thanks," Claire said.

"I'm sorry if I did the wrong thing," said Renya. "I didn't know what to do. I never know what to do."

Renya held her own drink to her forehead. This was her world. She hated it, but this was her world, and she participated in it. Even though it was wrong, even though she hated it, she still belonged.

That was the worst part of this toxic life with these toxic men. She was complicit. Even though every time she was in a room with them, she screamed inside her head, screamed and screamed and screamed and pictured herself smashing all the windows, throwing down the computers, still she played the doe-eyed girl, and still she acted demure. She was a scientist. She was an adult. She and Claire and Shantoo were smart, they had drive, they had vision, but still they had to pretend to be in awe of these powerful nobodies. They had to say nothing as they were made fun of and pawed at parties.

But what could she do? She could reject them, sure, but then she'd have to get a real job, and she wouldn't have access to the labs or to the libraries or to the millions of other things she got from the universities. She could strike out on her own. She could try to work independently. But realistically, walking away would end her research.

That was the thing that she and Nick never talked about. They made fun of those men, but quietly and behind closed doors. They never talked about what happened when Renya and others tried to defend themselves. They never talked about how women had to make themselves the brunt of all these stupid jokes, had to laugh the loudest as they were demeaned and groped, how they had to make themselves small. She never talked about how it was worse for others than for her.

But still, she lived in the world. She didn't bother saying anything anymore. She used to though. "I used to go to the department head in undergrad all the time," whispered Renya.

"I was always told to develop a sense of humour," said Claire.

"They wouldn't tease you if they didn't like you," mimicked Renya.

"They assume that you're mature enough to get the joke."

"You're a pretty girl, take it as a compliment."

"Mature people accept praise gracefully," said Claire. "Because touching without permission is just an acceptable sign of admiration if you think about it."

"You could always have said, 'No thank you,'" said Renya. "That was my personal favourite. Pulling away means no. Slapping someone's hand away also means no. Also, I say no. I always say no. I always say stop."

"Recognizing we have no power here should preclude saying yes," said Claire. "Not that they do ask. They just find ways to corner us in the dark."

"This should be obvious," whispered Renya, "but I hated watching that." She'd seen that happen before too. Men were bad with her, but they could get hyperaggressive with women of colour, with people they felt had even less recourse. There was her bestie Aisha in grade twelve, and the chemistry teacher who'd held her arm and shaken her. There was Janet in undergrad, and that professor who'd talked to her closer and closer as she'd sweated in discomfort. There had been more instances. Renya could feel herself sweating now, just the act of remembering bringing back that stinging shame. She hated it. "Again," she said, "I'm sorry."

"You did fine. I think I'll turn in early tonight though." And Claire turned and left her.

Renya sat for a while, and watched the vending machine. Eventually, she shuffled back to her room and worked until she couldn't keep her eyes open, as had become her habit here.

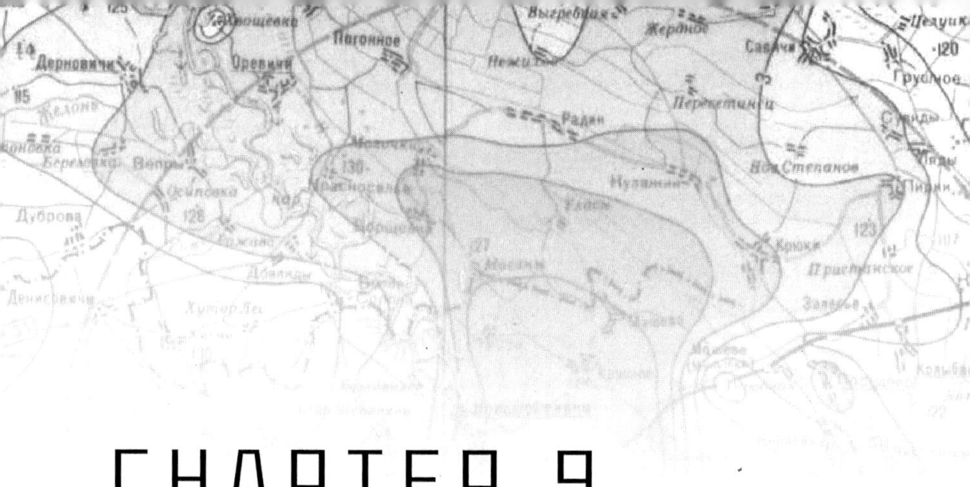

CHAPTER 9

RENYA WOKE IN THE MORNING TO MULTIPLE MESSAGES IN HER program. It had recorded fear tells in multiple situations. The duration of the displays was increasing. Alert the authorities, it requested. Who was the authority? She had a sick feeling that it was her, but she didn't want to act on any warnings right now.

Nick's Skype icon wasn't active. His computer wasn't even on, it seemed. She sat. She flipped through her notes. She didn't want to talk to Nick anyway.

She scrolled through the historical photo sets donated so graciously from those anonymous suits. There were still a few target sets she hadn't run. She found a set of liquidators and biorobots treated in hospital. They were covered in giant bandages that just barely concealed oozing sores. Their faces were obstructed. The program wouldn't help here, but common sense indicated there was probably fear there. She ran the pictures anyway. Inconclusive. Obviously.

Then she ran pictures of the so-called elephant's foot, the mass of radioactive fuel that dripped down under the reactor in an irregular shape that looked like the foot of an elephant. Inconclusive. That made sense. There were no faces.

Then she ran the photo sets of suited people working on the sarcophagus to cover the ruined reactor. In the distances, cranes could be seen assembling pieces. The project was massive, the sarcophagus hundreds of feet high and as big as a football field. The workers were forced to run, none allowed out in the air for more than a few seconds, and everyone's shift was meant to be just minutes. They were blurry, obviously. No faces could be made out, but some fear was found. Again, the program was more efficient than she was.

She checked Skype again, but still Nick wasn't there. She paced. She put on her shoes.

⊙ ⊙ ⊙

Renya was still rubbing her eyes when she crept into the dark dining room for breakfast and was surprised to see it occupied. She'd thought she could get up even earlier to be alone, but there were already people there today. Among them were Claire and Shantoo, who were sitting at a table by the corner, staring into mugs, saying nothing. Renya poured herself some coffee and picked up a biscuit. She brought her breakfast to their table and sat down beside them.

Shantoo was drumming her fingers against the tablecloth.

"Your nails are purple today," said Renya.

Shantoo looked up. She was frighteningly beautiful. "Do you like them?"

"I thought your sister did that for you."

"Oh no," said Shantoo. "She dresses me. She does the classy stuff. But even if she's not here, I paint my nails every time they need a touch-up."

"That's very classy," said Renya, looking at her plain fingers.

"It's the opposite, in fact," said Shantoo. "I study the earth, creepy-crawly things. I always have dirt under my nails. Now, poof! You can't see. My colleagues don't dig around in the muck as much as I do, but I like to feel the earth I'm studying. I like to be down on the ground."

"She also uses nail colour as a mood identifier," Claire said lightly.

"How did you know that?" said Shantoo.

"Nothing gets by me."

"What does purple mean?" said Renya.

"It means I reserve judgment," said Shantoo.

"But you're wary," said Claire.

"Yes," said Shantoo. She turned to Renya. "But don't be afraid. I'm often wary."

"You've been looking at albedo?" said Claire.

"You know *too much*, I think," said Shantoo.

"I heard you talking to the climate guys."

Shantoo turned to Renya. "I look at soil degradation, or how well the soil is working to house living things. Usually, I directly measure soil structure, and things like salinity, alkalinity, toxic chemicals and radiation, obviously, especially here. But I've been talking to the climate-physics team, and they're looking at soil albedo, reflectivity that is, so I'm starting to look at albedo too. I've started to ask how much of the sun's energy is being redirected by the soil, and how much is being absorbed by it, and, well, by any living things inside of it."

"The albedo is changing?" said Claire.

"This is climate change," said Shantoo.

"You didn't expect it?"

"Here is untouched," said Shantoo. "I thought nature might be taking it back."

"With the exception of the radioactive overload."

"This is more complicated when I stop hyperfocusing on radioactivity," said Shantoo. "It's so much more difficult when I zoom out. I thought all this was simple, in general. We burn fossil fuels. Those fuels stick in the atmosphere and trap the sun's energy. So we stop burning fossil fuels and fix the problem. But it isn't so simple."

"Nobody's going to stop," said Claire.

"And even if they do, it doesn't matter. Energy is trapped already. More is being trapped every year. And trapped is trapped. It still has to do something, go somewhere. And in the meantime, the other pollutants that we're sending up there, which are terrible for us, don't get me wrong, are in fact slowing the heating effect. Sulphur is one example. That's one that I've been looking at. We burn sulphur, especially in shipping. Sulphur in the atmosphere is reflective. The sulphur reflects the sun's energy back outward, so it cools us down in the short term, or, at least, it makes us heat less quickly. Also, unfortunately, it sticks in our lungs, and it affects the soil too, of course, so we should stop burning it. But if we do cut down its use, the sulphur doesn't last as long as carbon, and it falls out of the atmosphere quite quickly." She turned to Claire. "That's what I started telling you about. It's called aerosol termination shock. This region is perhaps experiencing this. There's less sulphur in the atmosphere overhead. That means more of the sun's energy is being directed at the soil. That in turn means that the soil is degrading much faster than I'd anticipated. This has consequences to more than just soil, as I've been learning."

"From the climate physicists," finished Claire.

"The chilling aspect," said Shantoo, "the part that I can't quite get past, is that perhaps this isn't just happening here. Perhaps this is a very widespread problem. I think I'm understanding anomalous recordings from back at home, and elsewhere. I can't believe I hadn't seen how very complicated these sulphur restrictions turn out to be."

"I can see why you're not sleeping," Claire said, and they lapsed into a long silence.

Suddenly, Shantoo turned to Renya. "How are we supposed to cope with the fear?"

Renya shrugged. "Not my specialty, unfortunately."

"What do you do?" Claire asked Shantoo.

"I paint my nails," she said. "I watch construction. I sit on swings. I don't know whether these methods will suffice anymore."

Claire turned back to the window. "I've started going to church," she said.

"I was thinking of going again when I get back," said Renya.

Claire watched her wordlessly.

"I'm going to go home to a life change," Renya went on. "I used to spend all my time with Nick's colleagues so I don't know how many friends I'll still have when I'm all on my own. It's hard to make friends as an adult! There aren't that many places you can go. But I don't know how that would work. I'm Jewish, for one thing. Except, I want to find a community, like I had in undergrad. I want to find a place that I can go regularly, where I know everyone, you know? I actually have really positive memories of church."

"I mean I've started going to church again because I believe in God," said Claire.

"Oh," said Renya, "maybe we could –"

"I just want you to know," Claire was saying, "I'd like to be friends. I'd like to keep in touch. But I feel you need to know this about me first."

"You talk like it's some dirty secret," said Shantoo.

"Lots of people –" Renya started.

"Before you get all shocked," Claire interrupted, "before you get all judgmental, please let me remind you that everything is belief. I ran to science because, after a whole childhood of smothering belief systems, I thought, finally, I'll have empirical evidence, reasons more than just this one book says so. But that wasn't there."

"Of course," said Shantoo.

"Science is just camps," Claire went on, "and you choose to believe in those camps too, and usually not for any good reason, either. I'm in my camp because I liked one supervisor more than the other one, and I only liked him because he joked around a lot and I wanted to live closer to my family. There was a third camp, but that guy worked at Michigan State, and I'm not a snow person, so that's not happening. So don't tell me that science isn't all based on belief too."

"I would never," said Renya.

"Me either," said Shantoo. "I would never claim otherwise."

"So then I really thought about it," said Claire. "After years of absence, after decades of not going to church, I realized that I really *do* believe. So I went back. Even if it's weird. I believe and I find comfort."

"That makes sense," said Renya.

"I'm going to need a lot more comfort now," muttered Claire.

"I don't think it's strange at all," said Shantoo.

"Most of Nick's colleagues believe," said Renya. "They go to church religiously." Her eyes widened. "Religiously. Get it?" She hadn't meant to make that joke.

"But your colleagues don't?" demanded Claire.

"I don't know," Renya stammered. "I socialized more with Nick's friends. That's embarrassing to admit."

Claire turned to Shantoo. "Do you believe in a higher power?"

"It's a very interesting question," said Shantoo, "but it's not one I care much about. I have a list of topics that intrigue me and that I think about all the time. That particular question isn't on my personal list. I couldn't explain to you why."

"So if you don't believe, what do you think about?" said Claire. "I mean, in the hard times, in the darkest part of night here when we're alone and questioning everything, what do you think about?"

"Ghosts," said Renya with a certainty that surprised even herself.

"Love," said Shantoo.

A silence settled across the table, disturbed only by the ghost of a breeze from the window nearby.

"I don't think that it's strange that you go to church either," Renya whispered after a moment.

"Do you think you could still respect me?" said Claire.

"Of course," said Renya.

"This conversation doesn't change anything at all," whispered Shantoo.

Believing in God wasn't strange. Looking for higher power seemed to be part of the human experience. Renya herself looked for ghosts more than she'd like to admit.

They lapsed into silence again. Renya turned to the window, hiding a smile, cresting a wave of happiness at the thought of remaining friends and staying in touch. A breeze rattled in through the window that was purported to be painted shut, and Renya shivered, her smile fading.

"Are you getting a lot of work done, Shantoo?" Renya asked, shifting in her seat.

"A frightful amount, yes."

Renya played with the tablecloth. Afraid. Frightful. Another mood identifier was language choices. The words leaked out, just as emotions did. Often, people didn't realize they were skewing that way. They were afraid here too.

She reached for her day pack, and organized it for the day.

⊙ ⊙ ⊙

As Renya crept through the woods to her third group of the morning, she scrolled through the day's photographs on her camera display. She saw the faces of scientists whose names she didn't remember, soil people, big-animal people, small animal, lichens, bugs. And they showed fear, almost everyone. Face after face showed fear, clearly visible and unhidden. So she'd found the seepage first, then some scattered anxiety and fear, and now, to confirm it, fear was most people's primary emotion. Every day, there had been more and more. She could show the transition quite clearly.

She followed her grid lines to another large group. When she found them, she stopped. She hid quietly and focused her camera. They were wearing masks. It didn't matter though. Here too, the fear was plainly visible. She could see the researchers' pallor and worry lines, the deep grooves down foreheads. She could see the sweat, despite the cold wind. These ones were arguing, one woman gesturing to the station.

"I've heard that this is an anomaly," said a man whose voice carried despite the distance.

"I heard it's to do with the weather," said another. "A recent windstorm churned up the soil."

"I don't care," said the woman she'd pinpointed before. "I don't want to be out here." The woman stomped back toward the hotel.

After a moment, the rest of the group gathered their things and followed.

⊙ ⊙ ⊙

Renya was left alone in the woods. She should follow them, she knew. She should go back. But she was close to her usual meeting place with Yuri. She even thought that she heard the familiar whir of a broken-down motorcycle engine. She reached into her pockets, but she'd forgotten the good masks again. She hesitated. She'd have to be careful. Fear was motivating. Fear made you think, made you do, made you move. Too much fear could be a problem though. Terror tends to make some people freeze. Too much sustained fear could make others burn right out. So she listened to her footsteps and forced herself to take deep breaths. She cleared her mind. She watched the trees dance in the breeze. She walked farther into the woods, where she somehow knew that Yuri would be waiting.

"You're always here when I need you," she said, when she saw him. "You're like my guardian angel, or a friendly ghost."

"Are ghosts friendly?" said Yuri, steering Renya toward the motorcycle.

"Why are you always here when I look?"

"It could be that I look for you," said Yuri. "I wait for you sometimes. I think that we can maybe work together for our same goal."

Renya didn't know what he meant by that, but found that she didn't care. She followed him.

⊙ ⊙ ⊙

Yuri leaned his motorcycle against a pine tree and walked quickly out into the forest.

"Where are we?" said Renya, smoothing out her hair, still trying to get her bearings. "Why are we stopping here?"

Yuri didn't pause. He didn't even turn around. Renya hesitated. She shouldn't just follow him. She shouldn't just let him lead her around. She should keep track of where they were. Consulting a map was hard while struggling to stay on the motorcycle.

Yuri turned abruptly. "What's the most radioactive place in this whole region?"

"The elephant's foot," said Renya.

"Of course," said Yuri. "Yes. But other than that."

Renya thought about it. There was the roof of reactor four, of course, but he probably didn't mean that either. There were hot spots on the ground where they'd buried irradiated rubble. There was also a forest that hadn't recovered.

"The Red Forest?" she said. After the accident, the smoke and ash from the fire had blown onto the forest, and all the trees had turned rust red, then died abruptly. Liquidators had bulldozed most of the pine trees, then buried them in trenches dug into the ground. They'd covered the area with new soil and planted new trees on top, but it was still highly radioactive. It was one of the areas she was not permitted to enter.

"It's a good one, yes," said Yuri. "But there's better. Come. Follow."

Renya ran to catch up. "I'm not allowed to go there," she said, the wind whipping her hair into her eyes. "I'm not allowed to go to the Red Forest. Have you been?"

"Of course," said Yuri, "but there's something even more dangerous."

"I mean, there are hot spots."

"The claw."

"Oh," said Renya. She slowed, then walked faster again to keep up. "I've heard of that." The claw was part of the crane that had been used to clear the roofs of contaminated graphite from the reactor itself. It had received immeasurable amounts of radiation, over a long period of exposure. Workers had taken short shifts, but only the one crane had been used. When the workers were finished with it, the story is that they didn't know what to do with it, so they dumped it in the forest. They abandoned it. There was nothing else they could do. "Nobody knows where that is."

Yuri's eyes flashed. "I know." And he waved her forward.

They crunched a few feet more. The trees, Renya noticed, were thinning out. Then, there it was. The claw. All alone in a clearing was the claw that she'd read so much about, whose picture she'd pored over. She froze, with one-half terror and one-half exhilaration, if she had to guess. Her dosimeter crackled like fire. Her heart raced. Her breath came fast and shallow. She took one step closer, and the dosimeter's alarm sounded. She looked down. She hadn't known that it had an alarm function. She stepped back, but the beeping didn't stop.

"That's it," she breathed.

It looked like the claw from a child's arcade, hand-shaped and sitting on its curved metal fingers, but it was big, taller than she was. It was covered in rust. The wind was picking up now too. The sound it made howling in the trees, plus the blaring dosimeter alarm, made her heart pound.

"Put your machine near it," said Yuri. "I dare you. That's a number you'll never see again, if the machine can even read it."

"Everything around it is dead," said Renya. But that wasn't entirely true. Several feet away, several trees poked spindly branches toward it, and on those branches were small specs of green and yellow. They were struggling, but surviving.

"We shouldn't be here." She turned and ran back the way they'd come.

"Anyway," said Yuri, hurrying after. "There's a cemetery too. They buried most things in dirt, but they couldn't bury that. Watch your machine scream there too."

"I don't want to go there."

"I'll take you back to the city. There's still much to explore. You'll see."

"Okay." But all Renya could think about was that she shouldn't have come *here*.

"I'll take you back to Prypyat. I'll show you some places that are even better."

He climbed onto the motorcycle and she climbed on behind him. She hid her head in the small of his back as they roared toward the dead city.

⊙ ⊙ ⊙

"What do you think?" said Yuri.

Renya struggled to catch her breath. She'd just walked up over ten flights of stairs, up to the roof of the building. At least it was open-air.

She looked up. The entire city was spread out in front of her, a postapocalyptic postcard.

"It's spectacular," she breathed.

They'd climbed right to the top of a residential building and were standing on the roof. She walked to the ledge. There was the Ferris wheel. There were the abandoned bumper cars. There was the Palace of Culture. Everything was cracked and breaking, and run through with veins of green as the forest crept in. And beyond this circle, this island, this mirage of humanity and civilization, there was the forest, the tide of the natural world closing in. You could see it. Renya felt like she could see everything.

"Come." Yuri was already pulling her back to the staircase. "Follow me. There's still so much I want to show you."

She looked up. Clouds long like fingers stretched over the sky.

⊙ ⊙ ⊙

Renya followed Yuri down again as the metal stairs they stepped on seemed to creak and scream under her feet. She held the railings tightly. The stairs yawned under her weight and she prayed for the staircase to last at least until she got to the ground floor. This building wouldn't last forever, she realized with a jolt that rocked through her. She grabbed the railing tighter. She thought of this ghost city as frozen in time. But it wasn't frozen. It was disintegrating. Cities needed people, to work on them, to weatherproof, to fix everything that broke. Renya looked out of the yawning hole that had once been a window as she swung herself down to the final landing. She thought she felt the building move under her feet. When she pushed outside, she was relieved to breathe the outdoor air.

She walked farther into the courtyard and looked up at the rows of buildings, at the sidewalks and streets. Prypyat would fall apart someday. All these buildings would crumble. The forest would overtake the place completely.

Yuri was running down the stone path. She sprinted to catch up.

⊙ ⊙ ⊙

"This is a better building," Yuri was saying, his cheeks charmingly pink. They were on the edge of the town, where it disappeared into the forest, first slowly, then quickly drowning in reclaimed wilderness. "You'll like this one." This was a side of Yuri that Renya hadn't seen yet, the excited one, the sincere one. He was like a little-boy adventurer. He was treating this exploration like trick-or-treating.

"I wanted to study history," he was saying, "but I didn't have enough good grades. But I'm studying it now. I study with my eyes and my feet and my hands. And I can show other people. I can tell people what it was like. It won't be dead now. The people who hide here now, they won't disappear completely when they die, because I will be a witness. You'll join me. You'll come back like me. You will be a witness too. This is something that we can do. I knew that this is something you wanted to do. I knew you wanted to do it with me."

He hurried through the cracked and broken streets. "This place I want to show you, it was a school. There are dolls and gas masks inside, yes? It wasn't because of the accident. All the classrooms had gas masks because this was during the Cold War that everything stopped here."

But then a high-pitched whine pierced the forest hum, and Yuri stopped. For a moment, he was silent. Renya looked out into the waving trees, the sea of sickly branches, and she was brought back to herself. She had no idea what that sound could be. She felt gravity pull her down. Her knees buckled, and she set herself down gently on a tree stump. The adrenaline she'd felt earlier, the drive to come, was gone now. All her forward momentum was momentarily gone. This passed. It was fine. She'd known it was coming, and she knew it would pass. She breathed slowly and counted seconds as she inhaled and exhaled.

Yuri knelt. His face was stubbly and handsome, and he was watching her solicitously. He looked like Nick – the old Nick – for a moment. "Are you not well?" he said.

Renya waved him off. "I'm fine," she said. "I just want to write up some notes."

Yuri nodded. "You're sure?"

She wasn't, of course. But before she could answer, he was already off, bounding down the old stone path. Renya felt herself droop, her shoulders relaxing and bending forward.

She took out her camera. She focused on the forest first, then on the cityscape, but she didn't take any pictures. She put the camera back in her pack. She felt for her computer. There was Internet here, for communication between security guards or something, Yuri had explained.

Nick's image immediately filled her screen. He must have jumped up to get the call.

"You weren't around," she said.

"I know, that's because I –"

"I came online and you weren't here."

Nick scrutinized the screen, his upper eyebrows raised, alarmed. "Where are you?"

"Prypyat. There's Wi-Fi so I thought I'd try you again."

"Prypyat!"

"Relax," said Renya. "I'm not inside a building."

"There's no –"

"There are tourists here." She'd seen a whole pack of them, all snapping cameras. Yuri had made her hide. That made sense though. Security personnel were likely not allowed to bring guests. "There are ecotours that run through."

Nick was running a hand through his hair. "That doesn't mean it's safe," he said. "There's a reason it's called the exclusion zone, the zone of alienation. It won't be safe for eight hundred years."

"I should go." Renya looked down the path. She exhaled. She was here. She wasn't planning to come back. She should explore.

"No!" Nick was standing again. He crouched so his face filled the screen. "Listen," he said. "Okay. Okay, listen."

"I don't know why I turned this on."

"No! Don't go."

"I should find Yuri," said Renya. "He's supposed to show me around."

"Stay," said Nick. "Tell me about the history."

Renya studied Nick's expression. It was blank. It showed no sign of that smug superiority he had sometimes, no sign that he was making fun. He knew how to make his face blank though, when he concentrated. He knew who he was married to.

"I'm serious," he was saying. "I've been thinking about it, and it's absurd that I know so little about the story."

Renya reached for her backpack and the computer wobbled.

"Wait!" said Nick. "Stay! After the explosion . . . what happened next? Please explain it to me."

Renya let the silence stretch. Nick's kind-eyed expression felt comforting. Suddenly, he looked like the old Nick too. "There were still people alive in the plant," she started.

"Inside?" said Nick. "They must have heard the explosion."

"They didn't know what had happened."

"So they had to find out," he prodded.

"Some of the scientists ran outside, up to the roof of the fourth reactor. The lid had blown off though. It had flipped and crashed back down. That's when they saw that there was a hole, and twisted metal, and they could see right into the core. They could see that it was burning."

"They must have been afraid."

"Yeah, because you're not supposed to be that close to the reactor."

"There has to be containment, lead, something between you and the core."

"It would be like seeing your own heart exposed." She shouldn't have said that. She moved to turn off the computer, but Nick raised his hand. His eyes were pleading. Renya paused.

"*My* heart is fine," said Nick.

"Sure."

"There's a latency period," he said. "With radiation poisoning."

"Yeah!" Renya sat back. "You feel fine. But you know you're dying. You know you won't survive it. So they must have known that was it for at least some of them, and they were in the latency period."

"Then what happened?"

"Then the fire trucks got there. A whole fleet arrived."

"Flooding the containment with water would have made it worse though, right?"

"Yes," said Renya. "Water is a moderator."

"So it would have made the reaction go supercritical. That could have blown up all of Europe."

"Firefighters died," said Renya, "some of them, lots of them, slowly, over the course of days and weeks. Then the helicopters got there next. The fire was still burning, and you're right, they couldn't use water, so they had to have pilots fly over it and have co-pilots throw sandbags of concrete and lead, and boron as well, of course, to absorb the neutrons."

"That's right!" said Nick. "They'd need the boron to absorb the neutrons and stop the chain reaction. Then they'd need to cover the core with lead. All the while, they were trying to put out the fire."

"They could only be up for minutes at a time," said Renya. "There was a rule that nobody could fly more than two flights too, but most went longer, and so many people went up again and again. And there were miners too, at that time. They had to dig underneath the plant to try to contain the core. It was still melting down and down through the basement. They couldn't let it hit the water tables."

"It would have –"

"It could have contaminated the drinking water."

"And caused a nuclear explosion."

"Water is a moderator," said Renya. "It would have started another critical reaction, and poisoned everyone and everything for miles."

"Imagine knowing that," breathed Nick.

"The miners couldn't ever be still. They always had to run. They were supposed to wear masks, but they couldn't."

"Why not?"

"It was too hot and they couldn't breathe. They couldn't catch their breath. There was a fire raging right above them. So they took off their masks. It was so hot some of them took off their clothes. Sometimes one or two would just drop dead. They must be the ones who inhaled or swallowed radioactive sources, but the rest would just keep working. They understood the situation was that serious, and their part in it was that critical."

Renya heard a sound, a scratching in the woods. She froze. The tourists were long gone. She was supposed to be alone.

"Renya?"

"Hello?" she managed to croak. Her throat felt closed. There were wolves close by. The sun was setting. She hadn't noticed. Wolves prowled here by night.

"Renya?" Nick's face was close to the camera again.

"Is someone there?" Some of the wild dogs seemed damaged, unhinged. She'd heard the small-animal guys talking. And there were looters. The scratching intensified. Renya stood, knocking the computer off her knees. "Hello?"

And then a voice emerged from the woods, a rough male voice. "Hello? Как поживаешь?" she said. But her Ukrainian was rough, unpractised and likely imprecise.

The scratching turned into footsteps, heavy ones. Renya crouched. There were renegades, if you believed the rumours. She could see Nick's face on the toppled screen.

"Ren?" Nick, through the computer, looked frantic. She didn't want to think about what this might be doing to his heart. "Sweetheart, what's happening?"

"Кто там?" called Renya.

"Who's there? Renya, who's –"

"Подождите!" she said, but there was no reply.

The footsteps stopped, and Renya heard an order to hold up her hands. She did. The world seemed to sway. She felt faint. She breathed deeply to keep herself from blacking out. "I'm allowed to be here. I have a visa. Do you speak English? I have a visa."

"Who is it, Renya? What's happening?"

There was another curt reply, something about a knife and self-defence. She couldn't make it out.

"Knife?" she said. "No. What? No. What do you mean, do I know how to stab a person?"

"Renya!" Nick sounded short of breath. What could she do? There was nothing she could do for him. Renya edged toward her computer and pushed the screen closed, cutting off Nick mid-yell.

She could shield him at least. Whatever happened, he didn't need to see it.

Just then, Dima emerged from behind copse of trees. He was grinning. He'd crept around the building, then hidden. He'd scraped the sides of the buildings with a fork he'd brought, he told her. He'd disguised his voice.

"You ass!" Renya rushed over but stopped just short of him. "I thought I was going to have a heart attack."

"Good," said Dima. "You should be more careful. I heard you talking. If you talk so loud, you should know how to defend yourself at least."

⊙ ⊙ ⊙

Dima's hands felt hot on her waist, and she could smell sweat and cigarette smoke. She hated it. It scared her. She loved it. They were in the abandoned city square. The light was bleeding out of the sky. In the light of the early-risen moon, the buildings and the cracked and broken sidewalk shone white like bones. The sounds of their scuffling echoed magnificently.

"Bend your knees," Dima growled. "Keep your centre lower."

Dima and Yuri were pretending to teach her self-defence moves. She was pretending to learn. She felt wild.

"I should finish that call," Renya said. She'd messaged Nick that she was safe right away. She'd clapped the computer shut after that.

"Later," Dima said roughly. Renya didn't really want to call anyway. This was fun. The relief of the averted disaster had made her euphoric. "Come on," he said, facing off against her again. "Weight on left foot, swing with right arm."

So Renya swung. Dima ducked and came at her. She lost her balance, and he grabbed her again. He held her to him as she half-heartedly struggled. She could smell the hand-rolled cigarettes on him. She felt enveloped in that smell and in the heat of his body. He tightened his embrace. He was attracted to her. She could feel it.

"It was a good try," he said softly, his breath tickling her ear. He held her a moment longer, then gently set her back on her feet. He made a big show of looking down at her, from high and from much too close.

Yuri, smoking, leaning against a nearby tree, nodded. "You did well," he said. "But I could show you better."

He was jealous. These rough men were fighting for her attention. She shouldn't love it so much, but she did. She thought about how she might spin this when she told Nick about it. At the thought of Nick, she felt a weight, a drop in her stomach. She'd slammed her computer shut. She should explain what had happened. She should reassure him. She would want to be reassured. She also wanted to experience this wild night.

Dima hugged her to him, so hard that she lost her balance again and fell into him. "Come," he said. "We will show you more. You should know this place completely. You need to be able to defend yourself anywhere."

Yuri straightened. He stamped out a cigarette.

Dima nodded. "Let's go."

⊙ ⊙ ⊙

Renya had been following Dima and Yuri around and through the abandoned city, in and out of buildings, for what felt like hours, when Dima stopped abruptly, back on the edge of the forest. He wheeled around. "We'll give the girl a rest."

Renya shrugged. They seemed to be breathing harder than she was, but she wasn't about to argue the point. She looked around. The light had failed. The darkness was absolute.

A scream seemed to rip through the city.

"Metallists," Yuri said simply.

"Who?"

"Doesn't matter." He nodded toward the trees. "We go to the woods now."

They walked a few miles farther, then the men stopped and shrugged out of their backpacks. Renya sat down on the root system of a huge, dying tree, and felt the wind whistle past her jacket and through her hair. She made herself rigid to keep herself from shivering.

Dima pressed a bottle into her hand, and she held it to her lips without looking at it. The alcohol burned down her throat. It seemed to tear at her esophagus. She coughed.

Yuri laughed. Renya felt the bottle being lifted away from her.

"What is that?" she spluttered.

"Vodka," said Dima. "I made it myself."

"Do you like it?" said Yuri, and both men laughed when she hesitated.

"Drink more," Dima said roughly. "It will help."

Renya shrugged. She grabbed the bottle back. Then she drank, and let herself be pulled to her feet, pressed against Dima's chest again. This was a terrible idea. But what was safe? Safe was faculty mixers, getting talked-down to and being groped in dark corners. She hadn't come all the way to Chornobyl to play it safe.

Dima took Renya's arms, held them out and in front her, then stood behind her. She could feel his breath on her neck. She could smell the sharp tang of alcohol, strong as disinfectant. The night was cold but his body was so hot. She felt her own body heating in reaction. She didn't let herself think about what that meant. Dima forced her knees to bend slightly. Then he hugged her close and pressed his face to her cheek. "This," he said, "is how you begin. You start low to the ground."

"Okay." And Renya got it. "Your centre of mass has to be low so you're harder to knock over."

Dima grunted. "I will show you." And he came in even closer, so Renya could feel his smoky breath on her neck again, blowing down her shirt. "I will try to make you fall."

"I don't think so." Renya wriggled away. She swung her backpack on and pulled to tighten the straps as she ran farther out into the trees, laughing. She heard Yuri take off after her, then heard the shush of Dima's sneakers follow. She couldn't see them in the sticky, inky, dark, but she could hear them crunching through the plants toward her. They ran and whooped and screamed into the night.

⊙ ⊙ ⊙

It wasn't until she was walking back toward the research centre that Renya finally felt the cold. Yuri had dropped her off a few minutes from the gravel path and the slow walk was helping her to clear her head and still her heart. The night air was suddenly stinging her hot cheeks. She took deep breaths, hoping that the fresh air would help her sober up, at least.

She sat down beside a tree, in the dust, and took out her computer.

Nick answered her call immediately. There was a window behind him. It was black. It was night where he was too, then. She had no idea what that might mean.

"Ren, where have you been? Ren? What happened? Are you okay?"

She held the computer close to her face and scanned his facial muscles, his eyelids, cheeks, and the muscles around the mouth. She saw something, for sure, but she couldn't concentrate on what it signified.

"Do you remember when you used to send me drunk texts?" she asked Nick.

"Are you drunk? Who was –"

"Who?" she said.

"There was someone in the city," said Nick. "He asked you about a knife. You talked about a knife!"

"Oh that was nothing." She moved her head and the whole forest streaked to the left. "It was just Yuri's friend Dima. They're security."

"I heard about that. There are security patrols."

"I know! Right?" When she swung her head around, the trees streaked black with dots of light and colour. She steadied herself. "There are looters here, that's the thing. These men, these people, they sneak in here late at night to steal things from the ghost city. There are metallists who take things apart to steal all their components. I think they sell it all."

"Everything there is contaminated."

"The new owners could potentially die slow and painful deaths, I know, can you imagine? But this is life here."

"Ren, where are you now?"

"Dima said you can bring vodka with you. You just have to keep the bottle tightly shut." She remembered the sloshing of liquid, a struggle to find her lips. "Can you believe it? He drinks here all the time. He says he's into radiation."

"Ren, are you safe?"

"Dima was a resident!" He'd called himself a resident. He said that he'd lived here before the disaster, but she didn't believe it. The math didn't work out. In any case, his accent was off, high-class, not of the working class anyway, not even Ukrainian, she'd guess. And his clothes, the shirt under his uniform, his watch, his rings didn't match the story. Unlike Yuri, whose clothes were threadbare, Dima was somehow wealthy. He'd likely grown up that way too. He had that air. She had no idea how he'd ended up here. "He said that, but I think he was lying," she amended.

"He asked you . . . Renya. You talked about a knife. I heard you before. You talked, you said, there was something about a knife."

"Dima's just intense. He wanted to know if I could defend myself."

"Why did Max, I can't believe –"

"The academic community eats its young."

"What?"

"And its wives too. Anyway, tomorrow Dima's going to teach me how to use a knife. Then I'm going to find a way to go to the sarcophagus."

"You can't go there. You need PPE."

"You don't."

"You need protection."

"I have what I need." And she'd heard rumours of dishwashers giving rides for cash.

"You have to take care of yourself."

"What is it to you?"

"What are you talking about? Please."

"Please what?"

"Please take care of yourself. For me, if not for you."

"I need to do this," Renya muttered, the alcohol suddenly souring in her stomach. "I have to go."

"Fine." Nick was pacing again. "But call me later."

Renya raised her eyebrows.

"Please," said Nick, contrite. "Please call. I just want to talk."

Renya repacked her computer, but instead of going right back inside, she took out her camera and scanned through the pictures she'd just taken: the night, the dark forest, the boys whipping through it, her flash illuminating their hair and making their eyes glow. It'd been a while since she'd taken pictures purely for fun. Then she got to the day. She stopped at Claire. She studied the emotional displays she'd found. Fear. Sometimes it was more than fear. She clicked from shot to shot. She'd found terror. And then, in the last shots, sadness. She tried to think about what it all meant, but she couldn't focus. She couldn't concentrate. Maybe didn't want to think about it.

⊙ ⊙ ⊙

Back in the centre, Renya found Claire sitting alone in the dining room. Her face was down. She was studying something, comparing notebooks. One of them, Renya realized, was her own. Claire was looking through her collection of radiation readings. She pulled up a chair.

"I'm buying a dosimeter when I get back," Claire muttered.

"For home?"

"For everywhere. You're smart to have one."

"I'm getting rid of this one though," she said.

Claire looked up.

"I'm not bringing anything back home," she said. "Radiation exposure and all that."

"Right!" said Claire. "Me neither. That's smart. Just in case."

Renya looked out the window. All she saw was the light fixture reflecting back at her. "What are the animals like?" she said.

Claire's smile didn't reach her eyes. She looked sad if anything. Or maybe the sight of Claire fighting off fear for her sake was making Renya herself feel sad. The difference between the emotions clearly experienced and the countenance expressed tended to pull at others' hearts.

"There certainly are lots of animals," Claire was saying, "well, birds anyway. Well, some birds. Some populations are dropping. I don't think that has anything to do with radiation though. That's a virus, I'm pretty sure. Anyway, I don't know what to make of any of the populations I've studied here. I don't feel like I completely understand what I'm seeing yet."

Renya ran the tablecloth between her fingers. She felt the rhythm of the threads as they rubbed together, remembering, suddenly, quiet dinners of her childhood, looking for anger, guessing at causes, watching the lights outside the dining-room window dance as cars hummed past.

"Tell me about fear," said Claire.

"It's caused by a perceived threat," Renya said by rote, not looking up. "It can cause different reactions depending on the circumstances: how quickly that threat is coming, if it's coming right away, if it's coming later, if you can get away, if you can't, if you know what to do, if you have any power over your circumstances. It can make you need to move, run, get away, or it can make you freeze. It can make you fawn. Or it can make you angry."

"There are times I'm happy and working. Then it hits me all at once."

"Textbook reaction to non-immediate fear stimulus." Renya nodded. "If you know what to do, then other parts of your brain take over. You can even feel happy. But every once in a while, you'll take a break, or even just a breath, and the situation will hit you. It's like that with all emotions, well, most emotional experiences. In general, emotions are more like waves than wading pools. There are, however, deep ends. Those exist too."

"My fingers tingle," said Claire

"Classic sign," said Renya. "Your face will show it too, but sometimes for only seconds at a time. I call that seepage or short displays. It's one of the things that my project is looking for."

"I'm packing up specimens to take back, but I've looked at some here. The birds' brains are diminished."

"Oh." Renya rubbed her forehead. She thought about what that could mean, what it might mean for them. "That's weird."

"That might be radiation," Claire was saying, "or it might not. There are viruses that will do that too. Again, I know there are those circulating viruses."

Renya was having trouble too. Her brain wasn't working. Her thoughts were cloudy. She was having trouble with memory. But lack of sleep would do that. Alcohol could definitely do that too, not that she'd been drinking much, well, tonight she'd had way too much. Brains diminish over generations anyway, not over a couple of days. And she was tired. She was so tired. She was hardly sleeping. She was processing a lot of things.

"They're these wonderful, graceful animals," Claire was saying. "They read the wind. They communicate in ways we can't figure out. They ride updrafts and understand weather and listen to pressure waves. One flew into a tree. I was just standing there. I was watching it. It flew into a tree trunk and died."

"Have you ever seen that?"

"Maybe," said Claire. "Yes, I have, at home, but only lately. That's chilling too. I also read all these different reports. Animals are better here. They are worse. There are more. There are fewer. There are tumours. The populations have adapted. They're dying off. They're susceptible to disease. There are viruses. They're getting decimated. They're surviving anything. I don't get it. I don't like that I don't get it. It's like we're all looking at a different place, all the different teams. It's like we're all studying different populations. But we're not. We're all looking at the exact same thing. It's the same at home. At home is more chilling, because I keep seeing damage here, and I find myself thinking, well, this is comparable to what I see back where I live, and maybe I'm understanding it differently now. I'm seeing it all in a new way because I've been *here*."

"That is chilling."

"Humans pointing guns I understand. At least, I would know where the threat is coming from."

"This is the worst kind of fear," said Renya. "Your body doesn't know how to react. The fear tends to trigger muscles and primes you to run. Your body doesn't understand what your mind does: Where could we go?"

"I was so sure," said Claire. "I was so certain in coming here."

"I was too," said Renya. "Now I don't know why." And then, after a silence: "Have you considered just working at a zoo?"

"Little kids throw stuff too."

"There are dangers everywhere."

"I wasn't honest with you last night," said Claire. "I've stopped being able to handle sadness too. My grandmother died."

Renya looked down at her fingers. Claire had told her that last night. Maybe they were all getting forgetful and zoning out, but they were also dealing with fear on a larger scale, and that definitely had effects.

"I got too sad all at once," Claire was saying. "I still do, when I think about it."

Renya didn't look up. She would be displaying sadness too, but she didn't want it to show, not now. Her grandmother had died too. It had happened when she'd been in high school, and she'd been cut down by it. "I'm sorry," she muttered. She could feel the flash of pain, in her torso first, then radiating outward. It wasn't as bad as on that afternoon in the school courtyard, as her dad told her, ushering her to the car. But the memory still triggered the actual expression. It still hurt. It created a kind of physical pain. She didn't want to be sad now. She wanted to put that memory away. Grief was not a top-five emotion. Sadness wasn't her favourite of the basic six at all. It might be under anger for all that.

"You're not supposed to be that heartbroken," Claire was saying, "but I spent most of my childhood with her. I wasn't latchkey. I never went to daycare. It was the two of us together. I knew her more than anyone."

"I miss my grandmother too. More than anyone else, she was the one who raised me." And again, Renya remembered the gut-wrenching pain that radiated down her as her father hesitated, one hand on her wrist, and whispered into her ear. What was memory except an echo of the real thing? "We were close too," said Renya. "My father turned it into a learning opportunity. My grandmother died because she didn't tell anyone about her symptoms. Always tell when you don't feel well." Hence the early awareness of fear and pain in others. Hence the need for early warning, that need that had multiplied with Nick's heart event. It wasn't something she wanted to tell people: the childhood fear turned into adult obsession. That might be part of her scientist origin story too, she realized. Her true origin might be more complex than she'd imagined.

"Well." Claire's voice had brightened. Renya looked up. Her eyes were haunted, the lower lids pulled up, classic fear, classic sadness, that classic back and forth between the two. But she was making an effort. Another classic sign of something or other. "I'm glad you're here," she said. "I'm glad I met you. At least there's that."

"I've been thinking about that," said Renya. "I realized that you're the first person in a very long time that I really liked and decided I wanted to be friends with."

"It's funny, isn't it?" said Claire. "We're thrown in with people. We don't decide on our social circles so much as we're assigned them. It's like we never left grade school."

"I like you a lot. And Shantoo."

"Ditto," Claire said brightly. She was trying to lift the mood. Renya appreciated it. "What were you like in grade school?"

"I don't know," said Renya. "I did what I was told. I saw all the dangerous kids, and I flirted with joining up with them, but in the end I didn't hang out with them very often."

"You were a good girl."

"I was."

"You didn't want to be?"

"My dad had something on me. They smoked. My mom died of cancer when I was a baby. That always brought me in line in the end." Maybe she hadn't actually wanted to experience fear even then. Maybe she'd always been drawn to watching other people experiencing it.

"Oh," said Claire. "I get it. You were the kid-wife."

Renya started. She'd never heard the expression. It fit the situation exactly. Even after her dad had remarried, she'd been in charge of taking care of him: she made the tea, brought the journals, tidied the office. Kid-wife.

"Matt, my partner I mean, he was the kid-husband," Claire was saying. "His dad took off. He took care of things."

Renya looked down at Claire's finger. No ring.

Claire nodded to her hand. "We never married. We almost did once, but I couldn't go through with it."

"Why not?"

"He thought I was obsessed with birds. He hated all the time I spend on them. It's not just at work."

"You bring it home with you." Renya was nodding. "But you have to bring it home with you. That's the point."

"Yes." Claire nodded. "That *is* the point. Otherwise it wouldn't be worth all this time and attention. It wasn't really an ultimatum but it was kind of an ultimatum. I chose the birds."

"Endgame birds?"

"Maybe. Maybe all of them. We had some pretty major rows. We decided not to get married after all. We're still together though."

"You can do that?" Renya had thought that was impossible. She thought you couldn't say no, or even just say later, and then be together anyway. When Nick had knelt down that day at the harbourfront, she'd thought it was a yes or a return to living alone.

"We live in adjoining condos," said Claire. "Not adjoining. Next door. It's what works."

"I would have done that if I'd thought it was an option. I'm like that, I think. I see two options when there's a spectrum."

"I'm glad we fought when we did," said Claire. "Otherwise, we would have lived the way our parents did, just because we thought we had to. I'm glad we found something that works for us."

Renya nodded, pretending to understand that. She wished she did.

"We've been fighting a lot since I've been here though."

Renya nodded again. This, she did understand.

"Tell me about fear," Claire whispered again. "Obviously, I need to understand it better."

"It triggers the amygdala, first of all," Renya started.

"I mean, what do you do when you have it?" Claire interrupted.

"I don't really know," Renya said, also by rote. "That's not really my specialty."

Claire nodded. She arranged her papers.

"I mean, I do have thoughts," said Renya quickly. "My advice is not to ignore it. We have emotions for a reason. Charles Darwin even thought they were adaptive, that they helped with evolution. So start by figuring out what the emotion is telling you. Fear means danger. First, get yourself away from the immediate hazard, if that's possible."

"Right." Claire turned to the window. Renya saw her shudder.

"In regular life, you can often not completely get away from the danger," said Renya. "You shouldn't block out the fear, all the same. You shouldn't try to block out any emotion. Try to feel the fear, but don't get overwhelmed. It wants to drown you, it wants to take you under, but don't let it."

"Feelings are more like waves than wading pools, you said."

"But there are deep ends," said Renya. "Stay afloat if you find yourself in the deep end."

"Any advice on staying afloat?"

Renya shrugged. "Same as in the water, I guess. Take deep breaths. Count to ten. Some people like to get away, metaphorically speaking: they think about a place where they're comfortable. Some people like to get grounded where they are: they touch something, and smell something. They like to talk themselves through it, through the immediate fear, that way. I like to count. I take deep breaths and count the seconds that I inhale, and count as I exhale. Your exhales should be longer than your inhales, so I count in for four and out for seven. I didn't get that from an expert, I should point out. I just read that on the Internet. It doesn't always work."

"Thank you," whispered Claire.

"I'm no expert, unfortunately." Renya bowed her head. "This isn't really something I'm particularly good at."

"You have insight," Claire whispered, "and it helps."

Renya looked up. Claire touched her hand. She squeezed. Then she breathed deeply, the exhaustion visibly catching up to her. She leaned back in her chair.

"Anyway," Claire said, now packing up her things, "I should turn in. I don't want to tell you what time it is. You'll be shocked, I'm afraid."

Renya waved as her friend shuffled toward the door, but she wasn't ready to sleep yet. A screech sounded outside the window. Renya jerked, her heart suddenly racing. She couldn't see anything out the window at all. It was likely an owl. Claire could have identified it, but she was making her way out of the room. Fear also caused cortisol, she should have told her: it gave you energy to run. It made you want to fight.

⊙ ⊙ ⊙

Back in her room, Renya had put her computer on the edge of the bed, and Nick's face in close-up took up the entire screen.

Renya crouched in front of the camera and held up her knife, in roughly the position that Dima had shown her.

"Stop it, Renya," said Nick. "I do not want to see your fighting stance."

This was less fun without the strength of Dima's hands and the heat of his body, but Nick was flushed, she noticed. He was upset. He was in a new room now, though it looked much like the last one. All she could see through the screen was nondescript wallpaper and a threadbare comforter on the bed. Their home was nicer. She swung out with the butter knife she'd swiped from the dining room.

"I don't need to learn how to defend myself with a knife," Nick said, his voice peevish.

"Weight on left foot," said Renya, "swing with right arm."

"This Dima, he's –"

"He's intense. He's not like anyone I've ever met."

"He's dangerous."

"He's –"

"He's damaged."

"You haven't even –"

"No, I'm serious, Ren. If he patrols in the exclusion zone, if he works there a lot, he's been damaged. Don't laugh at me, this is serious. I've been doing research, and if he works a lot of shifts there, then he might have abnormal chromosomes."

"You said I could –"

"Not with a man who has abnormal chromosomes. Don't laugh at me. There's nothing funny about –"

Suddenly, Nick looked down at his watch.

"Do you have to go?"

"Sorry, I have to –"

"Don't worry. It's fine." But maybe it wasn't fine. She liked talking to him. She missed him.

"I'll be around later," he said. "You can call. And thanks for calling me back. I'm really glad you're safe."

Renya sighed. When the call ended, she fetched a bottle of water from the vending machine and drank it quickly. Then she got back to work.

⊙ ⊙ ⊙

Late that night, Renya couldn't sleep. She covered herself with her blanket. She closed her eyes and listened. Something hollered out in the night, and a sad screech resounded as an answer. The sounds ricocheted off her walls like they'd come from inside the room. But they couldn't have. That was a ridiculous thought.

Renya curled in a ball. One thing caused another caused another. No matter how badly you wanted to rail at someone else for causing the avalanche, chances were that you could go back even further and find out that it was your fault all along. She wanted to tell Nick that she saw it now. She didn't want to tell him. She didn't want to talk to him again. All she wanted was to see his face.

It was very late at night for Renya, but she couldn't seem to calculate what time it would be for Nick. She felt listless. She sat up and threw off the blanket. She opened her computer and activated Skype. Then her Internet phone called out and she answered.

"Renya!" said Nick. "I've been . . ."

Renya pulled up the blanket again. Nick was in a new place with blank, sterile-looking walls. She pretended not to notice.

"I'm glad you came back," he said.

"I can't sleep."

"Are you –"

"There's something that I wanted to talk to you about."

"It's okay, Ren. I'm on my way –"

"God," she cut him off. "God. On your way where, I don't even want to hear it."

"I don't want to say too much, because I'm not sure I'll be able to pull if off, but –"

Renya waved her hand for Nick to stop. She'd imagined that she'd be thrilled to hear that he was leaving her for good. She thought she might at least feel vindicated, or at peace. There would be no more wondering. There would be no more not-knowing. She could be mad at him, if she felt like it. She didn't feel like it though, suddenly.

"I keep thinking about critical reactions," she said quickly. She was the one who'd left first, in any case. She'd flown here. And she'd asked him to be gone by the time she got back. There was that. She had to constantly remind herself about that part, and about how she'd have to look for a smaller apartment when she got back, and about how she'd have to move all her stuff. She thought, strangely, of the spoon on the table in that abandoned house. She remembered the clothes still folded neatly inside drawers.

"I've been thinking about how one thing causes another thing causes another thing . . ."

"Sweetheart," Nick started. She didn't want to look at Nick through the computer screen. She didn't want to see his expression. It would be pity, likely. She didn't need to see that.

"You were at the bar," she said. "You told me you were going out to play pool."

"It was a mistake," said Nick.

"The faculty club."

"No."

"Taps then, no, that other pub, where your colleagues always go."

"I thought we agreed not to talk about this again."

"I asked Teagan after you told me. He said you were playing pool."

"We said we wouldn't bring it up anymore, we *agreed*."

"I must have looked confused. He elaborated. Billiards."

"He shouldn't have –"

"There must have been one decision then another decision then another thing."

"I was just drunk."

There was a silence. Renya let it stretch.

"Do you remember the day we first met?" said Nick.

"No." But of course she did. It was a memory they often discussed.

"We were at your dad's house," said Nick.

She'd been wearing a blue dress, he a jacket, the sun radiant in a blooming backyard. But that was a very old self, the pre-married one. She'd lived in a tiny but neat apartment. She'd gone to yoga every day. She made sure to drink enough water. She used to miss that old self. Now she was agnostic. Maybe she missed her married-self now. That was funny. Her mind turned back toward that darkened bar. "You must have been talking about physics," she said. "Bose-Einstein condensation, I bet you anything."

"Your dad was hosting a faculty party," said Nick. "Remember? He'd invited you. He wanted you to hear the conversation and get interested in physics again. You're a rising star in your field but he wanted you to go back to studying physics."

"You were playing pool," said Renya.

"You were auditing one of Teagan's classes," said Nick. "You were doing it to get Max off your back, I realized."

"She must have impressed you. Clearly she's better than me, so she can follow your conversations better."

"We were all trying to get your attention that night."

"She must have said something really pithy, something really smart."

"We started playing with the cutlery, you and I. I dropped my fork under the table, remember? Then you dropped your fork. The party was going long. The sun was setting at that point."

"Maybe you went for a shot close to her. Or maybe it all happened after billiards. Maybe you both went to the bar and you scooted close."

"We were talking under the table. Your dad was trying so hard not to see that we were fooling around."

"Maybe your finger touched her leg."

"You were the person that everyone wanted to know, and you chose to talk to me that night."

"And then maybe you made the decision to let it stay there. That's just something small. A pinky finger isn't infidelity."

"You were electric, you were like a live wire –"

"Then you might have taken her hand. No. Your finger was touching her leg. You moved your hand to her knee."

"I told you I wanted to know you, remember? I took *your* hand. I'd never done that to a girl before."

"Maybe you kissed her fingertips too. Girls like that. It's a delicate gesture. It made me feel like you were paying attention. You stopped doing it after we were married for a while, but I used to love it."

"I'd never kissed a girl's hand, I remember."

"You can be charming, I know that. Then she probably said, no *you* might have said . . ."

Nick knelt in front of the computer, his face suddenly giant, taking up the whole screen. "Please stop," he said. "Please don't do this."

"What?" said Renya.

"Nothing happened."

"But it almost did."

"Not really!" Nick's face appeared in extreme close-up. "I had no intention of doing anything at all."

"There are logistical issues," said Renya. "There must have been some conversation, some planning. You ended up walking her home."

"I don't think that we –"

"Nick!" And it worked, somehow, Nick paused, and that must be what Renya had wanted? They looked at each other through the computer screens.

"Do you really want to know?" Nick said at last.

Renya didn't answer. She curled up in her blanket. The truth was that she didn't know if she wanted to know. She was so tired. She could just sleep. She could get enough sleep for once here. When had she last had eight hours? When had she last had five?

"I said I'd answer anything," Nick was saying, "but you said . . . remember?"

"Remember what?"

"You said you didn't want to know. You said! You wouldn't be able to get over it if you could picture it. Anyway, nothing happened. We went out to play pool, not just the two of us, but the whole department. Well. Not everyone. You know how it is. Then it was late and I said I'd walk her home. She came on to me. She kissed me, I admit that, but then I left. I shouldn't have let it get that far. I only did, thinking of you."

"Thinking you'd get my attention."

"I wanted to have something provocative to say," Nick muttered. "It was juvenile, I know."

But that wasn't the big problem anymore. It never had been in fact. The problem had always been that he'd felt he needed to get her attention in the first place. "I have to ask myself what was the decision that started it all. That's why causality is the worst. *Why* did you go to the bar? *Why* were you out on a Thursday night? You never used to do that. You teach on Fridays."

"It was a department thing."

"At first, you didn't want to go. Remember?"

"It was just pool!"

"But what started the critical stupid reaction?"

"Ren –"

"Where was *I*?"

That was the problem. That had always been the problem, even if she hadn't wanted to admit it to herself.

Nick didn't answer. He didn't have to. "Let's not do this," he said after a moment. "I don't see –"

"The apartment was empty," she said. "We both know that."

"Listen –"

"I wasn't there. I hadn't been there for weeks." Nick was scared, as worried about the event, the heart thing, well, the stent, as she'd been. He was still going from follow-up to follow-up to confirm that he was okay. He was, but the appointments had been stressful. She'd gone to the doctors with him, but checked out after that. And after that, she'd just left all the time. She'd been absent in mind first and then in body. She just kept coming up with reasons to go out. She'd left. She was a person who left.

"But –"

"I was auditing classes at night," said Renya.

"You were learning how to program."

"I was scared."

"Scared of –"

"*That* night –"

"We shouldn't –"

"No. We shouldn't. I guess not. I am sorry though. I'm sorry I wasn't there. I'm sorry I got so scared. I'm sorry I was gone first."

"Ren? I'm proud of you. Not that it matters. But I am. And you weren't as gone as you think."

Renya felt her eyes fill with tears.

"And you needed to learn how to program."

"Right." She cleared her throat.

"You'd been talking about it for years," Nick said lightly. "I didn't really understand at the time, but you were right. How much have you done with those programming skills since then?"

Renya wiped her cheeks. Suddenly, she couldn't keep her eyes open. "I have to go to sleep," she muttered.

"Okay."

There was a long silence. Neither closed their laptops.

"Is your computer plugged in?" said Nick.

"Yes."

"Can you leave it on?"

"Okay."

"Okay?"

Renya curled up and closed her eyes. That other woman would just have to deal with it. Nick was offering one more night, of sorts. She planned to take it. She closed her eyes and pictured the warmth of his arms around her, remembering Sunday mornings in the warm pools of sunlight, wrapped in blankets and pillows, drinking coffee, listlessly looking through crosswords until she could find a clue she could unravel. She knew that Nick was watching, likely remembering the same thing too. It had been nice while it lasted. They'd gotten angry at some point, competitive in a strange way, but for a while it had been nice.

⊙ ⊙ ⊙

Renya woke to an empty screen. Nick had cut the connection in the night. Or maybe it had just timed out. It didn't matter now. She threw off her blanket and stumbled to her feet.

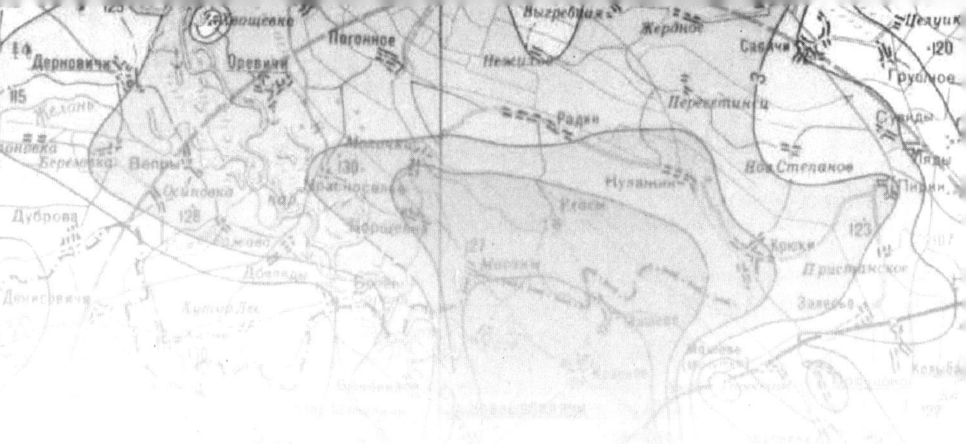

CHAPTER 10

"MOVE FASTER," BARKED DIMA. HE PUSHED HER FROM BEHIND, and Renya stumbled on the stairs in yet another unlit Prypyat apartment building. Her misstep clanged in the gloom. She grabbed the railing and hauled herself forward. She walked faster.

When Renya had found Yuri in the woods that morning, Dima had been with him, and they'd been different. Their responses had been curt and quick. They'd shuttled her onto the back of Yuri's motorcycle and wheeled around so quickly that she'd nearly fallen off.

"Move!" Dima hollered again now. Renya hurried.

They'd gone straight into a building in the middle of an apartment block that Renya hadn't visited before, one that she didn't recognize from books or pictures. They hadn't explained where they were or what they were after. Then they'd moved on to another, and then another. The time of patiently explaining what she was seeing was, it seemed, over.

"Pay attention to your feet," said Dima. "Let's go." He'd veered off onto a landing, and Renya hadn't noticed. She stopped abruptly, halfway up the next flight. She turned and galloped down the stairs to meet Dima and Yuri.

"You have to keep up." The steeliness of Dima's tone was chilling. The cast of his eyes twinkling dully in the pale light of a window made her breath catch. She stepped back. He was acting strangely, even for him.

"You're holding us up," said Dima. "Yuri, she's making us wait."

"Go on without me then," said Renya.

Renya heard a scream, and she, Dima and Yuri froze. She wheeled around. She saw a shattered window, and then she understood: the sound had been the wind. The scream had been caused by a broken pane of glass caught by the wind. Another breeze blew around it and made a shrieking sound again. Her heart hammered. She held her chest, imagining she could slow down its frantic beating.

Dima and Yuri seemed to have figured out the noise too. They turned back to her.

"Go on without me, for a few minutes," she said again, gently this time. "I have to take some notes."

"What do you need to write down for?" demanded Dima, his eyebrows pulled down, his eyes slits. In the gloom, she could see the dull shine of bared teeth.

"I'm a scientist," said Renya. "It's what I do. That's why I'm here." She turned to Yuri. "You go on. You can meet me outside when you're done." She made her tone steely too.

She wrenched her computer out of her bag. She didn't look up again. She didn't want them to see her fear. After a moment, she heard the crunch of footsteps over debris. She just needed a minute, she was sure. *They* just needed time. *They* just needed a moment for this emotional wave to pass. She opened the computer and immediately found a connection.

⊙ ⊙ ⊙

Renya opened Skype to Nick already online and pacing. He rushed to the camera. "Ren, where have you been?"

"Do you see where I am?" she whispered, holding the computer on the railing.

"Ren, wait, are you inside?" He stood still, blanching. "Don't, Renya, run, Renya, get out of there."

"Dima says it's fine." But she was already rushing down the stairs.

"Please, Ren –"

"Yuri too. They come here all the time and they're okay."

"They're gambling," said Nick. "They can gamble with their own health, not with yours."

"It's fine." But she wasn't sure it *was* fine. She wasn't sure *they* were okay. But she was being careful despite them. She made sure to stay inside buildings for a minute or two, no longer. She always found an excuse to leave early. "It's so still," she whispered, struggling to hold the computer upright as she ran down the stairs. The picture, she knew, would be wobbling. "Everything is so still. There are all these buildings with no people, but all the evidence of their lives. There are tables and chairs. Sometimes there are blankets spread out on couches, napkins and plates still set on dining-room tables. Sometimes things have obviously been taken and that's strange too. But still. It feels like everything is just waiting for people to get back."

"You can't stay inside, Ren, you can't –"

"I'm walking out now."

But Renya heard footsteps nearing. She closed the computer just as Yuri rounded the corridor.

"It's a really good one this time," he said, reaching down a slender hand. His fingers felt wiry but strong as they wrapped around hers. She let herself be pulled, tucking the computer under her arm.

⊙ ⊙ ⊙

Again, Renya followed, inside another wing, up another staircase. "Are you going to be long?" she said, her voice echoing hollowly in the gloom, in the streamers of dust. Yuri didn't answer. She looked at her watch. She'd wait two minutes then escape again.

Soon she found herself in a wide-open room. A tree was growing through the floor, and the windows, although streaked with soot and dust, stretched from floor to ceiling. Renya rushed over. The view was panoramic, and she could see so much, shades of grey from the buildings, sidewalks and low hanging clouds, and the dull green of trees growing up through the cracks in everything. There were the spindly trees, the crumbling buildings, the courtyards that she'd seen in all the pictures, all under a buckling limestone sky: it was breathtaking. The view reoriented her. She ran to a corner of the window. There they were, the merry-go-round, the Ferris wheel, all surrounded by desolate branches and a sky that threatened rain.

"You like this," said Yuri. "I knew you would."

"You always know," Dima said roughly.

Renya reeled around. She hadn't seen Dima in the room.

"He always knows, with the ladies," Dima growled.

"I just want to help," said Yuri. "I want to be a person who is helpful."

Renya turned to Yuri who was flushing and averting his eyes.

"Sit down." Dima's voice was a command. His expression was stormy, and Renya wanted to leave. He stared her down, and she concentrated on the view outside the window. She could barely see the gravel path that led away from here. She didn't sit. She didn't move either. She didn't look into Dima's face again.

"You're sure this is safe?" she said again to Yuri.

"Sure," said Yuri.

"You said there are looters."

"We are the looters," said Dima.

Renya froze. "You mean you protect from the looters."

Dima touched his jacket, stepped toward her. "Does this look real to you?"

"What?"

Dima bent down again. "This is what I do," he said, chipping away at the tiles on the floor. "These are beautiful. They will get a good price."

"You sell things from here?" She'd thought he might be doing that. She thought they both might be taking things. She hadn't really believed they'd go through with it. "Souvenirs?" People talked about souvenir sellers on the message boards. Renya had thought they were being funny. She'd thought the whole thing was a big inside joke.

"Souvenirs, yes," said Dima. "Tiles. Aluminum, iron sidings of course. Other things too. Mostly other things. I don't like to compete with the metallists."

Yuri barked a laugh. "You don't like to get caught."

"Workmanship is shit now. Nothing is made well. Things from this place make good money."

"But you could hurt people," she said. "This stuff is radioactive. They might not understand the risks. People are interested in souvenirs from here, sure, but they probably don't understand what it means to bring it into their homes."

"Don't condescend to me." Dima had stopped his work. Renya turned to find that he'd straightened, that he was glaring at her and advancing. "Don't you talk down to me, bitch."

Renya backed up into the glass, stung. She was used to rapid-boil emotions. She usually knew how to look for the signs of a turnaround, but there had been nothing to indicate *this* level of rage. Anger, sure. But not rage, not this marching, advancing aggression.

Dima stepped nearer. His hands were fists.

"Don't come any closer," she said.

"You don't like the tone of my voice?" said Dima.

"No," whispered Renya.

"Then get out of my country."

Renya looked down at her fingers. They were curled in. She pressed her knuckles against the window behind her. The glass was cool. She tried to breathe softly and silently. She tried to slow her breaths. She schooled her face while she thought about what to do next. Don't show terror. Some dogs can smell fear. People could sense fear too.

"We're not your pets," Dima spat, as if he'd heard her thoughts.

"No," Renya said quietly. She stilled her thoughts too.

There was a silence, and Renya was very aware of her physical presence, of her shape pressed against the window. The truth. The truth was that she wasn't dangerous. She didn't really want to be with the dangerous kids. She never had. They could sense it. And these two were more dangerous than the hooligans of her youth. What had those other boys gotten up to? Graffiti? These were men. And one of them introduced dangerous objects into people's homes. Was there a market for radioactive things? There must be. There were such strange and dangerous people around. But others could be hurt too, their friends, their neighbours. They wouldn't know about the poisoned objects. They couldn't give consent to this. Oh God. What could Dima do to her? She was alone with them, and who were they? She had no idea who they were, or what they were capable of. For all she knew, they could be monsters.

"You're worried about the idiots we sell to?" Dima was saying. "Why do they deserve more than me?"

Scratch that. They were definitely monsters. Renya pressed herself to the window, hoping the glass wouldn't suddenly give.

"I'm living a half-life. They should live half a life. You think I don't understand your physics? I understand your physics more than you and more than your bastard of a husband."

"How do you know about my husband?" she whispered. She must have said something, but to Yuri surely, not to him.

"I'm living the physics," said Dima. "I see it every day."

"It's so beautiful here," Renya stammered. Yuri was silent. He was watching her. He wouldn't look away. Renya averted her eyes.

"It's broken," said Dima. "And everything in it is broken. Don't you fucking forget that."

"Are you –"

"I feel pain that sears down my sides," said Dima. "It's nerves. It's flaring nerves. It's damage. It goes and it comes back and then goes again and then I go months and I don't feel it. But it's the beginning, I know."

Renya inched toward the door. "You know . . ."

"Of course I know. We all do."

She turned to Yuri.

"Of course I feel it too," Yuri said softly.

"You never told me."

"We're going to die a painful death," said Dima. "It's started already. Of course I know. I don't need any help from any Americans."

"I'm Canadian."

"I don't need you." Dima nodded toward Yuri. "He doesn't need you. He needs me. That's all. We were young when we started this. We were children and this was our game. We took the list of things not to do, and we used it as a checklist. It's not a game anymore though. Now it's real and now it's *ours*."

Renya slithered against the window, edging toward the door.

"We bring you here so you can feel it too, someday."

Renya stopped.

"No," said Yuri. "No, Dima. That's too much." He turned to her. "I wanted you to see. You said you wanted to see. I wanted to show you this so you could be a witness with me. I just wanted to help."

"You're a child," Dima spat.

"No, I'm not," said Yuri.

"Well, now she's exposed," said Dima, grinning.

"We came here years before the pain started," said Yuri, his hands up, placating.

"But who says when the damage was done?" said Dima. "Maybe it happened right away. Maybe it happened on our very first visit. *You* don't know."

Renya was shivering now, more and more violently. But she was safe. She hadn't been here for very long. It was all probability, all chance, and she was lucky. Her government had signed the papers. Her bosses liked her. Her administration didn't want her to die. Her father was cool with her coming here. God, she wanted to leave. She looked up, she didn't know why, and through the window she saw the sun low on the horizon, peeking out from behind laden clouds. The sun was setting. She glanced at her wrist. She couldn't make out the time. It was clearly late and she'd been inside here for more than two to five minutes. Why had she come here? How could she have stayed so late? She begged for this moment to end. Soon, she whispered inside her head, soon this day would be over, and this trip would be over. Soon, she'd be on the other side, looking back. She looked sidelong out the window, deep into the clouds that were gathering and shifting, blocking out the sun again, and she wished for a way to get safely back to the hotel, back home again, she didn't care who was in it.

Finally, she turned and looked at Dima and Yuri. "Why do you stay here?" she said, her voice shaking. They could hear the quavering lilt; they'd marked it. "Why do you keep coming back?" They could see her shuddering body, she saw. They were taller than her. There were two of them and one of her. She watched Dima make the same calculations.

"Too fucking late now," said Dima. "And we have work to do."

He was saying something, something under his words. His expression showed aggression. Channel Claire. Think wider than expressions. Find the context, the emotional world. Discover intent. Body language: jaw thrust out, leaning forward, eye contact with those narrowed eyes, lower ocular muscles activated, teeth bared. He was telegraphing antagonism, threat. He was hinting at violence. He was talking about hating outsiders. He was saying that she deserved to be hurt, as a representative, as a proxy. He was really saying that they all deserved to be hurt. What were they doing with the relics? Maybe they weren't only sending them to Ukrainians, to Russians, to people obsessed with the disaster. Maybe they were sending them away too, to other innocent people, maybe even without disclosure. They could be trying to poison people with radioactivity. He wanted to hurt foreigners. Dima wanted to hurt people. All that was conjecture, but of one point Renya was absolutely sure: he wanted to hurt *her*.

She looked around wildly. She could kick him if he came near. She knew how to claw at his eyes and target soft tissue. She could find a weapon in this broken place. They were strong, but she was smart. Well, she'd have to be smart now. She took a deep breath. She counted. She plotted an escape route. It wasn't as difficult as it had seemed at first glance.

But first, she needed to know.

"Do you tell people these things are from Chornobyl?" she demanded.

"Sometimes," said Dima. "Chornobyl?" he mimicked. "What are you? Ukrainian? Is that what I heard you speaking before?"

Yuri, Renya saw from the corner of her eye, wheeled around.

"No, you're not," Dima said. "You're not even Ukrainian, really. You're nothing."

Dima advanced. Renya crept ever closer to the door. She wasn't safe. She wasn't safe. The thought echoed in her head. But she would make herself safe. She stood taller. She steeled her face.

"Relax, American girl."

"Fuck off," she whispered. She could attack, then duck, then run out the door. She looked quickly out the window, but the last of the light was draining away in purples and blues. She didn't know the way back. The forest was irradiated, every plant, every tree a danger. How could she have come? How could she have been so unthinking? *Stop*, she told herself. *One step at a time. Get out of this room first, then worry about the rest.*

Renya looked around again, plotting her escape. She wasn't trapped. She'd just have to be fast.

"Relax and you'll enjoy it more," hissed Dima.

Take a deep breath, Renya reminded herself. He was trying to make her panic because she was less powerful when she was panicking. *Count*, she told herself. *Exhales should be longer than inhales. Visualize your next move. Get out of the limbic system and into the rational part of your brain.*

"Dima doesn't mean anything by it," Yuri said softly. "He isn't serious."

"I heard what Dima said," she hissed. "I understand what he means. He wants to hurt me."

"Sure," Dima said, walking nearer. "But you'll like it too. American girls like it rough."

"I'll take you home," said Yuri.

"Stay away from me," said Renya. If she ran behind Dima, then behind Yuri, she'd be out the door before they could react.

"You think you can find your way alone, little bitch?" Dima grabbed her arm, hard.

Renya shook him off with a strength that surprised even her. She ducked around him, fast, and fled, down the winding stairs, out into the dusk. She heard them stumbling after her. Dima might be strong, but she was faster. She was at the ground floor landing and out of the building before she heard Yuri and Dima bang into the stairwell.

She ran, hugging the side of the building to make herself less visible, but she'd be long gone by the time they made their way outside, she knew.

⊙⊙⊙

Renya retreated to the family district, to the apartment complex nestled away from the city centre and close to the edge of the woods. She found an alcove between two buildings and ducked inside. She paced, then she stood still, then she paced again. She had to figure out what to do next. *Think*, she pleaded with herself. The light was quickly draining from the sky. She didn't know how to get back to the research station. She didn't want to sleep here. She couldn't sleep inside a building for sure, and wolves prowled this place in the night. She paced more. She forced herself to stop and take a deep breath. First, she had to make herself safe *now*. She needed to be invisible.

Renya rooted through the trees and shrubs and found a hiding place with enough room for her. She sat. She'd sounded so strong for a moment upstairs. She *had* been strong. She'd gotten out of that room. Where had that strength gone? Why was the fear back again?

She heard a clang of metal on metal in the distance. Was that them? She shook herself free of her backpack, then took out her computer. Almost immediately, Nick's face filled the screen. "Ren, where are you?" She quickly turned down the volume on the computer. Dima had found her last time because of the noise.

"Relax, I'm outside again," she whispered. She couldn't ask him for help. He was so far away. What could he do? What could he have done if he'd been right here? It was fine. She'd figure this out on her own.

Nick hurried close to the computer. "Are you okay?" he said in a rush.

This was reminding her that she wasn't alone in the world. That was important. She could use this interlude to catch her breath, calm herself, restart her rational thinking.

"What's wrong?" Nick was demanding. Renya lowered the computer volume still more. "What's happening?"

A breeze howled through her little causeway, but that was good, that would hide the noises.

Renya put the laptop on the broken sidewalk, angled up the screen, then hid her face in folded arms. She was safe here. She was well-hidden. Dima had found her before, in his better mood, when he'd been teasing her and before he'd turned threatening, but she'd learned her lesson. He wouldn't spot her here, and the wind would mask her talking. Still, she whispered. "Yuri had to go for a minute," she mumbled into her hands. "He has to . . . he has to check in with –"

"Where –"

"I don't really know where he is. He said . . . I left, I left them, I'm scared. I shouldn't have come."

"Are you afraid of him?" whispered Nick. His face was pale. It wasn't colourless as it had been, but he was very pale nonetheless. She should lie. She couldn't seem to.

"Yes," whispered Renya. "I'm afraid. I'm afraid of him, well, of Dima."

"Do you have that motorcycle you were telling me about?"

"It's Yuri's motorcycle." She peeked out of the brambles. She was stuck here. She was well and truly stuck, she who never forgot to clean the apartment every Wednesday, who recycled, who jogged. How had her life wheeled so far out of control? "I don't know what I should do, exactly. I'll stay for the moment. I guess I'll just . . ." She looked around, at the gravel, at the crumbling buildings. She heard more shots ring out in the distance, at opposite corners of the plaza. She was safe right now. She could think her way through this.

"Yuri will come back for me." She wanted him to. She didn't. She never wanted to see him again.

Nick watched her. He opened his mouth, then he closed it again. Renya let herself cry. She just wanted to curl up. She didn't have time for that now. She didn't know what to do. She shouldn't have come, out to the city, off with these scary men, out of her country. Why had she ever left her childhood bedroom in the first place? She'd reached the unhelpful stage of fear, she realized. It wasn't motivating anymore. It caused sluggishness and apathy. She'd experienced too much sustained adrenaline, over too long a time period. Okay. Okay. She could work with this. As long as she understood it, she could work around it. She took a deep breath and held it. She counted.

"It's okay," Nick started.

"It is," said Renya. "It is okay." She'd just have to work around the emotional overload. One more fright could push her over the edge though, she thought, and now she had to stop herself from laughing, she didn't know why.

Just then, a wolf howl echoed through the abandoned city. Renya burst into laughter. She couldn't help it. She covered her mouth.

"Are you okay?" said Nick. "What was that?"

"A wolf," said Renya, wiping hysterical tears off her face. "Did I mention that wolves hunt here at night?"

"There are wolves?" Nick demanded.

Renya didn't answer. She looked around. The sun was truly setting now. It was getting dark. Soon, the laptop would be the only source of light, for however long the battery lasted. Then it would be that inky blackness that she'd experienced with Claire and the wolf researchers. Even if Yuri came back for her, should she get on a motorcycle with him? Nick was right. Yuri was damaged. Dima was certainly messed up, but Yuri couldn't be counted on either. Renya heard a bang, then a metallic echo. She wheeled around.

Another howl ricocheted off the buildings. The wolves were close. They lived in caves nearby, oh, and the wolf researchers had set traps close to here, and they were coming to dismantle or mark or tag or whatever every evening this week, Tiv had said.

"Renya, please –"

More noises followed. They were anvil sounds, metal on metal, like giant hammers swinging. The sounds were in stereo, from all over the city, now. Renya turned, then turned again. She couldn't see anyone close. Dima had mentioned metallists. People were stripping the city of all its component parts.

Another metallic sound echoed, close.

"What the hell was that?" said Nick.

"I have a plan," said Renya. "The wolf researchers have traps nearby, and they're prepping for hand-off to another team, or for when they have to come back. I don't know. I don't remember. I'll go find them. I know where they are, approximately."

She'd seen a map only briefly, and days ago, but she remembered the rock formations around them. She could find them. If she had to, she'd yell until she got their attention.

"That sounds like a great plan." Nick touched the computer screen. He looked so scared. He was so solicitous. She'd loved it, then hated it, now she loved it again. What strange creatures people are. She should study that next, how emotional reactions change. There's probably something profound there too, but Renya couldn't quite think of it.

"I'm going to go now," she whispered.

"Good luck," said Nick. "Call me back when you can. I love you."

"I love you," she said, unthinking.

Renya closed the laptop, crouched to put it back inside her backpack, then crawled out from her hiding place.

⊙ ⊙ ⊙

As Renya stood again, she heard a rustle by the building. She froze, looking around. The building's side door was hanging off its hinges. She ducked behind it.

"Renya!" called Yuri, his voice hushed as if he didn't want to talk too loudly.

"Girl," said Dima, an exhalation of breath more than a shout, but with anger unmistakable nonetheless.

Renya shrank even farther into the space behind the door. She held her breath.

"Do you hear those sounds?" Dima whispered. "The metallists own the city in the night. Saws and blowtorches. Even I wouldn't want to be caught by them. I wonder what they'd do to a little girl."

"She's not here," said Yuri, in Russian. Renya didn't have that much experience with the language, but it sounded accented to her. His voice wavered.

"The Palace of Culture," Dima responded in kind.

Renya listened as their footsteps retreated. They were still talking to her, but she could no longer make out the words. She ran, crouched low at first, and then just fast, all the way to the woods.

⊙ ⊙ ⊙

Finding the wolf traps wasn't hard. Renya picked her way along the cavern entrances until she found the whole team. They were almost finished dismantling the traps and loading them in the jeeps, and she even helped them pack and carry. They were happy to give her a ride back. If Tiv and his colleagues didn't believe her story, that she'd wandered too far and couldn't get back before dark, if they noticed her red and puffy eyes, they were too polite to say.

⊙ ⊙ ⊙

Back in her bedroom, Renya locked the door behind her and curled on the bed that had once felt so foreign, that felt like home now. *You get used to anything.*

She reached to the chair next to the bed, where she'd just put her computer. And suddenly, she was crying. She could feel tears on her cheeks. She wiped them off.

She couldn't talk to Nick again tonight. Instead, she wrote him an email. *I'm fine*, she wrote. *I got home. Thanks for listening, when I was by myself in that city.* She sent the same message through Skype.

She turned on her program. She had one last target set of historical photos. These showed teams of scientists studying the plant shortly after the accident. In the first set, they were trying to find out what had happened to the radioactive fuel. They were dressed in full PPE, their whole selves completely obscured by the protective equipment, walking carefully in what was clearly the basement. They couldn't get too close, but they needed to understand the damage. They needed to know what was happening. Where were the fuel rods? Was the reaction still out of control? Was it still melting down? The rods had melted, that they knew. They'd dripped through the floor and into the basement. They needed to know how far the core had gone. In the pictures, they fastened equipment to what was clearly a child's remote-controlled tank, and they sent it through a hole in the wall and into the reactor. Images of the destroyed core got recorded that way, by that little kids' toy that one of the scientists had brought. Renya ran the pictures. The program came back inconclusive. But that made sense. You couldn't see the scientists' faces through their protective clothing.

Then she wiped her face and got back to work, loading the present-time photographs she hadn't yet run.

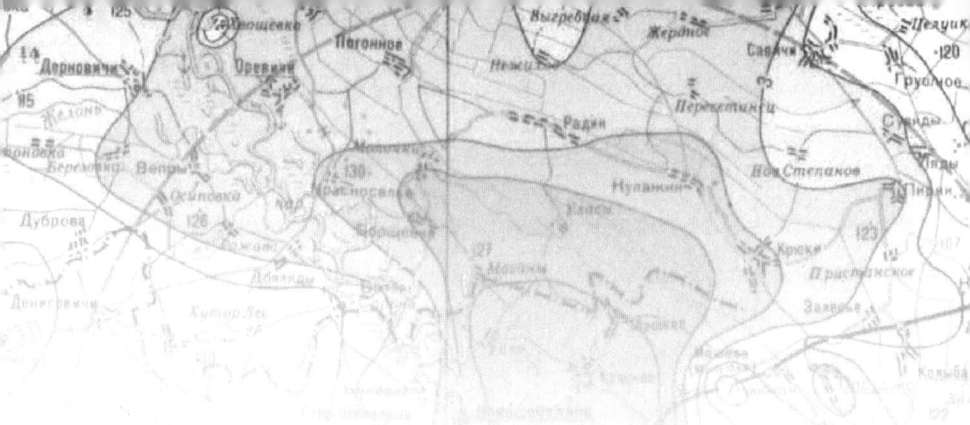

CHAPTER II

WHEN RENYA GOT TO THE DINING HALL EARLY THE NEXT morning, Shantoo was alone, scarily beautiful in the straining morning light. Renya sat opposite. She nodded to Shantoo's hands. "Your nails are red."

"Not so bright though," said Shantoo.

"Alarm?"

"A bit."

"Why do you do that?"

"I feel unequal to making myself understood sometimes. This, I feel, is something."

"I should do that for my husband," Renya said. "I mean, I should have done it. Before."

"Moods with loved ones change faster than one can paint."

"That's true," said Renya.

Shantoo motioned to Claire's empty seat. "Having a rough morning, I think," she said. "I suspect that she'll be here presently."

"Are you afraid here too?" said Renya.

"I think we're all seeing now that we should be spending time elsewhere as well. There are signs. They're getting unmistakable now. Maybe I'm understanding the world as a whole a bit better, and I don't like what I see."

"That's what Claire was saying," said Renya. She could admit it now. Her system had worked. The programming had to be worked out a bit, but the idea was sound. "What have you seen?"

"The soil is strange," said Shantoo. "It's strange in ways that I wasn't prepared for. There is less breakdown than I would have suspected. Organic materials are taking much longer to decay. You might have noticed the leaves."

"There are so many crackly leaves," breathed Renya.

"They're not breaking down as one would expect."

"The ground feels almost bouncy in some places."

"The regular life cycle seems to be suspended," said Shantoo. "I think maybe it's not just here. I'm waiting to get lab results. I'm waiting for my team to send me results from back home. I'm waiting to hear from colleagues in other countries too. Alarmingly, I'm seeing damage from populated cities, from big cities, even here. I'm seeing microplastics. I'm seeing PFAS, forever chemicals. They shouldn't be here, yet they are. And I don't need to be a veterinarian to see that all the life here is wrong. Yesterday, a wild dog followed me. I think it was mad. It was barking. I tried to radio for help."

"My radio didn't work," whispered Renya. She'd played with it her first day here. She hadn't been able to generate anything other than static.

"Nor did mine," said Shantoo. "In fact, I'm not clear who it's supposed to connect to. I walked slowly at first, and then I ran. Luckily, it didn't follow."

"I'm glad you're okay."

"Life is changed here."

Renya shivered, thinking of Yuri and of Dima. Life here had changed.

"Maybe life everywhere is changing," said Shantoo. "That's what scares me most. I'm looking now, I'm talking to colleagues in other fields, and what I'm finding out about is chilling. People talk about water cycles breaking down. People talk about life cycles struggling. I don't know how much soil will be usable for agriculture in the coming decades, or even centuries."

"So it's the whole world that's breaking."

"Even so, I'm not going out anymore. I'm staying put, and washing my hair often. I suggest that you do the same."

And then Claire was creaking toward the table, eyes averted.

"I wonder what readings I would get in the farms nearby?" said Shantoo. "I wonder what readings I would get in farms in my own country? I wonder how much monitoring there is, anywhere?"

"Yes," said Claire, nodding.

"This is why I want to leave," said Shantoo. "It's not so much that I'm uneasy here. It's that I'm anxious to see which findings are replicated everywhere else. I want to move on. I want to zoom out. I need to get on with it."

Shantoo turned to Renya. "What emotion are you reading now?"

"Anger," said Renya. "Your brows are lowered. Your nostrils are flared. Your lips are thinned, sometimes baring teeth."

"That's a good read."

"That's not seepage," said Renya. "That's no short display. That's a real emotional display."

Shantoo sat up stiffly. "I'm trying to decide who is at fault," she said. "Why are we not talking about what's happening? Why do we never discuss environmental collapse? That should be all we work on, and all we ever talk about. Why are we not talking constantly about the scope of this problem? Is it my administration? Is it the university as a whole? You'd think they'd be interested."

"They also like to make partnerships," said Claire.

"Can I continue to work for a university who has no regard for my safety or well-being?"

"Did you ever think that they did?" Claire was slumped farther now.

"I expected basic human decency," said Shantoo.

"Did you really?"

"Maybe not." Shantoo sighed. "People like their water bottles and non-stick pans. They like their vacations and air travel."

"Maybe they don't know," said Claire.

"The world is unsafe. Nowhere is safe to be. Maybe we might as well be here."

"Might as well go to North Korea," said Claire.

Shantoo sniffed.

Renya stood to leave.

"I have one more question," said Shantoo. "Were the ones who gave you the money for your research the same as who gave you the dosimeter?"

"No," said Renya. She felt herself stiffen. "Nobody gave me the dosimeter. I ordered it myself." She felt fear tingle up and down her spine, remembering. "I got the idea from them though." As she'd been leaving the strange funding meeting, she'd come upon two members of that unnamed committee whispering to each other in the hall. "I heard them talking to each other. One of the women said she'd bought air-quality monitors and soil-testing kits. Another said she bought a dosimeter. I bought mine soon after on eBay."

"These people," said Shantoo.

"Who though?" said Claire.

"Maybe everyone," said Shantoo.

"I don't think they were worried about radiation," said Renya, "or chemicals or chemical exposure. At least, for my project, that wasn't their primary concern." Renya remembered that first boardroom meeting. She'd paid attention to pauses, to intakes of breath, to attention and note-taking. "I'm not bad at seeing when people perk up. I mean, it's my training. It's what I do. They didn't care about the radiation. I talked a bit about chemical exposure. That didn't stop them."

"What did?" said Claire.

"What was their primary concern?" said Shantoo.

And Renya remembered the moment in which the whole room had held their breath. That second of nobody breathing, when everyone had leaned forward all at once, all eyes on her. "Viruses," she said. She'd just started talking about virologists and hospitals, doctors and experts on the news, and the stillness at that point of the presentation, the intake of breath, had surprised her. "They were definitely thinking about outbreaks."

"Viruses." Claire guffawed. "Let's add that to the list, shall we?"

"I will admit," said Shantoo. "I'm also getting worried about those international labs. I've been asking around this week. I've heard some frightening things."

"Maybe they're necessary," said Claire. "They say we're due for an event."

⊙ ⊙ ⊙

Renya locked herself in her room again. She paced until she found herself at the window. She wanted to go home. She wanted to go out there again. Why? To impress Nick? Maybe. To impress Yuri? To stick it to him? She needed to give Yuri the money she promised. She said she'd pay him, so she'd pay him.

Renya stopped herself and forced herself to look at her reflection in the window. What was she doing? What did she really want?

She sighed. She wanted to know why Yuri did it. She wanted him to know that she wasn't afraid, of him or of anyone.

In that boardroom that she'd told Claire and Shantoo about, she'd been powerful. She'd had a great idea, and she'd known it, and everyone in the room had known it too. And she'd been right. Her project would work. It would use scientists, sure, but it could save them too. It could indicate to good people that they were in over their heads. It could get them help when help was needed, when they felt unequal to asking, or when they were unable, for whatever reason. Yuri was in over his head, she realized. He felt unable to ask for help. She'd been too wrapped up in her own struggles. But he'd been trying to communicate, and she hadn't been receptive at all.

Renya paced again, then stopped at the window, feeling pulled outside once again, just like when she'd first arrived. She was feeling curious. It was a burning curiosity though. She hadn't been listening to Yuri. What had he been trying to say?

⊙ ⊙ ⊙

Renya walked out into the forest and into the silence. She'd been walking all morning and hadn't seen one scientist. None of them were in their quadrants. They'd all retreated now. It wasn't just Shantoo and Claire. Maybe they were all packing up. They were leaving soon, so it made sense. But maybe none of the party felt safe enough to leave the station.

Renya made her way to the downed tree. She stopped and looked around. She hadn't seen Yuri yet. She'd counted on him just being here. Before, he'd always just popped up when she'd wanted him. He'd been watching her, he said. Renya guessed he'd been waiting for an opening.

She leaned against a tree. She started her own write-up in her head. It would be impressive. This would get attention for sure. She'd found when the scientists had panicked. She could pinpoint the exact moment. That ability could be harnessed. She could program for it. They could scan for fear and other expressions on the news, whatever camera feeds those suits had access to.

She heard snapping twigs and froze. But then saw him, Yuri, his familiar lanky silhouette behind the trees. He didn't seem to have noticed her yet.

Renya watched him. He was bent today, not standing in his usual arrogant posture. He was leaning against a tree playing with a cigarette. When he lit it, Renya saw that his hand was shaking. There was a whole world inside him, and not the one that she'd imagined: the pool cues, clicking balls, bitter whiskey and angry laughter. There was pain there too. There was fear, clearly. Yuri reached out a hand and stroked a leaf. It was a remarkably gentle gesture. He had family, friends, probably all exposed like he was, and he probably worried about them too. He was more dangerous than she'd thought, but more human too.

Very quietly, Renya shifted to get her camera out of her pack. She took shot after shot. This wasn't for research. She wanted to remember. Then she put her camera away and shuffled noisily away from the trees. Yuri wheeled around.

Renya watched as he straightened and adopted the loping gait she was used to. He flicked his cigarette away and stepped on it.

"I'm sorry about what happened," he said gruffly, not looking up. She wanted to see his expression. His posture, his shrug, made him seem sincere though.

"I said I'd pay you," she said, abruptly holding out the bills she'd fished out of her suitcase.

He just watched her. He didn't move to take them.

She didn't lower her hand. "You might as well have it."

"You don't need to," he said finally.

"I promised," she said. "Anyway, I'll just burn them anyway. I plan to get rid of everything I brought with me. I don't want to bring contamination back home."

He took the bills.

"Come to my apartment," he said abruptly.

"Are you kidding me?"

"I'm not like Dima," he said, "not really. I still work here. I really do. He did too until he got fired. I explore after my shifts, yes, but I'm not like him. I'll show you some other people. I don't want you to think that all people from this place are like *him*."

Renya hung on to her tree. She didn't want any more danger. She looked at him, closely, but she couldn't get a sense of his inner life. None of her usual observations seemed to help. No muscle activation, no facial expression or breathing rate or internal temperature change would tell her what he was thinking. She felt like she was watching him through a dirty window, but every time she focused, she could only see her own fingerprints. In his place, what would she want? She would want absolution. But she was blindly reaching for answers. She was only accessing her own emotional life. That wasn't the same thing as empathy.

"Just please visit me for a minute," he said.

Renya just watched him. Why should she let herself be fooled again?

"It's not what you think," said Yuri, clearly understanding at least some of her worries. "It's an apartment block for all the security." He ducked his head. "When I'm not stationed here, I live with my parents."

Renya was about to tell him absolutely not, to rant, to yell. But then he looked up, right into her face, and that gesture made her pause. He knew that she studied emotional displays. He was daring her to study him. And what did she see? With Dima, there had always been an edge of anger. His jaw, she could admit that she'd noticed, had always been a bit clenched, his brows always drawn down and furrowed, even when purportedly happy or excited. She didn't see this in Yuri. She didn't see any evidence of anger or rage at all. She could see his corrugators, and of course his depressor anguli oris were activated, pulling down the sides of his mouth. This indicated sadness. He was sad about what he'd done. Well, he should be.

A breeze blew past, blowing her hair off her shoulders. She looked at him again, less clinically this time. There was something else evident on his face, something more complicated than the six basic emotions. She saw yearning, she felt. She saw a need to be understood. She felt a tug of sadness herself. She could relate to that. She wanted to be understood too.

"Okay," she said. "I'll go."

Yuri bowed, then gestured toward the motorcycle.

⊙ ⊙ ⊙

The residence, when they finally reached it, was a concrete block with tiny windows. Inside, it reminded Renya of an undergrad residence: hallways crowded with doors, faded wallpaper, shared washrooms and the smells of cooking and laundry and socks.

"I'll leave the door open." Yuri smiled lopsidedly. "When I'm at home, that's what my mother demands. When I call her later, I'll tell her the door was open when the pretty lady came to visit me."

Renya crept into the one-room apartment. She lightly touched the worn material of the desk chair, and scanned through the room, at the white curtains, brown carpets, threadbare rug, desk. It smelled like cooking oil and stale cigarette smoke. There was a little camping stove on the desk, beside a pen.

"It's not much," whispered Yuri.

"It's nice," said Renya. And she sat stiffly on the couch. He sat on the bed, across from her, bounced a bit on the creaky springs.

She felt like she was a teenager again. She had a fluttery feeling in her stomach, shyness, or awkwardness, maybe, she realized, but not fear.

"I'm sorry," Yuri said, the gruffness in his voice back again. "We were having fun. Then it all got out of control. Dima has bad days sometimes."

"Is it because he feels unwell?" Renya scanned her body. She felt some discomfort in her shoulder and her legs. But she'd been so active lately. It could mean anything. "He talked about an illness."

"We live out there sometimes. You're not supposed to drink from the streams or eat the berries. We do of course. That was the first thing we did when we first went out there. Still we do it. Why bother stopping now."

"Why do you stay?"

"Before, we were very reckless. It was a good job. Good money. It was the first time I had money of my own. We came back often. When we weren't working, we would sneak inside. We treated this place like our playground. All the things they tell you not to do? We did them all. Now, why bother taking care of ourselves? We've exposed ourselves too much already."

"I'm sure that's not true," Renya whispered.

She reached toward him. She touched his hand, but only for a second. He was scared. She could understand that. Renya watched him. She'd felt driven to come here. She'd been going through the history again with the photo sets, but she already knew it all. She had two dozen dog-eared texts at home. She used to talk about the disaster with her grandmother, her father, her weird bedtime story that she couldn't live without, that her family got passionate about as well. Something always drove you.

Something drove Yuri too. There was the weird, unhealthy friendship with Dima, sure, but there was more to it than that. Something must have brought him here.

"Why did you take this job?" said Renya. "I mean, at first."

Yuri shrugged. "It's work," he said. "It was a job. It paid really well. Well, I thought so at the time. I didn't have so many choices. I didn't do a very good job in school. I don't have choices, still."

Yuri coughed. The sound rattled around the small space. He ducked his head, and Renya turned away to give him privacy. She wondered whether he got scared at every cough too. She'd felt like that after Nick's heart attack. She'd panicked at every sound he'd made. She'd worried about every feeling in her own body. Yuri might be like her. He might worry that it's the start of something bigger, something worse. She touched a pen on his desk and twirled it. Then she saw a slightly open drawer, and pulled it open to find other items: the doll, the lamp, the teacups, the gas mask. She stood. She backed away.

Renya turned. Yuri had stood up too. He was close behind her, blocking her exit. For a moment, he didn't move. Renya felt her body fill with adrenaline. She eyed his stomach and planned her attack: knees to gut first, then gouge the eyes. But then she looked at his face. He was sad again. He moved aside.

As Renya walked past the desk, she saw the boxes piled underneath.

"They're Dima's," Yuri said quietly.

"They're here."

"He lost the security job so he sneaks back in and sometimes he stays here, with me, in secret. Sometimes he asks me to keep his things."

Renya turned and left the small room. Yuri caught up with her in the hallway. "It's complicated."

"I appreciate that," she whispered.

"I really am sorry," he said. "I want to make amends."

"What?" said Renya. "To me?"

"I want to be helpful," he said gruffly.

"You've said that before," said Renya. "What does that mean?"

"Nobody understands this place," Yuri whispered, steering them back to his doorway. "Nobody knows what it's actually like here. I want to make it understood. I could never study history. I didn't have good grades. But I can be a witness. Dima, he sends things away for money. Not me. I'm helping people to understand."

"You're hurting people."

"I try not to," said Yuri. "I just want to help. I don't send things away. Those are Dima's things. That's what Dima does." He held up a beat-up notebook. "I just make a list of things I find. I draw pictures sometimes."

Renya reached for the book. When she'd pictured Yuri at home, before, she'd imagined him sketching, but she didn't know why. She flipped through the pages. The pictures were beautiful. She stopped and looked closely at one of the pages toward the end. On it, Yuri had drawn a metal spoon resting on a table. She'd been in that house. She'd seen that spoon. She'd noticed it too. Yuri had captured the way it gleamed, the way it had caught the sunlight through the smudgy window and shone.

Yuri shrugged. "My family is poor," he said. "There's no university for me. There are only hard jobs and church people who give us things and clothes that a hundred people wore before me. You people, you study and you try to make things better. I want to be one of the people who helps. I have to find my own way to do that. Being a witness, that is something. That is something that I can do, and it's important. I thought, when I met you, when you were holding the camera, that you understood this."

Renya wanted to be angry, but she couldn't muster it. She found herself nodding instead. She did, in some strange way, need to bear witness too. She didn't know why. She didn't even know what she felt so drawn to bear witness to.

"Take me home," she whispered.

⊙ ⊙ ⊙

As soon as Renya got out of the airless apartment complex, she felt better. Yuri drove her back through the checkpoint and she asked to walk the rest of the way. She slid off the motorcycle and waved weakly as she sped into a run. He called after her, but she didn't turn around. When she was close to the research centre, she dawdled on her way back through the trees, picturing Yuri's room, what his room at his parents' house must look like, imagining what he must see as his future. For all the problems of her childhood, Renya had always felt she'd had many choices.

Then Renya heard a strange galloping sound. She stopped. Her muscles locked. Had he come after her? Had Dima? But no, the sound was coming from the wrong direction, from the direction of the research centre.

Then she saw Claire and Shantoo running through the trees toward her. They were masked, but even through the masks, Renya could see the panic in their eyes. In seconds, they were upon her.

"Clairesie?" said Renya.

"I told you that you'd know when to use the name." Claire grabbed her arm, and they were walking again, quickly, toward the hotel.

"Everyone has strange findings," said Shantoo. "Nobody is seeing what they'd expected to see."

"I understand that," muttered Renya, jogging after. "I'm not seeing what I expected to see either."

"The world hasn't bounced back the way I'd expected," said Shantoo, out of breath. "There's less deterioration. Nothing is going away. Nothing is changing the way it should. Also, everything is changing. The soil is not accepting as much carbon as I expected. It's losing nutrients, fast. My soil samples from home show the same, even in farmland, even in farmland we've been working on. I don't know what that will mean in the long-term. I don't like these patterns."

"We've talked with the rest of the teams," said Claire. "We've confirmed that they all have strange findings."

"It throws a lot into question."

Claire galloped faster. "It could also be that none of us is sleeping well, and we're all panicking."

"We could be using the precautionary principle," said Shantoo.

"Precautionary principle," said Claire. "Ha! Look where we are."

Shantoo eyed Claire. "It could be that we've been staying up late with those climate researchers too often."

"I thought about this," Claire said. "And it could be true. It could be that my new climate panic is informing other panic. It could be that in ordinary circumstances, I'd be less concerned with my findings."

But the climate panic sounded terrible too. Renya's fingers tingled and she could feel the blood pumping to her legs. "This is a classic fear response," she realized she was saying out loud. They were running now, all three, back down the path, faster and faster. The hotel came back into view.

"My hands feel funny," said Claire.

"That's it," said Renya. "That's fear. It's universal, across cultures, across everything. Your heart pumps faster. Blood doesn't flow as much to your arms. It all goes to your legs. It gets you moving, away from the danger. Of all the major emotional responses, I like it the most."

"What about love?"

"Well," said Renya, "that's not really considered one of the major six."

Maybe she did like that one more than she admitted to herself. Happiness was a sneaky one.

⊙⊙⊙

They reassembled in the dining room a little while after they returned, hair wet, wrapped in large sweaters, hugging themselves for warmth. It wasn't just them. Claire's and Shantoo's teams were with them, as well as Tiv and the wolf researchers, and some others she recognized as studying wild dogs. The flora people were here too. Renya looked around. There must be a window open somewhere. It was usually warmer inside. Then she stiffened. Was the staff really opening windows? She stood. She made her way around the dining room, checking the seals on all the windows. If her colleagues thought anything of her behaviour, they didn't say anything. The windows were supposed to stay closed after all. Although, how could an open window compare to her running through an irradiated city for days? She'd known the dangers. She'd gone anyway. As had her friends, she realized with a start, when they'd come after her. She rushed back to the table and sat down.

She looked at Claire first, then at Shantoo. "You came back outside for me."

"Of course," said Claire.

"We don't really know what it means, of course," said Shantoo. "There hasn't been time to analyze these findings, or to think about what they could portend. But we didn't want one of our own out there."

Renya ducked her head. She felt warmth spread through her body. One of their own.

"Cities could be just as bad," said Claire, her voice bubbling with slightly hysterical laughter. "I think they are, in fact. I think that we're in terrible trouble everywhere."

"Maybe we should stay inside at home too," said Shantoo.

"Do you know how many dangerous aerosols you unleash when you're cleaning?" said Claire. "Do you know how many chemicals are in the air just from frying butter? I've been spending time with the aerosol physics people so now I know too much."

"We're not safe anywhere," said a wolf researcher.

"To be honest, I don't know how terrifying my results really are," said Claire. "I know that I haven't been sleeping. It could be that I was just looking for an excuse to panic. My results are directing me to look wider than just here. I think that's the point."

"Right," said one of Tiv's colleagues. "We're looking at environmental collapse more than just degradation now."

"We're looking at much shorter time scales too, I think," said Tiv.

"What about here?" asked another of Tiv's colleagues. "Have we decided that it's unsafe outside?"

"We knew that at the outset," said Tiv.

"But are things so much worse?"

"I don't know," said Claire. "I suspect that they minimized the dangers. They're minimizing the dangers of non-stick pans and this glut of plastic too. I've heard the new electric cars are aerosolizing microplastics that we all breath in, since they're so much heavier than regular cars."

"The government told us all that was okay," said another man. "There are whole bureaus that look into things like that."

"There's a whole field called lobbying," said another, "where corporations pay money to convince the government of things, and it's legal somehow."

"If we don't trust the government, then who should we trust?" said another.

"We trust each other," said the first colleague. "We make a circle of people whose opinions we respect, and we trust them."

"But I don't know enough people in enough fields," said Shantoo.

"And I wouldn't be able to track them well enough," said another wolf researcher. "They may lose it and I wouldn't know."

"We're all animal researchers here," said Tiv. "We know about toxoplasmosis."

Claire leaned toward Renya. "That's an infection that invades victim's brains, and affects the ability to perceive danger," she whispered. "Famously, mice get it, then lose their ability to be scared. They stop running away from cats."

"What happens to them?" said Renya, picturing the cartoons of her youth, and Internet pictures of mice and cats snuggling up.

"The mice get eaten," said Claire. "Cats don't care whether they feel fear."

"Humans have been shown to suffer similar symptoms," said the wolf researcher.

"So there's nobody we can trust," said another.

"I was raised to trust my government," said another.

Claire and some others looked away.

"Maybe we just pay attention," said Claire.

"Was all this worth it?" said Shantoo after a moment. "Were these findings worth risking so many people? Scientists come here every other month. More and more of us use up our radioactivity allowance here, more quickly than we perhaps believe. I checked. There are no changes in any plans. Another crew is scheduled to arrive after we leave. Is this worth it?"

"It's not just us," whispered Tiv. "We affect our families too."

Shantoo turned her ring. Renya massaged her finger. She suddenly missed the weight of the ring that, until this trip, she'd never taken off.

"This sounds wild," said Claire, "but I think all this is worth it. It's been worth talking to people in different fields. It's been worth comparing notes. I think that the earth is communicating. I want to let it speak. I want to hear what it's saying."

"What do you think it's saying?" said Renya.

"Get off me."

Renya laughed. Claire's face was serious.

"In that way, maybe it was worth it," said Claire. "Renya, you talked about zooming out. I didn't zoom out as often before I came here. I didn't look for larger patterns. For some reason, I seem to think more broadly here. I see more clearly that the world might be in trouble everywhere."

"I think I might agree," said Shantoo. "The stresses that this world has been put under are perhaps overwhelming it, not just here. The winds are changing. The ocean currents are shifting. They're breaking apart into shallow flows and deep ocean undercurrents, so the stir mechanisms might not work anymore, eventually. The weather is mutating. It's slow now, but the changes are getting faster. Storms are intensifying. Tides are taking land back to sea. And there are die-offs. Plants and animals are dying quickly, not gradually, but in discrete events. A whole herd of reindeer was found dead in Iceland. Beaches keep filling up with hundreds of thousands of dead fish. This is only what I've noticed in the newspapers."

"And you're noticing patterns too?" said Renya.

"The soil isn't regenerating," said Shantoo. "That will be a problem for things that grow in it, and for organisms who depend on the material that does. So that's everything. Some of the effects seen in the soil here, which one would expect, are happening in built-up areas too, which one wouldn't expect. I found strange readings in my niece's playground at home. I didn't understand them until I came here, because I understand them in the context of a nuclear accident."

Well, there was a red flag, thought Renya. She'd yearned to zoom out, but that was perhaps further out than she could conceive.

If the planet were trying to talk, what could it be trying to say? The planet, Renya thought, although ailing, although uncomfortable and aching for change, was probably less concerned than they were. It had had fevers before. It had survived them. But it had survived altered. It was probably looking forward to its new incarnation, even if Renya wasn't.

Let the earth speak, Claire had said. It was, but Renya didn't want to listen to its message: Stop it. Claire was right. Chornobyl was maybe the least of its problems now. Maybe it was the least of their problems too.

"Anyway, it doesn't matter," one of the wolf researchers was saying. "What I'm doing isn't that deep. But I want to do it. I have questions, and I came here to answer them."

"Yes," said Tiv. "God help me, but I needed to know."

Here were some display rules being broken. You didn't talk about this openly with other scientists. You didn't mention that there was something in you, something broken, something not quite right, that drove you and drove you and drove you. Renya thought of it as a pearl of a thought deep inside her, that pushed and nudged and drove. While all around her, everyone else had normal hobbies, like playing the guitar and hiking, that they could pick up and let go as they pleased, she could get utterly consumed by her work. It was a curiosity, yes, but it was driving, and it didn't let up, and scientists weren't ones to talk about their own psychological oddities.

"And you?" said Claire, looking right at Renya. "Would you have come if you'd suspected?"

"Most definitely." Causality really was the worst. There were things she wanted to know. No. There were things that she wanted to see. There was a pearl of a thought that drove her research, yes. But what had the dust been, the speck, the impurity, that had caused the pearl to form? What was her origin story? Why did she need to see the reactor? Why did she need to see the site of the disaster? There were those stories, told by her grandmother over grilled cheese and rugelach. There were the late-night physics talks with her father. She needed to see it. She needed to come. "I wanted to be here. I would have come anyway."

Renya looked up, at Claire's worried face, at Shantoo who was twirling her ring. Scientists didn't talk about these things. It was verboten. Friends talked about it though.

⊙ ⊙ ⊙

Later, when all the others had packed up and moved to their individual rooms, only Shantoo, Claire and Renya were left in the dining room.

"Why *are* we here?" Renya said, absently flipping through the pages of her notebook. She turned to Claire. "I keep thinking about origin stories," she said. "Do you remember? You talked about some weirdness, some little moment, that started it all. What do you think was the moment that put you on the path to get to where we're sitting right now?"

"Mine was a bird," muttered Claire, "although that's not much of a surprise."

"What was it about the bird?"

"I cared for it with my grandmother. It was a joint project. When we first got it, she said I should get to know it, but it was a bird. Like you said, they don't explain themselves. So I started taking notes about it, what food it liked, when it was active, and my usually reticent grandmother praised my note-taking. And we became friends, the bird and I. It took work, but I started looking at the world through her eyes, and I kind of loved it."

"I watched engineers taking core samples," said Shantoo, "one time after school. I couldn't have been more than five. They were in a neighbouring property. They were going to build a high-rise; I found out much later. I watched them from the swings in the playground across the street, and I thought about the scene for years, yearning to know what it meant, what those men were doing. I played at doing it too. I had a spoon that I played with. I dug at the soil. I compared it from place to place." She turned Renya. "And you," she said. "Your husband had a heart attack. You wished you could have predicted it."

"And before that, my grandmother died," Renya said. "And before that, my father and my grandmother and I had a book about Chornobyl," she said, not bothering to correct the Ukrainian pronunciation. "We looked at it often. My dad explained the physics. My grandmother explained the ghosts. I pored over all those grainy faces. And before that, who knows."

"And after?" said Claire.

A breeze blew in through the window, and Renya turned to look outside. "Aren't the windows meant to be closed?" she said weakly.

Claire stood. "I've seen the cleaning staff open them from time to time." She pressed down on the window and latched it shut.

"What did you mean by 'after'?" said Renya.

"You got here," said Claire. "You came. Did you find what you were looking for?"

"Not at all," Renya found herself saying. Yuri thought he might be getting sick. Dima was convinced it was too late for them. Did they really know? Could she devise a program to find that too? "I still have things I want to do."

"Me too," said Shantoo. "I should be good. I should lock myself in my lab back home. I won't though."

"Nor will I," said Claire. "There's still a lot I want to figure out too."

⊙ ⊙ ⊙

"Ren!" said Nick, his face neatly framed by the Skype window. "Are you okay? Where have you been? You didn't sleep there. Please say you didn't sleep there."

"I found the wolf researchers," said Renya. "They drove me home."

Nick put his head in his hands. "Is Yuri . . ."

"I was teasing you," said Renya. "There's nothing with either Yuri or Dima. There never was. I paid them to show me the city."

Nick reached to the camera. He gave her a warm look. It was filled with either pity or love, Renya couldn't tell. She waved it away. She'd brought this upon herself.

"He took me to his apartment today," she whispered. "I shouldn't have gone, I know, but when I went back to give him the money, he offered, and I was curious. I wanted to see how he lives."

"What was it like?"

"He keeps stolen things. They're sending them to people. You were right. He's damaged."

"It's okay," said Nick. "We'll be together soon."

"How can we be together? I left. I went a world away. I can't even get out of here for another day." But she wished she could be with him. Renya waved all that away too. It was a ridiculous thought. She'd told him to leave. He was moving on. It was all over now. "I'm not fearless," she muttered, to him, to herself, she didn't know.

"You shouldn't be. Fear is adaptive. It forces evolution. See? I sometimes listen."

"I was afraid of Dima. I'm afraid of radiation. I'm afraid that the radiation might affect me."

"No, sweetheart, you've mostly been in the outer ring, and you're well within the recommended time. I checked it out, of course."

"I went farther."

"Not for too long. The accident was a long time ago. It won't be safe to resettle for a very long time, but you're not resettling. You're visiting. The allowance is very generous. I checked. You'll be fine."

"Are you trying to placate me?" said Renya.

"I went to the nuclear guys," said Nick. "I went to the real experts. You're going to be fine."

Renya raised a hand. "I should say something," she said. "I'm sorry I wasn't there."

"The heart attack. When I had the heart attack, it wasn't a major thing. There was no permanent damage. And it's okay to get scared. You were there when I needed you, and you can take some time to focus on yourself and your own work. That's just fine. We're going to be fine."

Renya nodded. But then she stopped herself. They weren't fine. Nothing was fine. She was here. He was there. She had no idea where he was. She'd asked him to leave, and now he'd left.

They talked briefly after that, but Renya mostly watched the window. She couldn't bear to look at the computer screen. She made excuses to end the conversation.

She lay down on her bed and waited for sleep to come. When it didn't, she sat up wearily and went back to work.

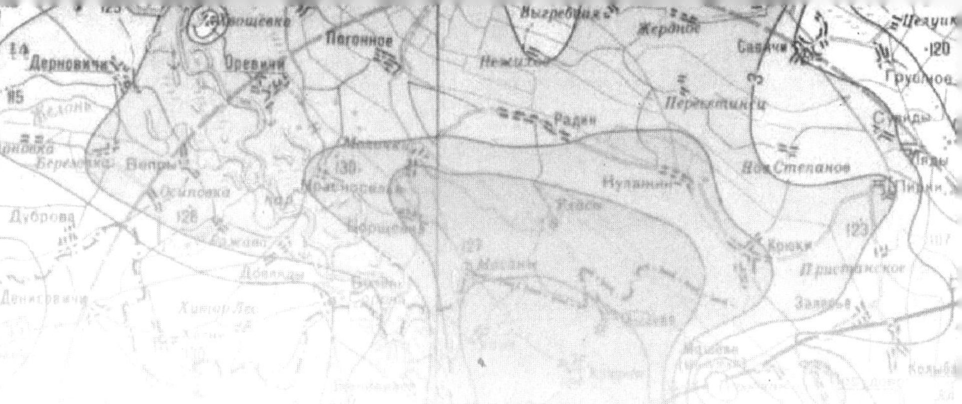

CHAPTER 12

RENYA WOKE THE NEXT MORNING TO A BLEATING ALARM. SHE turned away from it.

She touched the side table. She'd had a dream, she remembered. She'd dreamed, that night, of the liquidators, of walking with them, of spraying down dirt, and then, in the dream, she'd been in a boardroom, in charge of disaster cleanup. She'd wanted to un-explode the reactor. But she couldn't find a way. There'd been no good decisions to be made. There was no way out. There was just death upon death upon death whichever way you thought about it. One of the suits from her boardroom meeting had started sketching hanged men on the whiteboard.

She opened her laptop. The Skype chime started again. She found Nick against a blank wall again, another blank wall.

"Stay right where you are," he said. "I'm coming to get you."

"You can't *come to get me*," said Renya. "I'm in Chornobyl. Anyway, I don't need to be saved. I don't need you. I don't need my dad –"

"I'm not saving you."

"Good, because –"

"I want to be with you."

"Don't be an ass."

"What?"

She gestured to the dreary room, the threadbare blanket. "Look where I am."

"Without you, what do I have?"

"Your life," said Renya.

"You are my life."

"Your career."

Nick's face swam closer. "Seriously, Ren. I hardly even research anymore. I just answer other people's questions. I network. I'm good at that. You've made fun of me for it."

She turned to hide her smile. She had made fun of him.

Renya rubbed her face and realized it was covered in tears. "Now I understand it more," she mumbled.

"What?" And suddenly Nick was closer to the screen, his grey eyes shining. "What do you understand?"

"All my life, I heard these stories about this place that howls, these trees that turn red and die . . . Then I read on the Internet that at night, people swear the trees glow red. I wanted to howl. I wanted people to see that I was broken. I was walking around day after day and nobody saw any difference, I was still the department head's daughter, half of the cute little cross-departmental couple. I'm different. I want to look different. I want to grow extra limbs and have hideous deformities. I want to glow in the dark."

"That's not –"

"I know," said Renya. "I know that's not how it works."

"Does it help?"

"What?"

"Being there?"

"I had questions I wanted to answer. And I have, I'm doing it. And I wanted to see it. I needed to come here. I talked about it with my dad when I was a kid you know. My earliest memories are of looking through pictures of the disaster. My grandmother told me stories, set here, set in the disaster zone, about ghosts holding off accidents, about secret lives in the woods. So yes. Yes. It's ridiculous. I'm scared and I regret coming, but, yes, it helps."

"I should have talked to you more about it when you first had the idea. I should have offered to come. Your project is exciting. Everyone's talking about it. And that doesn't even matter: there's something you need to do, and I want to be there with you while you do it. You should have your adventure. I'll share it. I'll share the risk with you too."

Renya bowed her head. She felt tears stinging behind her eyes. This was what she'd always wanted. She'd wanted it so badly. She wanted to share this, the risk, yes, but the curiosity also, the experience, the way she'd worked at getting into Nick's physics. But it was hers alone. As was the damage that she'd already done to her body by taking risks in the forest, in the city. Nobody could share any of it with her. "But I'm not even the same anymore. You said that about Yuri, but maybe I'm the same."

"I didn't –"

"Maybe I changed on a molecular level."

"You didn't. Like you said, there are high-velocity particles that come from the sun."

"I have to go."

"What?"

"Despite it all, there's still more I need to see."

⊙ ⊙ ⊙

And that was it, she assumed. She'd let him go now. She'd asked him to leave, and he'd left. And they'd said their goodbyes. That would be the end of her marriage. She stood, wiping off her cheeks. She closed her eyes and pictured, for some reason, the house she'd seen in the woods, the glowing embers in the fireplace.

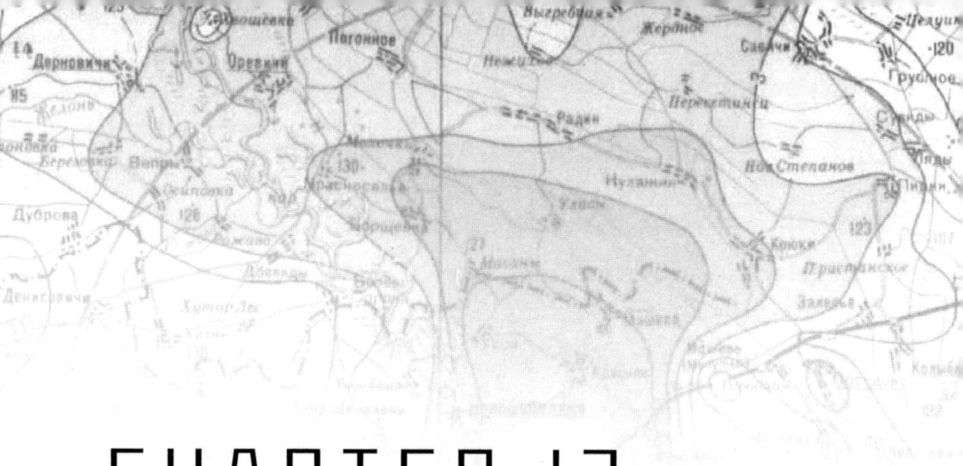

CHAPTER 13

RENYA STOOD IN FRONT OF THE FENCE, RIGHT AT THE FOOT of the sarcophagus. She'd heard rumours about a dishwasher who drove people out here. He wasn't even hard to find.

She sat the computer on the crumbling earth, then sat cross-legged in front of it. The Internet connection was strong here, for security patrols, she guessed, for monitoring what was still an earth-shatteringly dangerous place. She opened Skype, but nobody was there. She could record a video message anyway.

She leaned back and watched the sarcophagus. It was huge and visibly breaking down, pieces yawning open like giant mouths. She could hear birds trilling. The sounds came from inside. She wondered what kinds of birds lived there. She wondered whether Claire knew they lived right inside. She shifted to face the camera again. She turned on the recorder. "Hi, Dad! I can see reactor four now. I mean, if I turn around, I can see it. Can you see it behind me? I'm here. I made it right to the reactor. There are guards, and a fence, so I can't go farther. You need suits to get closer, to where those birds live. Now that I'm here, I don't know why I needed to see it. I don't know what I needed to do here. I don't know what I needed to see. You'd like it though. It's just the way you used to describe it, how Baba always talked about it."

She wanted to tell him something desperately, but she couldn't remember what. "I love you," she said into the camera. "I just wanted to say that it was a weird way to grow up, but I liked talking about Chornobyl with you. I liked talking physics. Even if I switched out of it and didn't study it that much in the end, I always liked talking about it with you. I still do. I don't tell you that often enough."

There was another long silence. "The stillness here is like a blanket. It feels like when I used to make blanket forts when I was little. I can't explain it. I can taste it. It's like metal. I feel like I bit my lip."

And Renya realized that she'd created a silence again. It was her fault. She was the only one here. These silences were her responsibility to fill. After the event, Nick had been her responsibility. She should have taken care of him and comforted him, but she'd been so scared. Her dad must have been scared too when her mom had died. That's why he'd gone away so much. That's why he'd found another wife so quickly.

She pictured Nick again, their lives together, the bed they'd shared, the kitchen table, the countertops, the arguments. She'd miss it all. Being married had been nice, for the most part.

She pictured her bedroom, hers and Nick's, the blankets they'd bought together, the pictures she'd made him hang and rehang. Anytime he went into the kitchen, he'd leave all the cabinet doors open, and she'd grumble that it was like living with a poltergeist. She remembered the blue drapes. She remembered sleeping in on Sundays, but then kicking his feet to get him to wake up when she woke up. She remembered yelling at him, how he left crumbs on the counters, she'd always hated crumbs on the counters, and that one time he'd eaten crackers in the bed and there were crumbs in the sheets and she'd lost it, and that had been the one time she'd slammed doors. They still laughed about it. They used to laugh about it, rather.

She turned to the camera. "This is interesting," she said. "And it's certainly cool to be one of the only people who's been here. But I think I'm sorry I came, all the same. I had questions, yes. But maybe I should have found some other way to answer them. And the questions themselves don't end. That's the thing. You answer one, and then you just find another. You lift one veil and you find another. On it goes. The more you understand, the more you need to know." She cleared her throat. "I found one lever I can pull, with fear, but I have more questions, more ideas now. What if emotions can presage illness? What if the same techniques I use can be harnessed to monitor for heart attacks, imminent strokes, autoimmune conditions? What if I can scan for body heat and muscle activation to predict medical crises? I keep thinking about that, as I take pictures of scientists here. Emotions are cool, but there are processes even deeper, physiological ones that could open a window to people's underlying health. Anyway. I love you, Dad. I wanted you to see that I was here."

She found she had nothing else to say, so she ended her recording.

Renya heard something, a rustle in the woods. She turned off the recorder. She heard a rumble that almost sounded like Yuri's motorcycle. Could it be Dima and Yuri? She scrambled to her feet. Maybe they'd come to prove their manhood. Or maybe it was the wild dogs that Shantoo had told her about. She'd been back and forth about all of her excursions thus far, but this one was most definitely reckless.

She turned and looked. Then she forced herself to look right at the sarcophagus. It looked like a harmless industrial landscape. The building was huge, covered by warped metal sheets that looked almost like clapboard, that were brown and rusted and decaying. She squinted. The structure was surrounded by scaffolding and ladders, it seemed. She could see huge gaps in the cover, where great pieces of sheet metal must have fallen away. A shriek pierced the air. She jumped. Just then, a flock of birds emerged from one of the gaping holes. There was life here. It seemed unimaginable. But animals lived here. They lived everywhere, even inside the sarcophagus, near the exposed fuel rods of reactor four.

There was a rustle from down the path, that same rumbling, intensified, and it seemed to echo now.

Renya turned to face the sarcophagus again. Her heart was beating so hard. She focused on the building in front of her. She wouldn't be coming back. She should really commit it to memory. This place was eerie in its plainness, in its ordinariness. It just looked like the industrial part of her city, near the waterfront. It could be any unused space. But the ruined reactor was inside. There was nuclear material in there that wouldn't be safe for thousands of years. It was sending out alpha and beta particles, that, if they hit any of her component parts, would cause a meltdown inside her. This still building, with its yawning metal sections and its singing nesting birds, was the most dangerous thing she'd ever seen.

The sounds got louder. Renya held the fence. She felt her body physically quaking. She looked around. She was scared. She was in the midst of terror. She had nowhere to go.

Just then, a shape emerged from over the hill. Renya's vision swam. She held the fence. She forced herself to focus on the actual threat this time.

Was that Yuri?

It was indeed Yuri, on that motorcycle cobbled out of pieces.

He stopped at the top of the hill, some feet away from her still, and balanced on his foot. He made no move to dismount, but then another figure emerged from behind him. Renya tensed, muscles locked, but it wasn't Dima. It looked more like Nick. The figure ran toward her.

"I wanted to make amends," Yuri called out. "I told you that already. I want to be someone who helps." He gestured. "And then I found him."

The man was coming closer. It looked like Nick. It couldn't be Nick.

Renya stood straight. It was. It was Nick. He was running toward her, cheeks red, eyes filled with tears. She ran toward him and threw herself at him when she got close enough.

Nick grabbed her into a tight embrace. She closed her eyes. Suddenly, her mind cleared, just like that. She wasn't broken. She hadn't been exposed for too long. She was tired. That was all. She hadn't slept more than a few hours a night in weeks, and that would make anyone disoriented.

Nick was sobbing, shuddering against her body. "I booked an ecotour," he was saying. "I wanted to prove that I could be supportive of you like you're supportive of me. I wanted to prove to you that we can be a team. I wanted to be part of this."

"Okay," she said.

"I love you," he said.

She loved him too. She hadn't stopped.

The cloud cover suddenly shifted, and the reactor seemed to blink. Renya heard a rustle. Seconds later a flock of birds emerged from a hole in the sarcophagus and fanned out, a giant sheet waving through the sky. An errant breeze lifted her hair, and Renya pulled away. She saw it all differently all of a sudden.

⊙ ⊙ ⊙

And the forest spirit let go of Renya's hair. She walked back to the other ghosts.

A person's life is played out on the planet, and in the end, that person is absorbed by it, by the earth, by the atmosphere, by water. Sometimes they break down and rejoin the cycle. Sometimes they don't. Memories can be reflected back outward again. Sometimes, some of what made that person remains.

The ghosts of the town were indeed here, lined up by the fence, but they weren't protecting Renya, at least not in a way that she'd understand. They were watching. They were watching the high-velocity particles. They were watching the plumes escape the still-used reactors. They were watching the smoke rise all around the world, from coal-fired power stations, from wildfires, from fireplaces. They were watching oil spills, and chemical processing, and manufacturing, and waste collection. From where the ghosts stood, unmoored from life and time, it all looked the same, because what they saw was the trajectory, started well before Chornobyl's explosion and continuing inexorably onward, toward a febrile world that was completely changed, toward a time that none there would recognize. They whispered in the scientists' ears from time to time, telling them to look up, asking them to zoom out. They blew in their faces to make them feel unsettled. They ran toward the birds to make them all take flight at once. They made them afraid, of what the scientists didn't quite know. In that way, they offered what protection they could.

ACKNOWLEDGEMENTS

EXCUSE THE CLICHÉ, BUT SOME GROWN-UPS NEED A VILLAGE just as much as children do, and I'm grateful that I've had a village.

Thank you to everyone at Wolsak & Wynn. Thanks specifically to Paul, Noelle, Ashley, etc.

Thank you to editors such as Emily Schultz, Scout Rexe, Janice Zawerbny, etc.

Thank you so much to my teachers (including but not limited to): Carolyn Smart, Linda Spalding, David Young, Judith Thompson, Catherine Bush, Shyam Selvadurai, André Alexis, Connie Rooke, Thomas King, Janice Kulyk Keefer. I still think about so much that they taught me. It turns out that I didn't even have to take notes. It's just always there.

Thank you to writer friends and long-ago classmates (again very much not limited to): Mia, Amina, Dave, Blain, Melanie, Kimberly, Abby, Motion, Jaime, Nila, Sheniz, Sandy, Dave, Jeff, Jordana, Carolyn, Zoe, Lana, Erin, Duncan, Leigh, Sam, Aisha, Katherine, Hollay, Andrew, Leah-Jane, Nuzhat, Ellen, Elizabeth.

Thank you to friends who helped me. I hope that you know who you are. I hope that I make it clear how much your presences matter.

Thank you to the people who helped me when this manuscript was in play form: David Young, David Young's TPL group, She Said Yes and the fantastic Louis Brown.

Thank you to literary heroes who didn't need to be supportive but were supportive: Kathryn Kuitenbrouwer, Kate Cayley, Kerry Clare.

This might read like a list of all the amazing writers who have ever been nice to me in any way, and that's okay. I appreciate it. Their kindness mattered to me.

Thank you to my family, especially my dad who suggested science as a jumping board to anything. It is a jumping board to everything.

Thank you to Oliver and Jake. People sometimes ask who I write for. I write for you.

NOTES

THIS BOOK IS A WORK OF LITERARY FICTION, AND THOUGH the streams of science described are accurate to the best of my understanding, great liberties have been taken with both timelines and the scientific research described for the sake of storytelling.

There is indeed research conducted in the exclusion zone. There is no research centre (at least not in the way described). I made all that up.

Renya's work was inspired by Dr. Paul Ekman. His work is incredible and worth looking at.

The climate/fauna/flora/soil science is very, very loosely based on real science that is also very interesting and very worth looking up.

The environmental concerns are real and terrifying.

ALEXIS VON KONIGSLOW is the author of *The Capacity for Infinite Happiness*. She has degrees in mathematical physics from Queen's University and creative writing from the University of Guelph. She lives in Toronto with her family.